LOST TREASURES

BARB GOODWIN
DOUG PENIKAS

SECRETS
OF THE
TOTENKOPF
RINGS

To our family for all their love and support.

A secret organization foolishly operates under the flag of a fox
To partake in such organization
Let alone be a leader of said organization
Is an abominable crime

Nineteen-year-old Becca Romanov stood by the fireplace and watched the crackling flames. Two bodyguards stood a few feet away allowing her a private moment. She couldn't help but think about how much her life had changed in the past year since she and RC had uncovered the secrets of the Royal Danish Egg. Nor did she ever expect to have a target on her back.

"Becca...Becca?" she heard from behind.

Becca turned from the fireplace and saw Brittany Hewes weaving through friends and business associates dressed in dark colors. Brittany wore a stunning black dress that made her stand out from the crowd in the grand living room. Colorful flowers and the calming, peaceful scent of rosemary filled the air. Becca's bodyguards made room for Brittany to approach.

"Thank you for coming to Germany for my grandfather's funeral," Brittany said. She gave Becca a tight hug and shook as she fought back tears.

"Of course. What are friends for?"

"He was very grateful for your assistance in acquiring the Vermeer painting for him a few months ago. I still can't believe it was in a garage in Madrid all these years. I don't know how you found it."

"I knew a guy," Becca said, hiding the difficulty it had taken to find the lost painting. "How are you holding up?"

Brittany dropped the strong persona she had been using to cover her sadness and was honest with Becca. "I don't want to be Brittany Hewes, CEO of Hewes Fashion Empire right now. I'm not ready. I just want to run away from everything. Come with me...just us girls. Maybe we can find a map that leads to the real Treasure Island or something? Hopefully, somewhere far away from my life?"

Becca sighed, disappointed. "That would be amazing, but I have upcoming guest appearances at different charity events."

"I know how much you hate those. But that's what happens when you find you're related to a famous, long-lost Romanov."

"You don't know the half of it." It pained Becca that she couldn't share the full truth with Brittany, but it was for her own safety.

"If there's anything I've learned from being your friend this past year, it's that your adventures are way more fun than mine. I just hope the next one requires scuba diving for two."

Becca smiled and squeezed her friend's hand. "One can only hope."

Brittany sighed. "All right. Back to mingling." She returned to her guests, and Becca admired how strong Brittany was during this time of grief.

Relieved to stand alone, Becca noticed people moving out of the way of a man wearing disheveled clothes who was headed toward her. Her bodyguards blocked his path, preventing him from getting any closer.

"Ms. Romanov," the man said with an urgent tone. He pulled up his right coat sleeve and revealed a flesh-toned tattoo of a feather on his wrist. It was a feather from a griffin, showing he was a member of the League of Griffins, a centuries-old secret organization. "We need to talk...privately."

The bodyguards looked at Becca for approval to let him pass.

She knew she was safe. Becca had a different griffin tattoo on her right wrist.

"It's okay," she told her bodyguards.

The guards moved out of the way to let the man pass but kept a close eye on their charge.

"Come with me." She led the way to the study. "Guard the door," she told her bodyguards, and once inside she closed the door behind her.

Becca sat on the sofa and studied the man. His nervousness was impossible to miss. He glanced around the room. Becca knew he was looking for surveillance cameras, as that was one of the first things League of Griffins initiates were trained to do. He stared for a long moment at the window overlooking a patio. He had facial tics, a sure sign of extreme anxiety.

"Please sit down, and tell me why you're here," she said.

The man's face was plain but not ugly. Actually, he was mildly attractive, the perfect person to be overlooked in a crowd.

She waited for him to speak. When he didn't, she said, "We're safe here. The guards are right outside the door."

He closed the window and pulled out a small instrument. He pushed a red button and said, "Jamming device."

She didn't say anything.

He pulled an object out of his pocket and handed it to Becca. It was a surprisingly heavy pure silver ring. Becca's eyebrows rose. The ring had a skull on top between two matching runes that appeared as a backward *N* inside a triangular border. Three other runes were embedded in oak leaves on the outside of the band. She twisted the ring around in her fingers and saw one of the runes contained a swastika inside a square. Becca looked up with shock.

"This is a Totenkopf ring. I've heard of them but never seen one before."

She studied the inner band of the ring and saw a name inscribed. "Heinrich Himmler, the head of the Nazi SS." Next to Himmler's name were numbers. 38.07.23. They could have been a date, but they weren't in the usual American format of month, day, year or the European format of day, month, year. "Is this authentic?"

"Yes. Find the others, learn their trueness. Don't stop until light is upon you."

Becca looked up from the ring. "What does that mean?"

"I have no idea," the man confessed. "I was told to deliver the ring to you and repeat the message. That's it."

"By whom?" she asked, intrigued.

The man didn't respond. He opened the door and walked past her bodyguards.

"Wait, please. I don't understand." Becca shoved the ring into her purse and ran out of the room after the man. He had disappeared into the crowd.

"Find him," she said to her bodyguards.

The three of them hurried through the crowd. She studied the gathering, looking for any burst of movement, but she couldn't locate him. Basic evasion tactics had taught her that if you wanted to make a quick escape, you must ensure your pursuer sees the direction you intend to go, then quickly move in the opposite direction. It was an escapist version of sleight of hand. If he'd gone the way she thought he had, then he was most likely going in the opposite direction. Becca turned around.

People were milling around, eating, and talking, blocking her way out of the grand living room. Something caught her eye, and she spotted the man on the far side of the room. He crossed the threshold to the back patio. Suddenly, his head snapped back, and blood splattered onto a couple drinking cocktails. The man's body fell limp to the ground.

The woman screamed, and her husband stood still, shocked into silence as he saw the blood on their clothes. Others turned to see what had happened.

"Shooter!" one of her bodyguards shouted.

The crowd panicked, screaming and running in all directions. Becca crouched between her bodyguards. They readied their weapons and covered her from the front and back. Becca had a pistol strapped to her inner thigh, but she couldn't use it in public without blowing her cover.

The guests continued to panic and run away. Patio chairs were knocked over as they fled.

"I don't have eyes on the shooter," one bodyguard said into his coms.

"Evacuation protocol one-eight-eight," said the other bodyguard.

Becca and her bodyguards moved as one unit. She knew the protocol, as it was one of the first drills she'd learned when she had been recruited into the Griffins. It was code for how a small team, four or less, could help a valuable asset escape a public area, right under the nose of the enemy. Normally, it was more challenging when protecting an innocent bystander. The fact that Becca knew the protocol helped them escape more easily.

Mass panic surrounded Becca. She saw Brittany being escorted out the front door by her security, while many others ran to their cars.

Becca and her bodyguards exited through the front door to a black SUV that hopped the curb to pick them up. Once inside the bulletproof vehicle, Becca kept her head down as they raced away from the mansion and the frightened crowd.

2

Becca arrived at the Griffins' headquarters in Heidelberg, Germany, about an hour from where the attack happened. The compound had been a school campus for troubled youth. On the outside it looked like any other school, but inside it concealed a super-network establishment. A massive reinforced wall surrounded the disguised compound's campus, protecting it from the outside world. Tall, thick trees shielded the perimeter. Extreme security protected the grounds. Not even Seal Team Six could infiltrate. Lines of invisible lasers crisscrossed the top of the wall to deter anyone from climbing over. Each building had multiple hidden satellite dishes on top. The compound held everything any Griffin member might need for treasure hunts and training.

The tech building was dedicated to developing new high-tech equipment, ten years ahead of military and public release. Hundreds of engineers and scientists worked around the clock to invent new, better gadgets. Becca had recently completed her mechanical-engineering degree and knew every piece of tech would fascinate her.

The armory, across from the tech building, had two large training areas, one indoors and one outdoors. A gun range stood on the other side of the armory with a room next to it that held every conceivable weapon, ancient and modern, as well as an archery range.

A world-class high-rise, dubbed the "Bunkhouse," held room for one thousand Griffins at a time. Basically, it was a five-star hotel that housed members on temporary and long-term assignments.

Becca went into the main building and entered the information-database level. It took up the whole second floor. Fifty slim laptops that projected holographic information in the cubicle sat on tables in rows of individual booths with high barriers to allow privacy and secrecy for those searching records.

Becca sat at one of the computers and spoke to it: "Show me only male, feather-tattooed members." The fact that the man had a flesh-colored feather tattoo on his right wrist helped Becca narrow down her search. The tattoos represented the status of every member within the organization. There were five levels, starting with Feather, then moving up to Wing, Talon, Claw, and Beak. Each level had four tiers the members needed to complete in order to advance up the ladder, should they so desire.

The only way to have this kind of tattoo was to have been inducted into the League of Griffins. The organization had a way of giving authentic, flesh-colored tattoos that only they could provide. The tattoos could not be faked.

When Becca was inducted into the League of Griffins last year, she had been awarded the Wing-level tattoo as an information gatherer. She'd skipped the Feather level because her discovery of Faberge's lost Royal Danish Egg had been applied to the requirements for a Wing-level status, even though she hadn't been a member at the time. She still had a long way to go before fulfilling her first-tier accomplishment within that level.

Being a Wing-level member allowed her access to certain information within the League of Griffin's database. Since the man who had given her the Totenkopf ring had a feather tattoo with four marks inside, she searched the database for all feather-tattooed members at the tier-four level. Feather tattoos, the first tattoos an initiate is given, represent the trusted-advisor status within the League. A trusted advisor was pretty much a normal bystander in the world who knew of the existence of the Griffins. Their job was to report any unusual intel to the organization.

Calculating, DIANA, short for Data Interactive Algorithmic Network Application, responded. DIANA was the Griffins' supercomputer. The number of search results that came up was in the thousands.

"Refine search," Becca said, and a new window popped up. "All Caucasian men between the ages of forty and fifty, average height, five-ten, lean build."

The search narrowed to a few hundred, and Becca worried this wasn't going to be as easy as she had hoped.

Requires more description to identify individual, DIANA suggested.

"I'm open to other search ideas," Becca said and sighed.

I can ID any individual from the following; fingerprints, addresses, social security, birth certificate, maiden name, blood type, retinal scan, dental records, bank account, facial recognition, and fifty more options. Would you like me to list them?

"Facial recognition," Becca said, deep in thought. "Can you get that from a sketch?"

Most likely. Depends on how accurate the sketch may be.

Becca grabbed a pencil and paper and roughed out a sketch of the man's face. It wasn't perfect, but she figured it could help her narrow the search. She wasn't the best artist, but her photographic memory had helped her in all her art classes.

"Scan image." Becca held up the sketch to the holographic window and watched as the computer laser outlined her drawing and then projected it in a new window in front of her, next to all the remaining names.

One moment, DIANA said.

The computer eliminated hundreds of names and photos,

narrowing it down to five in a split second. The man's face appeared as option four.

Becca was relieved that the sketch had worked. "Number four. That's him. Access file."

A big red warning sign flashed on the screen.

Access denied. Claw level required, DIANA said.

"What? For a tier-four, Feather-level member? That doesn't make sense."

Claw was the highest level in the organization underneath the actual leader, Mason Carter, who was a Beak. Being a Wing, it would take her years of excellent results before she would reach the level required to access the file.

"End search," Becca said, frustrated, and left the holographic-computer station.

Becca went to her supervisor's office. Brady Washington was the only person she knew with the required level to gain access to the file she needed. A former attack-squad member, he was now designated tier four, Claw-R, which meant he'd retired from the field. Brady had years of experience behind him and had chosen to train and manage new members. If anyone could get her access, he could. He'd been her assigned handler ever since she'd joined the Griffins.

"Hey, Brady," Becca said after she knocked, then entered his office. "I'm blocked from using part of DIANA. I need your help."

Brady was hunched over his computer. He looked up from his screen and gave her a suspicious glance. "I'm glad to see you're safe from the shooting at the funeral. We're looking into the matter now. It doesn't appear to be an attempt on your life."

"I know. The man was the target, and I'm denied access to his file. It requires a Claw level. But why does a tier-four, Feather-level member have the highest restriction on his file?"

"What makes you so sure the target wasn't you?"

"He was killed after he gave me this." She pulled the ring out of her pocket and placed it on his desk.

Brady picked up the ring and looked at it.

"It's a Totenkopf ring," Becca said. "The man was terrified and said he'd been instructed to give it to me. I don't understand why a Griffin would be killed over this. That's why I need access to the file."

Brady was a good handler. He was a tough instructor, a bit gruff and blunt, but Becca always knew where he came from and appreciated his directness.

"There are thousands of other more experienced Griffins he could've given the ring to, so why me?"

Brady handed the ring back, sat up in his chair, and opened a search engine on his computer.

"DIANA, pull up my last search result, please," Becca said.

The man's face appeared on Brady's holo-screen with the access-denied restriction.

"I don't recognize him." Brady shrugged. "Claw-level override; Washington, Brady," he said to DIANA. A light scanned his retina.

Access granted, DIANA replied.

"Antonio Herrero," Brady read. "Forty-six, a member of the Griffins since 2008, advised on over sixty recon assignments, lived in Sweden, Brazil, Kenya, and Japan." Brady sat back in his chair. "I'm not sure what you're hoping to find here, Becca."

"I don't know what I'm looking for, but I have a feeling I'll know it when I see it." Becca searched through Herrero's last two missions. "Located Lucas Santos's kidnapped daughter, Marcia. He was a Brazilian diplomat. Reported last known money-laundering movement for the Le Diable Rouge gang in France. This doesn't help at all."

"I don't see anything in his file about a ring." Brady continued scrolling through the reports. "I'm sorry."

Becca sighed. "It was worth a shot. Thanks for checking for me."

She returned to her suite on the third floor of the Bunkhouse. It consisted of a large living area with a view of the grounds and an elegant bedroom with two windows overlooking a beautiful landscape of trees. Her bathroom had double sinks, a marble countertop, and a rain shower. Next to her bedroom was a small sitting area she'd converted into an office. She'd placed pictures of her mom and her late best friend, Barry, on a side table. A colorful bouquet of fresh carnations sat on her dresser.

"DIANA, please access any information about this ring." Becca held up the ring, and the holo-screen appeared. It snapped a 3D shot, then a whirring sound began. The Griffin AI could scan both the inside and outside at the same time and finished in a few seconds.

DIANA found tons of information about the ring. Pages scrolled down the screen. It stopped, then showed an index of subjects, from the ring's history to the meaning of the symbols to its metallic composition and, finally, the legend behind how they went missing.

During World War II, Heinrich Himmler was the head of the Schutzstaffel, also known as the SS. The organization terrorized not only the German people but also German-occupied Europe. All SS officers received a Totenkopf ring. In 1938 Himmler ordered the rings of all the dead officers to be returned. He stored them in a chest in Wewelsburg Castle as a memorial to the dead officers. In 1945, when Himmler accepted that the Nazis were losing the war, he ordered all the remaining rings to be given back and then blast sealed them inside an unknown mountain. They have never been recovered.

All this history was fascinating to Becca, but she didn't understand what any of it had to do with her.

The cryptic message Herrero had relayed to her before he died haunted and frustrated her.

"Find the others, learn their trueness. Don't stop until light is upon you," Becca said, still unsure of the meaning.

Now that the ring was scanned into DIANA, Becca enlarged the screen to study the fine details. The ring was expertly crafted.

"Tell me about the runes, DIANA," Becca requested.

Five runes, DIANA replied. *Two Sig runes inside a triangle that represents the power of the sun and control of the universe. One Hagel rune inside a hexagon, which means faith and camaraderie, as well as bring the universe in you and you control the universe. One swastika rune inside a square standing on the vertex, which is the symbol of the power of the Aryan race and, lastly, a double rune in a circle that indicates signs of the salvation of the past.*

Becca waved her hand around the digital scan of the ring. The ring rotated with her hand motion. She pondered the meanings of the runes and how the rings related to the message she'd been told. She divided the message into three parts. Each sentence might be a clue.

"First part, 'find the others.' That must mean the rest of the lost rings. But that's obvious. DIANA, how many rings are still missing?"

There are approximately eleven thousand five hundred Totenkopf rings, also known as SS Honor Rings, still missing.

"Whoa." Becca didn't expect that.

No one has an exact count.

"How much are all the rings worth if they're found today?"

Approximately $60 million. But if they're found and given away separately, the value can drop to zero.

"Aha," Becca said. To any regular treasure hunter, $60 million was motivation enough to kill, but if Herrero was murdered by the organization Becca hated the most, the Brotherhood of the Fox, $60 million would be chump change to them. If the monetary value dropped, and the rings were worthless, there had to be a different meaning, a deeper one, a reason so compelling that someone would kill to learn it.

The second part of the message, 'learn their trueness,' could be just what she'd discovered, the true meaning. She'd eliminated one possibility, money, if it was Brotherhood related. So, what other meaning would be worth a man's life? She had no idea.

Whenever Becca was stuck on something, she always went on a short walk to clear her head. She took the elevator down to the first floor and stepped into the courtyard in the center of the compound. Tall pine trees scented the air, calming her.

She wished Barry was here with her. Her best friend since they were eight years old, their friendship and laughter had kept her grounded. Barry had been a computer geek, and last year he'd been a big help to her with finding the Royal Danish Egg. Memories of the two of them flooded her mind. When they would be on her bed doing homework, he would show her some new hack he'd discovered instead of focusing on the assignment. The multiple times he'd forced her to use her photographic memory to win other students' lunch money so he could get more food. He would have been extremely useful now.

Deep sadness overcame Becca, and she hunched into herself as she remembered her last moments with Barry in the coffee shop. She sank onto a nearby bench under a tall pine and looked up to the stars peeking through the branches. To her dying day she'd regret getting Barry involved. He didn't deserve to die so horribly by the Brotherhood of the Fox.

A tear slipped down Becca's cheek. Barry was gone but always with her. She heard him in her head. It was like he'd told her to figure out this new puzzle of the rings.

"I will, Barry," she said to the heavens.

Her walk cleared a bit of the sadness away. Back in her room, she activated DIANA in the little office in her suite. A see-through form of a pretty woman floated in front of her desk.

You rang, Becca?

"I see someone's given you a personality upgrade, DIANA," Becca said, surprised.

The computer geeks were playing around with a new script earlier today.

"I like it. Makes you more personable."

Thank you, Becca. You're very kind. How can I help?

Becca got right to the point. "Please do a statistical probability of where the SS honor rings may be."

On it.

It still felt weird talking to a computer, as if she were having a conversation with a friend. She hoped DIANA's supercomputer brain would be able to give Becca a new direction in order to solve the mystery.

One theory is that the rings are buried under Wewelsburg Castle, DIANA said in her soft voice.

"Use LiDar to scan under the castle, see if there's a crate buried there," Becca said. She waited as DIANA made her calculations.

Scanning using UV light and radar.

A three-dimensional map of Wewelsburg Castle hovered in the middle of Becca's room as DIANA ran the LiDar scan. Becca had learned about LiDar in her basic training with the Griffins. It reflected light from objects to detect them, like a visual sonar. Archeologists have used it in their profession before.

She saw the hill the castle was built on turn transparent as the scan processed every angle and its foundation.

No objects of the size and shape of a large crate found under Wewelsburg Castle.

"Not surprising. That would've been too easy," Becca said. She stretched, then went back to her desk, disappointed. Now she had to start over again.

What was the origin of the ring? Who was Antonio Herrero, and why had he been told to give it to her? How could the ring have ended up with him? And who gave it to him?

"DIANA, please scan the ring for DNA."

Scanning.

A few seconds later, DIANA gave the results.

DNA found for Rebecca Hunter Lake Romanov, Antonio Herrero, and Christianne Fischer.

Becca had never heard of Christianne Fischer. "Search Christianne Fischer," she said.

Searching. Christianne Fischer, born in 1930, still living. Ninety-two years old. Lives in Seesen, Germany, near the base of the Harz Mountains. One son, Stefan Fischer. One married daughter, Emery Schmidt.

"Search anything on the internet and government databases

about Christianne Fischer, please." Becca watched as a few pictures and local articles hovered in front of her.

"Any mention of Nazis or an honor ring?" Becca asked.

One article appeared: "World War II Horror Story. The Early Life of Christianne Fischer." Becca noticed the article had been posted by an Emery Fischer-Schmidt, possibly Christianne's daughter.

Becca took a breath as she read the article. Dated May 15, 2006, the article said that Christianne was fifteen in 1945 when four men came into the local tavern she'd been working at. All of them were miners working at the nearby mine in the Harz Mountains. They were elated with drunken excitement and talked among themselves. They boasted about some ultrasecret mission they had just completed for Heinrich Himmler and the Nazis. All the men were Nazi sympathizers.

One of the men waved a ring at his buddies. Christianne heard him bragging to the other three men about having stolen it as a token for completing their secret mission. After serving the men a few rounds of drinks, the man with the ring cornered Christianne near the bathrooms. He threatened to have her killed if she ever told anyone about the ring and then attempted to rape her. She fought back and accidentally killed the man with a carving knife. The ring fell out of his hand, and Christianne scooped it up. During the attempted rape, the other three men had fled. Not knowing what she had, Christianne took the ring home and put it away. The article said she'd kept the ring as a reminder of what she'd survived during the war. It also said no charges had been filed against Christianne.

Becca now held Christianne Fischer's ring. Knowing that Christianne still lived in Seesen, Becca pulled up a map of the town on her holo-screen and saw it sat at the base of the Harz Mountains.

"DIANA, how far can Griffin GPRs reach into the earth?"

GPRs are specifically calibrated to go three miles deep. The Griffins really souped theirs up, and it scans ten miles deep.

Becca smiled at how real DIANA seemed. "I'm still not used to your upgrade. Remotely use a GPR to scan the mine at the base of the Harz Mountains near Seesen, Germany, please."

Scanning.

Becca tapped her fingers on her desk.

An object matching the size and scope of the possible crate of rings does appear in this part of the mountain.

The screen revealed an area outlined in red.

Coordinates sent to your phone.

Becca's heart jumped as she studied them. The area was about four hours away.

Becca initiated a video chat with Brady. His hologram window appeared.

"I've narrowed down a possible location for the remaining rings to an old mine in the Harz Mountains near a town called Seesen, in Lower Saxony. I'm asking permission to be assigned with a team for an investigation and possible artifact extraction."

Brady responded like it was business as usual: "Granted."

3

The Harz Mountain terrain was somewhat rugged. Beech, oak, and sycamore trees were found at the lower levels of the range. Mining had been a big industry in the area for centuries, until the 1980s, but was borderline extinct now.

Becca hiked up the mountain with four other Griffin team members. She did her best to hide her excitement from them. This was her first official assignment in the field after being part of the Griffins for over a year, and she didn't want to appear inexperienced. Plus, it was way more exhilarating to be solving mysteries than doing her public appearances as Rebecca Hunter Lake Romanov.

Cornell, the Scottish team leader, led the way. He'd been in America for years but still had a thick Scottish accent. Considered one of the best team leaders, Becca was thrilled to be on her first mission with him. Red, so-called because of his bright-red hair, spent more time with technology than people. He was classified as an engineer. Hawk, a medium-sized Asian American, was one of two men brought in for protection. His size in no way indicated his skill. A master in multiple styles of martial arts, he was deadly. And Axel, originally from Samoa, was a beast when it came to strength and the second man used as protection. Little did anyone know that Axel was a big softie when you got to know him.

Sweat poured down Becca's face and back. Her quads were killing her as she walked up the lower part of the mountain. She slipped on some uneven dirt but regained her footing without assistance. She was determined not to let this mountain come between her and her prize.

A notification dinged on her phone. Their location matched the coordinates DIANA had calculated. Becca noticed the other team members had also received the notification.

"Okay. Now the only question is, which way do we go?" Axel said from the front of the squad. He seemed unfazed by the hike. "Look around for any kind of a sign or marker that could've been left for an SS soldier."

They searched the area multiple times and didn't find any hint or a clue where they should go next. Becca sat down to rest near a rocky outcrop. She drank water to hydrate and wiped away the sweat rolling down her face. A cloud blocked the sun, giving them a much-needed break from the heat.

The treasure hunt was thrilling and fed Becca's adrenaline. She knew they were close. She felt it in her bones. The rush always enhanced her abilities to focus and see puzzles out of thin air. She watched a shadow cross the mountain base as the sun peeked out from behind a cloud. A beam of light illuminated a rock embedded in the mountainside. Something about the rock caught her attention. It didn't look like a natural part of the mountain but more like someone put it there. Becca walked over to it and rubbed away dirt hiding an embedded skull.

Excitement kicked in. Becca studied the carving. The skull was small and appeared to be a match to the skull on the ring she'd been given. She pulled the ring out of a zippered pocket and looked at the top of the band. She placed the skull into the carved indentation. It was a perfect fit.

"It's a key," Becca said as Cornell came up to see what she was doing. She turned the ring. Nothing. She pressed a little harder. Nothing. "Damn. It's got to work. Why else would this be here in the middle of nowhere?" Instead of twisting the ring, she toggled it up and down. A hard click sounded, which caught everyone's attention. Small rocks tumbled to the now-shaking ground and revealed a door made of different-sized boulders and mortar.

"Nice work, Romanov," Cornell said. "You're up, Red."

Grinding and creaking mechanical sounds were heard from inside the mountain.

Becca took the ring out of the indentation, put it back into her zippered pocket, and stepped back. Her heart pounded with anticipation.

Dust and dirt blew into their faces forcing them to move away and cover their eyes and mouths as the opening cleared.

"Well, I'll be damned," Cornell said.

Becca smiled with delight as she stared into the entrance of an abandoned mine shaft.

Red did a thorough scan of the entrance with his enhanced phone. "I don't see anything that can set off a potential booby trap. We're good to go, Boss."

Cornell turned to Hawk and Axel. "You two stay outside and guard the entrance. Keep the emergency supplies close. Becca and Red, we're going in."

The three of them walked into the cave. Dust mites floated through the air. Becca waved them away and put on a respirator mask to protect herself. So did the other two. Large headlamps stared like a single eye from the front of their hard hats.

Rails and rotting wood planks lined the pathway deep into the earth. Stones lay on the ground covered in cobwebs that stretched down from the creaking wooden beams. The team cautiously walked down the tunnel looking for weak spots in the old wood framing. Becca held her Griffin-designed GPR, or ground-penetrating-radar device, in one hand. Cornell led the way, followed by Red and Becca. They reached the end of the tunnel and stared at the scarred rock and dried mud that blocked their way.

"It's a dead end," Cornell said. "We're in the wrong spot." He and Red turned to leave.

"No, we aren't." Becca studied the diagram DIANA had created of the mine on her phone. "This tunnel should continue for a few more meters, then go deeper to the right. Looks like the result of an earlier cave-in."

Just as she finished talking, a slight rumbling shook the mine. Rocks and dirt fell from the walls and rolled down the floor. Cornell held up a hand for the team to stop.

Becca's heart sped up at the thought of the mine collapsing. She wasn't claustrophobic, but she was very afraid of being trapped inside the mine.

"Wait a few seconds," Cornell said.

The three of them looked around the mine shaft for any clue as to whether they should stay or run. The rumbling faded, and the mine shaft stabilized.

Becca took a deep breath, then ran her hands over the tunnel blockage. The rocks were loosely piled, as if they'd been there a short time. "It should be behind here."

Red held his GPR near the blockage. "Radar pulses show more of the tunnel on the screen behind the rubble, just like Becca said."

"Clear it," Cornell ordered, then spoke into his com to inform Hawk and Axel. "We have to clear an old cave-in. Keep you posted."

Becca and the two men used their tools to clear an area wide enough for them to pass through. After an hour, the area was clear. They continued down the mine shaft.

Becca turned on the thermal-imaging feature of her GPR. The layout of the tunnel appeared in various shades of blue.

The mine rumbled in the distance. The squad heard small rocks hit the ground farther down the shaft. Becca stopped walking and waited for the mine to settle. She didn't like being underground. The mine's instability worried her.

Once the sound of falling rocks disappeared, Becca kept her attention focused on the GPR. She turned and scanned the tunnel wall. "I see something on the monitor." After some minor screen adjustments, she saw a green-highlighted box-like shape with a white-hot spot inside.

Becca's pulse sped up. "I've got an object matching the size we're looking for," she said to Cornell and Red.

Cornell glanced at his GPR. "I've got the same reading on mine. Time to dig."

"Wait," Becca said as she stared at the screen. "There's some sort of device between us and the rings. You guys see it on your GPRs?"

Red looked at his screen. He studied it for a few long seconds. "From their shapes, those look like two possible German-engineered charges, one on the left and one on the right side of your screen. The devices may be unstable. If we attempt to create an opening, the devices might blow. It's a crapshoot."

"So, we need a way to bypass the explosives without damaging the rings or having them spewed all over the mine shaft," Becca said. "Not to mention, we have to keep us safe."

"Becca," Cornell said in a stern, steady voice. "How certain are you these are the SS rings?"

"Ninety percent. The dimensions of the box and its location fit DIANA's calculations to a tee. Also, why would there be German explosives in front of the crate, if not to protect it from looters? Then there's the fact that the GPR shows a white-hot spot, which indicates a metallic substance inside."

Red turned to Cornell. "Your call, Boss. Are we digging or leaving? We could laser around each of the devices, keeping the triggers intact, and that would take no time at all. Then we laser out a larger opening to reach the crate."

"Do it," Cornell said. "Set up the trolley. We didn't come all this way for nothing."

They operated like clockwork. Becca and Cornell assembled a collapsible trolley, then helped Red cut out the two sections of wall that held each explosive device. They laid the devices on the ground a safe distance away from where they were working. Red lasered out more of the tunnel wall, making an opening large enough for them to access the crate. Once the wall section was removed, Becca, who stood closest to the opening, shined her flashlight into the hole. She smiled as she saw a large wooden crate with a swastika stamped on the side.

"Guys…" she said with a bit of triumph in her voice. "We found it."

Cornell stepped closer and shined his light on the crate. The black swastika, although smeared with dirt, was marked on the side of the box. "Open it."

Becca and Red each grabbed a crowbar. They pried the top off and placed it to the side. Becca shined her flashlight into the crate. The beam illuminated a faded, falling-apart, burlap-type material. She pinched the edge of the cloth, feeling the scratchy material disintegrate at her gentle touch.

Tarnished, silver, identical German rings filled the crate from top to bottom. Becca picked one up and studied it.

Cornell stared at a ring he'd picked up. He had a look of wonder on his face.

"It's identical to the one I have," Becca said as she pulled out her ring. She didn't try to contain her joy. "Grab a handful of rings to see if they're the same."

"You want us to look through these, right now?" Red asked.

"Just a few," Becca said. Her cheeks ached from smiling so much. "We'll look at the rest when we're out of the mine."

"There's at least a thousand of them here," Red said with wonder.

"There should be approximately eleven thousand five hundred." She didn't see the startled look on his face, as she was too busy staring at a date, 18.10.44, inscribed on the inner band of the ring next to Heinrich Himmler's signature. The layout on this ring used the European format for writing a date and was different from the one she had been given. On her ring, the year was in the wrong place. That had to mean something, but Becca was too excited to delve into it at the moment.

They grabbed a few handfuls of rings and sorted through them. Each one had all the runes on them in the right places and the date written in the European format.

"Let's get these babies back to headquarters where they can be scanned and sorted," Becca said.

"Nail the top back on the crate," Cornell ordered, "and we'll move it out." He typed a text on his phone. "I'm ordering the helicopter to pick this up outside." He sent the message, then helped Becca and Red.

After Becca finished nailing the top back on, Cornell and Red picked up the two-hundred-plus-pound crate and loaded it onto the trolley. Red laid his hammer and GPR on top as he moved to the back of the crate and prepared to push.

"Becca," Cornell said, "pull the handle. We'll push from the back."

Becca had trouble steering the unwieldy crate as they moved it out of the hole they'd created. The trolley hit the corner of the opening and shuddered as they continued to push the box into the mine shaft. Red's hammer and GPR slid off the top of the crate, bounced away from the trolley, and tumbled toward one of the old German charges they'd left against the wall. Every muscle in Becca's body tensed as fear encapsulated her. She skipped a breath while watching the GPR roll into the charge.

Cornell ran for the GPR but was too late. The GPR bumped the charge. They all froze. She feared this was the end of all her training and hard work over the past year, gone to waste, over this clumsy mistake.

Nothing happened.

"Shit." Becca stared at the charge.

"Hear any clicking?" Red asked.

"No," Cornell said, still stopped in his tracks.

"We have to move," Red said. "Now. That charge could blow any second."

"You're the expert," Cornell said. "Move!"

Becca pulled while Cornell and Red pushed the crate as hard and fast as they could. Her arms screamed with pain. Her legs tightened as she pulled the crate around the tunnel corner. She felt her quads spasm as she used all the power she could to move the crate faster.

"Keep going!" Red said.

Boom!

The blast thundered throughout the mine, sending clouds of rock-laden dust and shrapnel in every direction. Becca lost her footing and fell. She looked back and saw the mine begin to cave-in. She pulled herself up and went back to the front of the crate. "Come on!"

They all coughed while they regained control of the trolley.

"Push!" Red yelled.

As they made steady progress toward the entrance of the mine a loud rumble sounded, and the mine shook more violently than before.

"Move it!" Cornell shouted.

Becca put every ounce of strength into pulling.

The tunnel walls cracked and crumbled behind them as large rocks fell from the ceiling. It sounded like a massive wave of debris was bearing down on them. Becca didn't look back. They had little time to get out. She knew they must be close to the entrance, as the floor of the mine became an incline. Large chunks of the ceiling barely missed them as debris fell all around them.

The warmth of daylight hit Becca's skin just as the mine imploded behind her. They pulled the trolley out of the opening one second before the entrance filled with rocks, splintered beams, and dust.

They'd made it out alive. Just barely.

Becca, Cornell, and Red fell to the ground around the crate, exhausted. A large cloud of dust surrounded them, impairing their vision. Becca's heart pounded as she attempted to slow her breathing. The only thing she thought about was what RC would say to her when she got back. No congratulations for her completing the first real mission she'd been assigned. Knowing him, he'd hold the mine collapse over her for amusement. It didn't matter to her. As long as she got to see him again.

As the dust cleared, they looked at each other without saying a word. Cornell started to smile, then chuckle, and eventually laugh. Red joined in, as did Becca. It was tension-releasing laughter from the pure joy of being alive.

Cornell's laughing stopped abruptly as his upper body fell into his lap. A second later Red fell from a sitting position to his side. Blood ran down his neck.

"What the—" Becca looked around as the dust and debris from the cave-in had fully cleared and saw Hawk and Axel lying on the ground, dead. Becca grabbed her gun, got to her feet, and turned to see fifteen men pointing rifles at her. She didn't know who they were or how they'd found her and the team.

Then she saw him.

The man walking toward her, clearly their leader. The walk, the combat boots, the overly confident demeanor, and the cocky smile.

She'd know him anywhere. He was the last person she'd ever expected to see.

"RC?" She gasped.

His men wheeled the crate of rings to one of their trucks and loaded it into the back.

"What the hell are you doing?" she asked.

Becca watched Reed Alexander Carter, her protector, friend, and total pain in the ass, raise his gun, aim it at her, and fire.

Becca stood in disbelief and confusion. She felt a dull pain in her stomach. She looked at her hands, now covered in blood. Becca dropped to her knees and looked back to RC who continued to aim his weapon at her. She tried to muster the strength to speak, but no words came.

The sound of the helicopter Cornell had called for reached them. RC swiveled to watch it approaching in the distance.

A battle ensued, but Becca lost focus and clarity. Through blurry eyes, gripped with the pain and despair of betrayal, she saw the helicopter fly over and shoot at RC and his men.

The last thing Becca saw before she passed out was RC jumping into the back of the truck that carried the crate of rings and disappearing into the dust, leaving her to die in the sun.

4

Becca looked up at her best friend, Barry, who sat across from her at the small table in their favorite New York café. The daylight was unnaturally bright. Barry talked, but she couldn't hear a word he said. For some reason, he seemed muted. Everything moved eerily slow for Becca. Barry poured ketchup on his scrambled eggs. Lots of ketchup. She knew what was going to happen and tried to warn him, but no response came from Barry as he continued to draw something in slow motion. He turned the plate around, and Becca saw the word *run* on top of his eggs.

Boom!

The café exploded, followed by a bright light that enveloped Barry in a white oblivion.

Becca jolted awake, unaware of her surroundings. The bright ceiling lights shined in her eyes. She needed to focus, and it took much longer than she expected. Machines beeped and clicked. Pain radiated from her abdomen. Her hands went to her stomach, and she felt a thick layer of bandages. She looked down and saw an IV attached to her hand and realized she was in a Griffin hospital.

Then everything flooded back to her.

RC, the man she had trusted most in this world, shot her

without hesitation. After all they'd been through, how could he have done that to her? She remembered the cold look in his eyes and wondered how he could have done such a thing. Her heart sank.

A nurse came into the room and saw she was awake. "Good! You're up," she said in a cheery voice.

Becca had no tolerance for cheeriness. Pain overwhelmed her. Anger rushed through her, cleansing away thoughts of momentary depression.

"RC," Becca said as the reality of her situation sunk in. "It was RC!"

"Take it easy, Ms. Romanov. How are you feeling?" the nurse asked as she put a hand on Becca's shoulder.

"Where is he?" Becca was so focused on her pain and RC's betrayal that she didn't hear the nurse. "Why did he do this to me? What the hell happened?"

The nurse smiled. "The EMTs reached you just in time. They saved your life. You'd lost a lot of blood, but luckily, the bullet missed your vital organs." The nurse checked Becca's vitals on a hologram monitor. "You were very lucky."

Becca's mother, Vivian Lake Romanov, rushed into the room. "I was notified as soon as I landed and came straight here."

"Seeing her mother brought Becca to tears. She let out all her sadness, fear, and relief knowing she was there to comfort her. Becca's stomach burned with excruciating pain. She shifted, letting out a guttural moan.

The nurse held up a little device with a button on it and handed it to Becca. "Push this button to administer a dose of morphine. Don't worry, you won't get addicted. The Griffin machine has been calibrated not to let you take more than you should."

A tall woman in a white coat entered the room. "Good morning, Becca. I'm Dr. Anita Russo. How are you feeling?" Dr. Russo took Becca's pulse, read the monitors behind her, and checked her chart.

"Pissed off," Becca said as she shifted in bed.

Dr. Russo grinned. "Between one and ten, how bad is the pain?"

"Nine."

"That will lessen in an hour or two," Dr. Russo said as she wrote on Becca's chart. "I gave you a new version of our expedited-recovery serum."

"The Griffins modified it recently," Vivian said. "It's safe. I should know, a previous version had been administered to me before. You'll be all healed in about a week." Vivian smiled at Becca.

"By this evening your pain level will have dropped to one or two," Dr. Russo explained."Tomorrow, you'll be up and walking the halls. You'll see a miraculous recovery each day after."

"Awesome. Thanks, Doc." This news brightened Becca's mood a bit.

Dr. Russo nodded and left the room.

Vivian turned to Becca. "Are you sure it was RC?"

"I'll never forget the look in his eyes before he pulled the trigger."

"Did you speak with anyone before you went on the mission? See anything out of the ordinary? Something that might have compromised the squad?"

"No. Nothing." Becca realized her mother was debriefing her. "Are you asking me as my mom or my superior?"

The look in Vivian's eyes told Becca she was acting as her superior for the moment. "Why would Mason have you debrief me?"

"Because I'm your mother."

As annoying as it was, Becca was glad her mother was assigned to debrief her, considering she was the only one she felt she could trust at the moment.

"Becca," Vivian said in a calm and understanding tone, "you're the only one who survived. If RC did this, then that's a major breach of our entire organization."

"You don't believe me?" Becca pushed up on her elbows, wincing through the pain as she leaned as far forward as she could. "Why would I lie about something like this?" Her blood boiled at the thought that her own mother didn't believe her. She never expected she'd have to deal with such a heinous betrayal from RC. "He was the only person I recognized. I don't know how he found me. I hadn't heard from him in months, and he shot me and left me to die."

"Okay." Vivian grabbed Becca's hand. "I'll talk to Mason." Vivian helped Becca lay back down. "We'll figure out the next steps after you've rested and the serum has taken effect."

Vivian ran her hand through Becca's hair, as she used to when Becca was a little girl.

Becca felt the morphine kick in and drifted into a deep sleep.

During her recovery, Vivian came back every morning for a week and brought Becca coffee and a cheese Danish. Her abdomen had healed, just as Dr. Russo had said. She couldn't believe how much better she felt. Becca still had bouts of tiredness and a lot of down moments thinking about RC.

She began physical therapy three times a week. Her core muscles needed to be strengthened. The physical-therapy sessions were brutal. Becca's therapist, Maria, worked her hard. That, too, cleared her mind from dwelling on the reason for her injury. Pelvic tilts, supported leg extensions, inside and outside thigh lifts, and other torturous exercises, all reminded her of how far she still had to go. Her muscles ached, but she always felt stronger after the sessions. Becca was determined to get back to complete physical and mental health. As each day got better, Becca's mood lightened, and she began to feel like her old self again.

She went to the gym three times a day. Maybe it was overkill, but she had to block out the memory of when she'd been shot. Whenever the memory came to her, unannounced and unwanted, her gut would turn. But exercise gave her focus. She had no appetite for any kind of betrayal and was determined to find RC and confront him.

The grief she felt from the loss of the team seemed endless too. Becca hadn't known those guys long, but they were good people and great Griffins. Their skill had been something to watch, learn from, and admire. So she relentlessly worked out on the machines, ran the free-running obstacle course, and went to the armory to work with ancient weapons, her favorite thing to do. Tossing throwing stars at a target helped her hand-eye coordination and was one of the more difficult skills she had to perfect. Shooting a crossbow at targets was her absolute favorite. It came easily to her, and she always practiced with the crossbow at the end of her workouts.

While Becca recuperated, Brady assigned her to research other missions. Normally, she loved doing the research, but instead, she'd rather locate RC. She used what knowledge she'd discovered from the assigned research missions to conduct her own investigation into RC's last reported movements as she sat in her quarters.

Unfortunately, RC's trail had gone ice cold six months ago. His last reported mission was classified, and Becca hadn't figured out how to bypass the restriction level. She wasn't going to go to Brady or her mother about it, because she knew they wouldn't help her. She was too close to RC and the Griffins never condoned grudge missions. Becca needed peace of mind, and she wouldn't stop until she got her answers. She figured Mason would know, but it was practically impossible to get a meeting with him. You didn't go to Mason Carter. He came to you.

She had sent off her most recent assignment to Brady and now had a little free time. Becca decided to see if she could find any more information about Antonio Herrero, the man who'd given her the ring, and how he'd acquired it.

Becca heard a knock at her door.

"You decent?" her mom asked.

Becca waved her hand, and all the holographic research disappeared. "Yes. Come on in."

Vivian entered wearing a beautiful navy, long-sleeved wrap dress. "You ready?"

Confused by her mother's attire, Becca asked, "Ready for what?"

"You have a press briefing for the Hunger Relief Program charity in an hour."

Becca had completely forgotten. She'd been so focused on her research, she had neglected her Romanov responsibilities.

"Get dressed. We've got to get going," her mother said when she saw the look on Becca's face.

Ever since it had been discovered that Becca and her mom were Romanov descendants, they'd set up a nonprofit organization to raise money for Russian children who lived on the streets and had no way to get food. It was a great cover operation to conceal what Becca and Vivian really did and raised money for a good cause. It was also extremely boring.

Becca searched her closet to find the right dress for the occasion. She chose a midcalf, sapphire-blue, figure-hugging dress that was classic and simple, yet elegant. Sapphire stud earrings complemented the dress. Matching stilettos elongated her legs. Minimal makeup and a natural hairstyle finished off the look. She knew she looked good and wondered why she didn't care.

Maybe it was the aftermath of the shooting. She still hadn't shaken the fact that RC had shot her. So why did she wish RC was here to see her all dressed up? Why, in the back of her mind and heart, did she hope RC would show up?

Right now, there was no way she could answer that question, and not knowing if she would ever be able to scared her.

5

The Grand Bridge Hotel, close to Heidelberg, was noted for its swanky conferences, auctions, weddings, and other high-profile events. Situated along the River Neckar, famous for its four-star catering team, as well as its extremely professional and discreet staff, the hotel had a one-year waiting list to book one of its six venues. Celebrities from around the world stayed at this hotel because their privacy was never violated.

Becca stood with her mother and two Griffin security men backstage and surveyed the room from the wings. High, ornate ceilings were topped with gilded wallpaper. Black, round-backed, leather, cushioned chairs were arranged in five rows of ten across a highly polished parquet floor. Members of the press settled in their seats and prepared their cameras for Becca's report about the current state of her charity.

The GSD, Griffin Security Division, had chosen this hotel because of its many potential exit routes in case of an attack. This conference room had four exits and backed up to the employee hallway, which led to all areas of the hotel.

As Becca surveyed the room, she wasn't sure if she had butterflies in her stomach or a bit of pain from where she'd been shot. She still dealt with the remnants of healing. Even though the wound was healed, she'd occasionally have twinges of tenderness and soreness.

Becca had never been afraid of public speaking. Her nerves came from the unknown and always seemed to manifest in places she'd been wounded. She pushed the apprehension aside. Her training had taught her to face the unknown with calm and a practiced eye— never waver, don't back down. It wasn't easy to cope with, as every time she went out in public there was a chance the Brotherhood would try to kill her. It had been her new normal for a year, and although she was prepared for it, she never thought she'd get used to it.

"You're fine," her mother said with a confident nod. "We're right here."

Becca trusted no one more than her mother and her twenty-two years as a highly trained Griffin. She was glad her mother had been put in charge of her security detail during all of these "Romanov events." Since the funeral of Brittany's grandfather and the murder at the gathering, no event was safe.

"Thank you." Becca held her abdomen.

"Come on, let's get this Romanov stuff over with," Vivian said.

Becca turned to the event planner who stood nearby. "Everything looks great." She put on her Romanov persona. "This venue is so beautiful."

The event planner glanced at her watch. "They're ready for you, Ms. Romanov."

As Becca stepped onto the stage and made her way to her mark, she heard the murmuring of the press quiet down as they readied their recorders. Her mother and bodyguards stood behind her as she stepped up to the podium.

Becca spoke in fluent German. "Good afternoon, ladies and gentlemen. Thank you for coming to the briefing for the Romanov Relief Program," Becca said reading from the transparent prompter. "Today, I'll be updating you on the charity's progress and plans for the rest of the year. To date, the Romanov Relief Program, along with its partner charities, has fed two million children, found them housing, provided free medical services, and enrolled them in educational programs." The members of the press clapped in approval. "The Russian children range from six to fifteen years old. Since this is only the first year for the program, we look forward to compiling the results of our successes in the future and releasing them to the public. The rest of the year we plan to—"

The words on the teleprompter flickered away and were replaced by a black symbol of a fox head.

Becca froze. Her heart raced, and the pain in her abdomen throbbed, as fear filled her body. For a second, she saw Barry in front of her at the café having just drawn the word *run* with ketchup on his eggs. Becca's hands shook, and her eyes went wide as she looked at the evil emblem on the teleprompter.

Becca heard her mother's voice in her earpiece. "We have a silver breach."

Without drawing too much attention, the bodyguards stepped closer to Becca and created a circle of protection around her.

Becca looked at the crowd knowing she had to wrap this up. "The rest of the details can be found on the charity's website, theromanovreliefprogram.com. Thank you very much for coming." She gave a wide, professional smile before turning to leave the podium.

A murmur of confusion rose from the reporters who were startled at the abrupt ending.

Vivian, the bodyguards, and Becca all moved into the wings of the stage. Vivian spoke urgently into the coms: "Protocol four-five-eight."

Becca couldn't believe she had to be escorted out of another event due to a threat. Her bodyguards formed a line with her and her mother in the middle. The four stood for the four-person team, the five was the route number to take for extraction, and the eight was the exit door they were to use when leaving the hotel. There were sixteen exits, and eight was the closest.

The first guard held his weapon in front of him. Becca put her hand on the back of his shoulder to let him know she was there. Her mother put her hand on Becca's shoulder. The last guard lined up behind Vivian, his hand on her shoulder. All weapons, including Becca's, were held at the ready.

Vivian tapped Becca's shoulder, giving her the signal to move forward.

The four of them proceeded like a caterpillar, slow and cautious, through the employee hallway that led to the employees' entrance of the hotel, which was exit eight. All of them scanned the area for enemies.

As the team proceeded to the exit ahead, Becca heard some employees coming toward them from their right. The Griffin leading the team held up his hand, then closed it into a fist to inform the team to hold. They stopped just before the hallway crossed with another. Two female employees came from the right, but they were so focused on something on one of the girls' phones that they walked straight past the team without seeing them. Once they were clear, the team headed for the exit.

As they left the building, one team member covered the north side of the employee parking lot, the other covered the south. An SUV pulled up in a hurry. Vivian opened the rear passenger door, and Becca safely entered. As soon as Becca was inside, Vivian and the rest of the team climbed in, and the car sped away.

Not knowing if they were being hunted or tracked, Becca and the team wiped all the data from their phones and tossed them out the windows. A trail of useless electronics littered the side of the road.

They were nearly to Autobahn 656 when Vivian shouted, "Brace yourselves!"

Becca caught a glimpse out the left rear window, just in time to see an all-black Camaro with a vicious-looking ram grate slam into the rear fender of the SUV. Their car spun rapidly.

Luckily, their driver regained control and floored it. Becca looked back and saw the Camaro resume its pursuit.

The team members lowered their bulletproof windows just enough to shoot at the car as it approached. The Camaro had some sort of souped-up engine and roared closer to their rear.

Becca and team fired on the Camaro, but the bullets just bounced off its armor-plated exterior.

The Camaro slammed into the back of the SUV, causing it to swerve.

Becca grabbed the handhold over the window with a tight grip while trying to get a good aim at the tires with the gun in her other hand.

"I have no shot," Becca said, waiting for an opportunity to present itself.

"Their armor is impenetrable," Vivian responded. "Even the tires are protected." She reloaded her weapon after grabbing another magazine of bullets from inside the center armrest. "We have to lose them a different way."

The SUV roared past at eighty miles an hour on the narrow road, swerving in and out of other cars. The Camaro plowed through a few of them, not afraid of using its ram cage.

"I've got an idea," the driver said.

The SUV continued to swerve through cars, passing them at a rapid speed. It eventually made its way to an opening and changed lanes, allowing the Camaro to come up on the left next to them.

Becca realized what the driver intended to do—he was going to use the SUV as bait for the Camaro.

The Camaro raced up to the SUV, and as soon as it was along the left rear of their car, the driver made his move.

"Hold on!" He slammed on the brakes.

Becca and the others braced themselves as the SUV screeched, allowing the Camaro to get ahead of them. Then the driver swerved the SUV into the right rear fender of the Camaro, using a classic PIT maneuver and causing the car to spin into oncoming traffic.

Becca watched the Camaro get trampled by three cars and burst into flames.

The SUV continued onto the ramp of Autobahn 656. No other threats were in sight as they drove away from the accident hoping they were safe for the time being.

6

The tech building at Griffin headquarters in Germany, also known as Tech Central, was on the other side of the compound. Becca strolled the park-like grounds and listened to the birds singing as she walked to the building. She found the sounds soothing after her recent close call with the Brotherhood. She took in the beautiful orange sunset for a moment, allowing her body and mind to relax. Narrowly escaping frequent attempts on her life by the Brotherhood didn't make it any easier to breathe. All she could do to distract herself was keep focused on the task at hand—replacing her phone.

Each time Becca entered Tech Central she was awed at the scope and size of the building. The large airplane-style hangar took up over an acre of land. The building was made from graphene, the strongest material in the world. Testing proved graphene to be very effective, and the Griffins decided to use it for their other headquarters around the world.

The door Becca entered through seemed tiny compared to the scope of the hangar. Bright lights illuminated the cavernous room. Electrical, mechanical, chemical, and geotechnical engineers filled the space, along with hundreds of men and women who worked in the subcategories to those fields. It was like walking into a small city.

She approached a human-looking robot and put her right wrist under a light.

Scanning, the robot said. *Welcome, Rebecca Hunter Lake Romanov. My name is Manny. What can I help you with?*

"I need to replace my phone."

CTL division, aisle thirty, row fifteen, workstation twenty-seven. Manny brought up a map on his "face," a screen that had the route to her destination highlighted in bright orange. A big, red dot and the words, *you are here*, pointed the way. *The technician is waiting for you.*

The door clicked and slid open. The noise level in the cavernous room was amazingly low considering how many people worked in it.

Becca walked past everything a person could want or need. Each area was separated by five-foot walls but had no front or back panels to block the workers or members of the organization from entering or leaving each cubicle.

She passed a large area with guns, rifles, rocket launchers, and more advanced equipment she couldn't identify. Becca was sure that what looked like scrap pieces were converted by the engineers into the most ingenious items.

Tech Central had a separate building where vehicles were bulletproofed, souped up, loaded with the most advanced equipment and weapons, and supplied with the highest technological communications used anywhere in the world. The official name was the Vehicle Improvement Division or VID. New stealth technological advances were being developed for human, weapon, and vehicle trials. The world's governments and militaries didn't even have these items and wouldn't get them for another ten years.

Becca passed the exit to VID on her way to get her phone.

One of the things she liked most was that Tech Central took

ancient weapons and modernized them for field use. Becca saw weapons engineers testing grenade bolts in a three-person shooting range. The bolt had been modified to travel four times the distance of a normal crossbow bolt, and once it penetrated its enemy, the bolt could be detonated and used to kill other surrounding combatants and destroy structures.

Becca continued past the weapons-testing area and saw engineers teaching field agents how to use the latest model of the G-Shuriken, also known as the Griffin throwing star. Much like its predecessor, G-Shurikens were made from a highly secret metal that was strong and sharp but were modified with hidden compartments that housed a sticky, poisonous substance inside the pointed ends. The poison could be remotely activated into the bloodstream of the enemy, if needed. Once the stars were embedded in a person they had to be surgically removed. The star also had a remote responder built in that allowed it to be recalled to its user. Becca liked to call it the "boomerang" feature.

She walked underneath a sign that said CTL, short for Cells, Tablets, and Laptops. Every item came in a variety of sizes and colors. Small enough to hold in your hand, there were also big mainframe computers that lined a large room. All were powerful and connected to the Griffin satellites that circled the globe, allowing every tech item to work anywhere in the world.

Becca entered the large cubicle, labeled Workstation Twenty-Seven, and saw a pretty Asian woman who looked as if she was sixteen but was probably in her early twenties. She wore a wild print T-shirt and cropped pants with the same colors but different patterns. She wore a bright-yellow scarf tied around her ponytail. Dark, straight bangs covered her forehead, and she wore rings on the first finger of each hand, as well as her thumbs.

There were six monitors at her workstation. All were on, and even though the woman wore headphones and played a video game, she frequently turned to the other monitors and plugged in information. Then she'd go back to her game. From the numbers Becca saw on the game, the woman was winning.

Becca watched the woman multitasking with fascination. Then she said, "Hello."

The woman didn't answer. There was a strange object with a button on the counter and a handwritten note next to it that said, *Push me.* Becca pressed the button, and a vibration sounded near the woman, who jumped out of the chair.

When the woman saw Becca, she said, "OMG! It's really you." The woman pushed some files on her desk from one place to another, then put them back in their original place.

Becca could tell the technician had recognized her and was nervous. Becca smiled, unsure of how to handle the situation.

"I'm Cassie Lee. I didn't see your name come up on my screen notifying me that you'd arrived. I'm a really big fan, Ms. Romanov." Cassie rushed through her sentences. She couldn't quite look Becca in the eyes. "I've followed you since the Royal Danish Egg op. I can't tell you how impressed I am with what you did. Oh, gosh! I can't believe you're here at my workstation and caught me playing a video game. Don't tell anybody. I really like my job."

Becca smiled. "Please, call me Becca."

Cassie had a bright, beautiful smile. "I can't believe I can call you Becca." Then her hand flew to her mouth. "Oops. I didn't mean to say that out loud."

Becca laughed. "All my friends call me Becca."

Cassie's eyes widened with pleasure before she turned to read the notification on her computer screen. "Manny says you need a new cell phone."

"Yes. I had to ditch mine out the window earlier today."

"If I had a dollar for every member that said that to me. Let me just access your file, then I can download everything from your previous phone onto a new phone of your choosing." Cassie's fingers worked lightning fast on the keyboard as she pulled up

Becca's profile. "That way you won't have to do it yourself. Plus, it's a much quicker download time."

"Love that, Cassie."

"Let's go down to this table, and I'll run you through your options."

Becca followed Cassie to a display case of different phones. "Do you want an Apple-style phone or a Samsung-style one?"

"I'm used to the Apple-style phones."

"No problem," Cassie said as she pulled out twenty phones of multiple colors and sizes from the table. "All your standard requirements, DIANA 15.8 upgrade, eighteen terabyte hard drive; the thirty-two terabytes won't be available for another six months. With 12G signal, night vision, and thermal-imaging cameras. Facial-recognition software, GPS, yada, yada, yah."

Becca was overwhelmed with color options but chose a metallic, midnight-blue color. "

"Hey, a non-pink lover." Cassie grabbed the phone and went to one of her computers. "That's why you're a badass, Becca Romanov." She plugged the phone in and began downloading Becca's info. "Should take about five minutes and twenty-eight seconds."

Cassie reminded Becca of Barry. He'd had the same fascination and enthusiasm for anything electronic. Except Cassie was more socially awkward.

Becca looked at all the unusual items on Cassie's desk. She had no idea what anything was. Becca figured creating new, unheard-of devices and applications was Cassie's safe space.

Becca picked up an oval object with scored lines on it. "What's this, Cassie?"

"It's a supersonic sound stunner built into a belt buckle. Aim that baby at the enemy, and they'll drop to their knees with excruciating pain in their ears."

"And what's this?" Becca asked as she picked up an item that looked like a flat rectangle.

"It's an infinity battery. It never runs out. I'm still trying to get it to be compatible with different tech. Say goodbye to the days of charging."

A notification beeped on one of Cassie's screens. She turned to read it. "Crap!"

"What's the matter?"

"Oh, I'm working on this new software app, and it's not doing what I need it to do." Cassie moved between two monitors typing furiously to input data.

"What's it supposed to do?" Becca was amazed at how fast Cassie could move between the computers.

"It's an algorithm that's meant to narrow down the radius of a missing operative to one mile after their tracker has been removed or deactivated. Leave-no-one-behind kind of thing."

"That's ingenious," Becca said with respect for Cassie's intelligence.

"Problem is, the app does way more than that. It's become a privacy invasion on the world, able to bypass all firewalls and be completely undetectable. Let's say you want to find your parents or your friend. I'm able to input their info into the algorithm, then it hacks me into the last known camera that person used. Say their phone or laptop. I can pinpoint street cameras and access where they may be within a mile radius, find them and all their private information." Cassie leaned back in her chair, frustrated. "It's the ultimate invasion of privacy and not at all protective. I can access their bank accounts, secrets, web history, and even calculate what their next meal will likely be. So, I haven't figured out how to keep their privacy protected and make the software focused on just missing operatives. Once I crack that, then it will most likely be uploaded as an update to DIANA."

"What else do you need to do to fix it?" Becca asked.

"I need to beta test it in the field, but it's too dangerous to let out."

"Why can't you beta test it yourself?"

"I know how to use it. So, I need to see how others would use it to fix the kinks."

Becca thought for a moment. "I'll beta test it for you. Can you add it to my phone?"

Cassie hesitated. "You serious? I mean, really? Wow. Ummm. No, I can't. I shouldn't. I really need the data, but if you're caught, and someone steals it, you can say goodbye to the world's economy and hello to some prison that makes hell look like Hawaii." Cassie stood up and paced back and forth.

"I'm still willing to give it a shot," Becca said. "In order to make progress, one has to take risks."

Cassie stopped pacing and faced Becca with a smile. "I knew you were cool. Okay, I'll let you do a trial run for three days. No hacking into bank accounts or stealing personal information to sell to some terrorist organization. In three days, I'll remotely delete the app from your phone."

"Works for me."

Cassie's fingers came to life on her multiple keyboards as she installed the app on Becca's new phone.

"What's that symbol? An eye?" Becca asked while looking at the app icon.

"Yes. It's a griffin's eye. My own design. Meant to be a protective eye on the world."

"Love it," Becca said as she held up her phone and waved it to Cassie. "Our little secret."

Cassie nodded.

Becca left Cassie's workstation and began the long walk back to the entrance of Tech Central.

She had absolutely no intention of using the Eye to hack into random people's private information, steal money, or spy on them. She had every intention of using it for one purpose and one purpose only: to find RC and make him answer for what he had done to her.

7

Becca jolted awake in the middle of the night. Her hand flew to her chest as her heart pounded. Sweat lined her face and the back of her neck. She struggled to slow her breathing and fully wake up from her nightmare. She saw Barry, and behind him, something moved in the shadows. The movement came closer and prowled into the light. Not one, not two, but an entire skulk of foxes surrounded Barry and took him into darkness. All that was left behind was the symbol of the fox head. She couldn't escape the terror of the Brotherhood. Nights like this made her wish she'd never learned about the League of Griffins and the Brotherhood of the Fox.

She wondered how the teleprompter at the charity had been hacked. Proof, again, that nothing was safe, no matter how hard she and the Griffins tried to keep it so.

Wide awake, Becca went to her kitchen to make a soothing cup of chamomile tea. While it steeped, she splashed cold water on her face to wash away the rest of the nightmare. She took the cup back to bed and put it on the nightstand, then opened her laptop. Plumping up the pillows behind her, she positioned the computer on her lap and took a sip of tea.

Her mind turned to RC. How could she find him? She had no

idea what could give her a clue without knowing anything about his last assignment.

She opened Cassie's new app. A holographic 3D interactive globe hovered above Becca's phone. An eye icon appeared at the bottom left of the projection. She tapped the icon to display a window of options. It was a high-tech search engine. A wireframe surrounded the hovering globe with letters connected to different strands. One was CIA, another Interpol, and every other worldwide government network you could imagine. The main strand was the "search all" option. She tapped that, and a new menu appeared. She typed in "Reed Alexander Carter," RC's full name. Once she pressed enter, the globe spun and zoomed in on Germany. The hologram continued to zoom in until a satellite image of RC and the truck he had jumped into when he'd shot her appeared. The words *Last Known Whereabouts* were visible beneath the image of RC.

"That doesn't help," Becca muttered.

A widget appeared with a *Use Algorithm* button. Becca pressed the holographic button and watched the app calculate a one-mile radius of a likely recent location for RC. This took a little bit of time as the app worked its magic. While the app searched for RC it made a 3D model of his facial features. Once the 3D rendering of his face had finished, the search stopped at an office building that was for sale near an urban area of Wiesbaden, Germany, about an hour from Heidelberg. A bunch of red and green dots filled a one-mile radius. Red was audio and green was video. Becca zoomed in and pressed a green dot.

All the video feeds from street cameras, ATMs, cell phones, and tablets popped up as separate windows at the same time. Becca jumped, startled, as all the audio feeds went live for each video, creating a cacophony of noise.

"Mute," Becca said while covering her ears.

The audio disappeared, and the videos continued to play. She was amazed as she watched real-time feeds of people and understood Cassie's warning of how dangerous this app could be.

Each video feed showed the person's basic information, home address, phone, Social Security number, and all accounts along with how much money was in each one. She could access their photos, videos, social media, everything.

The neat thing about the app was it highlighted all the tech within each video feed. All Becca had to do was tap whatever highlighted piece of tech was in the frame, and she would be able to hack that device and gain a new perspective on the area she was searching.

Becca tapped onto different devices in the video feeds to see what perspective they gave. It was truly an impressive feat of engineering. Becca could spy on an unsuspecting public by hacking into any device that had a camera and see everything going on around them. She watched a woman reading a recipe from her tablet as she cooked the dish in her kitchen. Becca tapped on another video feed. This time, it was a teenager sitting on her bed by a window doing her homework. The Eye scanned the frame and located a bunch of cell phones of people at the street level going about their day. She chose another random person's phone, a woman, who was FaceTiming her boyfriend while walking on the sidewalk. The woman stopped to cross the street and an out-of-focus reflection caught Becca's eye.

Becca froze the frame so she could enlarge the image. It was a blurry profile of a man Becca partially recognized. The app scanned the image and filled in a wireframe sketch of the man. It showed a 75 percent probability that matched RC. Becca opened other feeds in the nearby area to try to find a clearer image of him.

The first video she jumped into was from a street camera. Becca hoped to get a wide angle of the man from the front, but he moved too fast, and all she saw was his left shoulder as he rounded a corner. Then she jumped to a security camera from a dress shop. The camera pointed straight out the window, and as the man walked by, he didn't look into the window. Becca only saw his right side from head to toe. The next camera aimed from a building across the intersection and, luckily, he had to stop for traffic. She finally got a glimpse of his face. Becca froze the frame and zoomed in.

"Gotcha," Becca said with anger toward RC.

With renewed enthusiasm she tapped the devices in the crowd of people near RC, searching for his cell phone. Nothing came up on his person or in his hands that she could hack.

"Damn you."

The freeze-frames Becca had taken to identify RC still hovered off to the side of the active video-feed window. Suddenly, all the freeze-frames pulsed like a notification. She focused on the new type of notification as the algorithm highlighted a man in the distance behind RC. The same man appeared in each freeze-frame, making it look as if he was following RC. The Eye scanned the man and showed Becca that he wore an earwig. A small body camera was hidden on the lapel of his coat. Becca tapped both the earwig and the body camera and watched a new video and audio feed appear in front of her.

"Target appears to be heading to the building on the northwest corner," the man said into the earwig.

"Proceed with caution, Hawk team," another voice responded.

Becca knew that voice. It was Mason Carter, RC's father and the head of the League of Griffins, instructing the man following RC.

Becca sat up on her bed, realizing she'd just hacked into a highly classified Griffin operation. The fact that Mason was involved told Becca something big was going to happen.

Becca read all the basic information on the Griffin following RC from the heads-up display that surrounded the frame. *Randall King, Griffin ID: G122645223, Tier 4, Claw. Hawk team leader. Two kids, Stephanie, ten years old; Janae, eight years old. Married to Allison King for twelve years.* Becca didn't finish reading the rest.

"Eagle team has eyes on the target. Moving in," another voice said.

The fact that two teams were following RC indicated there was way more going on with RC than she had originally imagined. She tapped Randall King's audio device again. The Eye app did its thing, and the Griffins' base-of-operations video feed appeared. She saw Mason and a few others monitoring the mission in real time. She had just hacked into her own organization's base of operations by accident. No one knew Becca was watching, and they didn't know she could hear them. She closed out all the other windows and left only the body-cam feed of Randall King and the Griffin base.

Becca watched on the hologram as RC entered the building.

"Target now inside, heading up the elevator. Elevator stopping at seventeenth floor," a member of Eagle team reported.

Becca watched the thermal image of RC as he exited the elevator.

"Where are you going, RC?" Becca muttered. She didn't like this at all. Her mind couldn't calculate any logical reason why he was there.

"Let's try and avoid unnecessary casualties and bring my son in as quietly as possible," Mason said.

"Copy that, sir," both teams responded.

"Hawk team, move in," Mason ordered. "Eagle team, cover the rear exit. Prepare to enter."

Becca watched Eagle team position themselves at the back entrance while Hawk team readied themselves at the front. Five men on each team had surrounded the building with RC inside.

"Operation is a go," Mason said with a more concerned tone than Becca had ever heard.

With raised weapons, the teams made their way to the seventeenth floor.

In the left popup window, Becca watched Mason pace back and forth in the communications room. His men took remote control of the electronics in the building. They froze the elevators on the seventeenth floor, and both Hawk and Eagle teams used motorized ascenders to rapidly scale two different elevator shafts to reach the sixteenth floor. Then the two teams went to opposing stairways and made their way to the hallway on the floor above to box in RC. They lined up against a wall of the business RC had entered.

"Hawk team in position," Randall whispered.

"Eagle team in position," the other leader responded.

"Move in," Randall commanded.

All the lights in the building went dark, and both teams entered through their designated doors, moving quickly toward RC. There was no way he'd be able to escape. He was surrounded.

Becca adjusted the video feed so she could see everything happening clearly with thermal vision. RC leaned against a conference table, unfazed by the power outage.

"Hey, fellas," RC said to both teams as they entered the conference room.

Suddenly, a bunch of heat signatures appeared on Becca's screen. Two, then five, then twelve. All had strangely shaped heads.

Gunfire filled the audio feeds. Broken German words were shouted as Becca watched both Griffin teams topple to the ground. She jolted at the sounds of horror and leaned closer to the video feeds, covering her mouth in shock.

"What the hell just happened?" Mason shouted at one of his tech guys.

"We've lost control of the building," the man replied.

The lights turned back on in the conference room, and RC stood with twelve other men, all dressed differently, each wearing a pure white fox mask. Every one of them had been invisible to the Griffin radar, even Cassie's Eye app.

Becca watched in horror as RC walked over some dead bodies to Randal King, who struggled to breathe. His armored clothing had been penetrated by whatever bullets were used by the Brotherhood.

RC bent down over Randall and looked into his eyes, not at him but at everyone who was watching through his eye-lens video feed.

RC's image froze, and a low-battery symbol appeared.

"Shit!" Becca shouted louder than she realized. Cassie's app had eaten up all the battery on her phone. Becca quickly grabbed her laptop and typed in Randall King's Griffin ID to access the feed once more. The image of RC reappeared. It didn't seem as if RC had said anything.

Becca continued to watch, completely stunned. A man dressed like a janitor wearing a fox mask walked up to RC and put his hand on his shoulder, showing how proud he was of him. He spoke to RC in German. Becca translated it in her head: "Welcome, brother." He handed RC a pure white fox mask.

RC donned the mask of the enemy and aimed the gun at Randall King, who lay helpless on the conference-room floor.

Bang!

The video feed went dark, and the words *No Signal* appeared on the screen.

8

Becca sat on her bed in shock. Only one word repeated itself over and over in her mind: *why?* She couldn't fathom any reason for RC to kill the two Griffin teams.

Her apartment door slammed open, startling her, as men flooded her bedroom. Bright lights blinded her, and she put her hands in front of her eyes.

"Shut down the computer! Now!" one man shouted.

Becca slammed the cover shut as men wearing bulletproof vests swarmed her apartment, ripping open doors and drawers.

"Stand up! Hands in the air," the man ordered. Becca jumped out of bed and complied.

"What the hell is this?" she asked, unable to see past the lights in her eyes. Her heart pounded with fear.

"Do not move!" The man pulled her arms down and zip-tied them behind her back. Then he pushed her into her desk chair. "Suspect in custody."

"Suspect? Suspect for what?"

Two Griffin squad members pulled her up from her chair and shoved her out of her room. She struggled and caught a glimpse of one squad member as he commandeered her laptop and phone. She overheard his report: "Yes, sir. We've found the device."

Becca's heart raced. Device? Oh, no. Her laptop. They'd traced her laptop signal and knew she had hacked the video feed of the recent catastrophic mission.

The Griffins roughly shoved Becca out of her apartment and into a midsized vehicle. They drove her to the main headquarters where she was placed in a fully paneled room with one chair in the center and no windows. Two Griffins shoved her into the chair, cut the zip ties from her wrists, and exited the room, slamming the door behind them. As Becca rubbed her wrists, she looked around the interrogation room. There were no light fixtures. The light that illuminated the room came from within the ceiling panels. The floor had the same panels. They were hard as cement to walk on as Becca paced the room. She touched a wall panel, and when she looked closer, she saw filaments running through the panels like circuitry on a motherboard.

"Your computer was pinged," a voice said from behind, startling her.

Becca turned and saw a full-body projection of Mason Carter standing in the middle of the room. Different ceiling and floor panels illuminated as Mason's hologram paced around the room he was in as he talked to Becca.

"A tech operative working the mission found an unauthorized computer had accessed our audiovisual feed. The technician followed the ping back to you. What I don't understand is, of the few people qualified to gain access to that private feed..." Mason's hologram pointed at Becca, "somehow you managed to do it." Mason walked around the room as if he was in it.

"I wasn't trying to hack any feed." Becca moved closer to the hologram and was impressed by how lifelike he seemed. "I swear."

"Then how the hell did you get in? If there's a flaw in our system it needs to be fixed immediately."

Becca leaned away from the hologram. She had never heard Mason this close to shouting.

"I was doing an unsanctioned beta test of a new app that's meant to be part of a future upgrade for DIANA," she explained as she walked around the hologram. "It's being developed by one of the techies, and I thought I'd give it a try to locate RC."

"You just compromised our entire security system with your careless beta test, Becca. You let emotions drive your decisions."

"The app did find RC." She stepped back from the hologram and studied Mason's face. The clarity of his image showed just how ticked off he was. "I had no idea I'd accidentally eavesdrop on a live op."

"I have people checking out the system now to make sure the Brotherhood didn't hack your signal to access our secrets," Mason said.

Becca didn't answer for a few seconds. "It seems the Brotherhood doesn't need me to give away our secrets. All they need to do is ask RC."

Mason's eyes narrowed, his lips thinned, and his face paled. Becca thought she saw grief in those eyes, despair on his face. But it didn't last long, and she wasn't even sure it had happened.

Mason didn't back down. "Even so, your signal could have led them here to this compound." His hologram stepped closer. Becca stepped back, feeling cornered, even though Mason wasn't in the room. "You've opened us up to discovery. The German facility isn't secure anymore."

In hindsight, she'd blundered, badly. Before she could apologize, Mason said, "You're now restricted to only doing Romanov-related activities."

"What?" Becca wasn't happy with his decision and annoyed she had to abide by it.

Mason leaned forward again. "You will not be part of any Griffin operations for the foreseeable future."

"Mason, I can still help," she pleaded.

"You're effectively blindfolded until further notice."

Becca's stomach churned. The decision was final.

"Tell me who developed the app you used to hack our signal." Mason crossed his arms.

Becca dropped her head knowing she had no choice. "Cassie Lee," she said, defeated.

"Report back to your living quarters, and await further instruction. Don't deviate, or I'll know. You'll receive your phone as you exit the building. We're keeping the laptop to make sure it wasn't traced by the Brotherhood."

Mason's hologram evaporated, and the door opened.

Blindfolded. That was the right word. She should have turned off the video when she'd stumbled upon it. The area where she'd been wounded throbbed, her anger resurfaced, and a desperate desire to find RC came with it. Fueled by hurt, she had only one goal in life right now: to get answers from the man who'd betrayed her. But without access to Griffin resources, she had no idea how to make good on her promise to herself.

On the way back to the Bunkhouse, Becca walked the perimeter of the compound to clear her head. Letting her mind wander, she tried to see the bright side of her situation. She loved this way home for its solitude. That's what she needed and wanted.

Becca knew the perimeter of every Griffin headquarters had invisible, electrified fences that surrounded the compound. One touch would electrocute the person while sending an alarm to the security building. Undetectable lasers crisscrossed the grounds outside the compound and the tops of the buildings at night. Even infrared cameras wouldn't see the lasers.

Becca dwelled on the impressive security measures the Griffins used in order to distract herself from her punishment. Fire-suppression systems were built into every building, which included pressurized hoses that were accessed right off a wall in each room. Handheld fire extinguishers were also in every office and at every cubicle and desk. Laminated PVB glass, a double-layered glass with polyvinyl butyral in between the layers, resisted bullets and was the material used in every window in the compound. There was also an access-control system, which limited member access to certain buildings, and a Griffin-designed property-surveillance system, which worked around the clock. Guards walked the perimeter every ten minutes.

She pondered how she could fix things with Mason. Following his rules was a good start. By accessing the feed, it looked as if she'd gone rogue, which she hadn't intended. Thankfully, Becca knew Mason didn't think of her as a traitor.

A twig snapped behind Becca, and she turned. Before her was a large man dressed in black, wearing the mask of a Fox assassin with a silenced pistol aimed at her face. Her body filled with adrenaline, and her training kicked in.

The man was strong and fast, but Becca was faster. She prevented the assassin from firing his gun as she moved into his space. Using swift, mixed-martial-arts attacks, she neutralized his movements. They struggled for his gun, and Becca was able to grab it from him.

She tried firing at her attacker, but the gun wouldn't work. Some sort of mechanism prevented her from pulling the trigger, and it wasn't the safety. She changed her grip to use the gun as a club. Becca focused on his body language and paid attention to his movements hoping that would give away his next attack. One year ago, she would've been helpless against a trained assassin, but her rage at RC and her recent Griffin training had turned her into someone who could hold her own.

The Fox assassin pulled out a knife. That didn't phase her. What did worry her was that she was still wearing her pajamas. She had two objectives: use her assailant's body movement against him and get a better weapon.

The assassin sliced and jabbed his knife at her, barely missing. She used the butt of the gun to deflect a few oncoming stabs and tried her best to hit her opponent in as many pressure points on his body.

They switched sides and circled each other, dodging the other's attacks. Becca tried to capture the knife and the assassin's arm, but she couldn't get a locked hold, and he was able to reposition himself.

Sweat poured down her temples and back as she watched for his next move. She kept her hands out ready to redirect any oncoming strikes.

The assassin lunged at Becca with a violent flurry. He knocked the gun out of her hand and it landed out of reach. His knife caught the midsection of her pajama top but didn't penetrate her skin. She regained her footing and ripped off the bottom part of her top. She twisted it around her wrists, pulling it tight, ready to use as a weapon.

Becca was able to avoid her assailant's attacks using the bottom of her ripped pajama top. She captured the man's knife arm by wrapping the shirt around it, then spun and ducked under his arm. She pulled his arm over her right shoulder, immobilizing him. She now had control of the man's arm and forced it to move opposite its natural direction.

Snap!

The assassin screamed, dropped the knife, and backed up. His arm was broken and useless.

Becca moved between the assassin and the fallen weapons. She wasn't going to let him get away, and she knew he knew it. Becca rewrapped the shirt around her wrists, ready for the next attack.

The assassin attempted to kick Becca, but it was easy for her to avoid his feeble attempts. She could tell the pain of his broken arm was too much. She kicked back at his leg, which threw him off balance. Then Becca aimed at his other knee and drove her foot into it, breaking it instantly. The man screamed again and fell to his good knee. Becca found the gun and picked it up ready to use as a club again and returned to her attacker. He was finished. Even though he attempted to attack with his good arm, it had no effect.

Becca took a deep breath, gritted her teeth, and bashed the butt of the gun repeatedly into the fox mask. The mask cracked more and more after each impact. She felt her opponent's resistance lessen as she continued to break the mask on his face. The grip from his good arm on hers released. Becca stopped her onslaught and took in a couple of deep breaths. She removed the remaining pieces of the mask from his face. Blood from cuts dripped down to his chin. Becca didn't recognize him. She curled her fingers into her palm and drove her hand through the base of his nose. The man fell limp to the ground. There was no more life in him.

Becca unraveled the torn pajama top from her wrists and pulled out her phone. She moved to get a better view of the man's face, broken nose and all. She turned on the flash function and snapped a photo. Becca took a couple of deep breaths and searched the body for any possible clues that could help her identify the man and how he'd gotten inside the compound. Nothing.

She searched the area and found the man's knife and gun but no sign of his phone. She bent down to pick up the gun.

Boom!

The violent jolt from the thunderous explosion sent Becca to her hands and knees. She turned in the direction of the sound and saw a wall of flames and smoke rising from the training and weapons buildings.

Becca shook her head for her eyes to refocus from the shockwave. An alarm sounded throughout the compound as she watched Griffin members hurry toward the burning buildings. Becca grabbed the assassin's gun and knife, got back to her feet, and ran toward the inferno

Becca could feel the intense heat from the flames. As she got closer, she heard more explosions from other buildings within the complex. Fire shot out of windows, doors, and the roofs of the armory and Tech Central buildings. Alarms wailed throughout the compound as Griffin firefighters roared up in their trucks.

The firefighters set up their hoses and shot fast streams of water toward the blaze. Becca watched them struggle to put out the fire. The flames weren't being extinguished, and she heard the fire chief directing his team on how to attack the growing inferno. He talked into his Griffin phone, and his voice sounded over loudspeakers throughout the compound.

"Initiate evacuation protocol. Repeat. Initiate evacuation protocol."

People streamed out of the burning buildings in droves. Dirt and blood were smeared on their faces, arms, and legs. Many helped others that were more severely injured move away from the blasts.

Becca saw three men carry a woman out the front entrance. She wasn't moving. They took her a safe distance away from the burning buildings and did their best to resuscitate her. Unfortunately, she was unresponsive.

Becca's protocol instructions kicked in. Each Griffin had been assigned a specific exit in case of an evacuation emergency. Becca's designated exit was D tunnel beneath the commissary building, two buildings away from the Bunkhouse. Once in the tunnel, she'd be given instructions to report to safe house D along with other information from Griffin high command.

Becca raced toward the Bunkhouse to gather her evacuation essentials, which included her handgun, knife, laptop, and a change of clothes. As she ran, she saw masses of Griffins leaving their buildings in an effort to get to their exits. It was controlled chaos. People carried backpacks, small suitcases, and messenger bags as they scrambled through the crowd. Surprisingly, there wasn't much screaming among the horror. Instead, there was yelling, not out of fear but for direction. Friends informed each other where they'd be or asked where another colleague might end up.

Becca weaved through the people as fast as she could and made it onto the walkway that led to the entrance of the Bunkhouse. She controlled her breathing to maintain her speed as she approached the front door.

Time slowed, and she saw a bright-yellow cloud appear within the Bunkhouse's entrance. The front doors blew out, spraying shards of glass everywhere. Becca felt as if she had run into an invisible force field that carried her a good twenty feet back. She landed on one of the grassy patches and tumbled over and over. Her brain was dazed, but the touch of grass beneath her palms made her grateful she'd landed there instead of the concrete pathway.

She looked up and saw the entire Bunkhouse covered in flames. The Griffin compound had been breached, and no building was safe. She had to get out of there. Becca gathered her strength and forced herself to her feet. Her equilibrium was off, and it took a good while to level out before she regained control of her center of gravity.

She made her way to the commissary and took the large, wide stairway down to the entrance of D tunnel, where she followed the crowd to the exit. When they were near the front, they were divided into groups of ten to exit the tunnel so they wouldn't draw attention as people streamed into the nearby community. People dispersed in different directions. Becca turned left at a street corner and went west, against the flow of most evacuees.

Becca glanced at her phone, and the GPS guided her down a safe route to avoid as many pedestrians as possible. Darkness covered the early morning hours. She walked through alleyways, small streets, and sometimes stopped, hiding so the few people out at this time wouldn't see her disheveled state.

Becca climbed a fence and dropped into the alley behind it. She walked a short distance and turned onto the main street of a neighborhood. She stopped. The safe house across the street was on fire. A local crowd had gathered away from the burning house with their phones out, livestreaming the destruction.

Now what was she supposed to do? She'd followed all her protocols and ended up here. She had no idea where to go next, who to contact, or if there was even a safe place for her now. She scanned the crowd to see if there were any threatening or unduly interested looks coming her way, but everyone was focused on the fire. She had to decide where to go and couldn't linger much longer.

Somehow, someone knew the Griffins' every move and had been a step ahead of them this entire time. It wasn't a coincidence. The Fox assassin, the attack on the compound, now this. Someone was hunting her, and she knew it was the Brotherhood of the Fox. They could be anywhere, waiting for her to slip up. For all she knew, everybody videoing the fire could be a follower just waiting for her.

"Don't react, and don't turn around," a voice said from behind her.

"Mom?" Becca said as relief flooded her system. "What the hell's happening?"

"Come with me. Don't make any sudden movements."

Becca followed her mother until they were well away from the burning safe house, then walked alongside her. They did their best not to draw attention, aside from the fact that Becca was in her ripped, bloody pajamas.

"I thought the compound was secure." Becca kept her voice low and walked with her arms crossed and hands tucked in her armpits to contain body heat.

Vivian didn't face Becca. She just kept moving and waited until they had turned the corner before responding. "Nothing is secure. Difficult to breach, yes. But nothing is ever secure. In time, you'll understand that."

"I'm relieved you found me." Becca looked back to see if they were being followed. "For a moment, I wasn't sure what to do."

"I never lost you, honey. I've been monitoring you ever since you joined us. What kind of a mother would I be if I didn't keep tabs on you?"

As much as Becca enjoyed hearing that, she felt annoyed by the fact that she hadn't seen her mother in months, other than the time she woke up in the hospital after having been shot by RC. "Where've you been, Mom?"

"Ever since you prevented the Brotherhood from obtaining the Royal Danish Egg, and eliminated one of their top brethren, it was only a matter of time before they retaliated. I didn't give Mason much of a choice to sway me from not protecting you. I kept my distance, as you needed to learn to fend for yourself, but you got the Brotherhood good last year. This is just the beginning of their revenge."

Becca wanted to protest, but her mother was right. Deep down she knew they would come for her, but she wasn't sure how they would and never expected they'd be able to infiltrate a Griffin compound.

"How did they know about the safe house? Why didn't they wait for me to get in there before setting it on fire?"

They continued down an empty street.

"They don't want you dead yet. Mason texted me about the attack. For all we know the assassin wasn't out to kill you. He could have been sending a message. It's classic Brotherhood of the Fox tactics. When you become a mark, they do everything they can to terrorize their prey before dealing the final blow. Barry was the start."

"Tonight, they almost got me."

Becca took out her phone and pulled up the photo of the assassin that had attacked her and handed it to Vivian. "He somehow got inside the compound and nearly killed me. I've never seen him before."

Vivian stopped walking as she stared at the photo in utter disgust. "Pete Donovan."

Becca wondered if Pete had been a friend of her mother's, but there was something else, and Becca couldn't decipher the look on her face.

"Who is he, Mom?"

"The mole I've been investigating. One of the three I had narrowed it down to. I really didn't want it to be him, but now it all makes sense."

They resumed walking down the street.

"Care to explain? Don't tell me he was your friend."

"Two years ago, Pete lost his wife to a rare case of pneumonia. Left with two children, his focus changed to putting the kids first."

"That's to be expected. Hardly a reason to become a mole for the Brotherhood."

"True. Might've been grief. But Donovan was a tier-three Talon and one of our best assassins. He had access to restricted tech, weapons, and all over the grounds. He could go anywhere. Made him a perfect candidate to be used by our enemy."

"A grief-stricken deadly assassin, and the Brotherhood of the Fox got their fangs into him? I wonder how."

"If I knew that, the compound wouldn't have been attacked. Text me his photo."

Becca did as she was told.

"I'm sending it to Mason." Becca watched Vivian's thumbs fly on the phone keyboard. "We're here."

They arrived at a complex of luxury townhouses. Six buildings with four units in each. They approached the door of a townhouse in building B. Her mother placed the palm of her hand above the doorknob. A beam of light scanned her palm and disappeared. A tiny click announced the door was unlocked. Her mother, gun at the ready, handed Becca her phone.

"Touch the green app on the home screen," she whispered.

Becca did, and the phone sent out a wide beam of light that outlined the entire townhouse. The light returned, and the phone projected a 3D-wireframe image of the walls and every room in the house.

"We're clear," Vivian said and put her gun away.

"I want that app on my phone," Becca said.

They walked into the townhouse and sat at the kitchen table.

"It scans the walls for explosives and heat signatures. A two-in-one application."

"So, what do we do now?" Becca leaned back in her chair, letting the pressure off her feet. She hadn't realized how sore they were during all the commotion.

"We wait for Mason to contact me with orders."

Vivian made a sandwich for each of them.

"Eat up. Don't expect to get much rest tonight. We have to stay on guard. Might've been more than one mole at the German headquarters."

Becca scarfed her sandwich, cleaned, and put away her dishes. Then she moved to the corner of a window and looked out into the early dawn. The sky had barely lightened behind the other buildings in the complex. Becca took a deep breath, knowing that at any second, she could be attacked again.

The next time she might not be as lucky.

10

Becca fought to keep her eyes open as she continued to peek out the living room window. The street was still dark and empty. She hadn't seen a soul walk by in two hours. She glanced at Vivian, who peered out a side window, keeping an eye on another angle of the street. Becca wondered how her mother stayed so calm and wide awake. She was jealous of her mom's focus. One day she hoped to have as much energy as her mother in times of crisis.

Two silhouettes moved past her window. She sat up, trying not to draw anyone's eye in her direction. The wireframe map of the townhouse activated on her phone and projected a holographic image of two men outside the front door. Her mother had also seen the notification.

Vivian readied her handgun and moved to position herself behind the door.

Becca hurried to hide behind the little wall that separated the entryway and living room. It provided the perfect cover from the two men about to enter. She heard the hand scanner hidden in the front door activate. The latch unlocked, and the door opened.

The men had to be Griffins in order to know about the scanner. That didn't mean they weren't part of the attack on the compound, though. Becca made sure her footing was grounded. She knew she would have to engage these men and needed perfect balance to do so. Luckily, she and her mother had been in the dark for hours, so their eyes had adjusted to see better.

The door creaked open. The men didn't speak. She heard a boot step onto the wood floor of the entryway.

Vivian grabbed the man's gun as he entered, trapped it between one arm and her body, and twisted inward, forcing the man to lose control of his weapon and stumble inside. She shoved herself backward into the front door, using it to slam into the second man, making him unable to fully enter. Vivian disarmed the first man and kicked him with full force, causing him to fall to the floor and slide in Becca's direction.

"You take this one!" Vivian shouted as she opened the door and attacked the second man.

Becca lunged at the man on the ground and grappled him, making it difficult for him to get up. She trapped his right arm and was able to wrap her legs around him and pin him to the floor. She caught a glimpse of her mom fighting the second man in the doorway. She even used the door a couple of times against him. Becca was impressed.

Becca felt herself being picked up, even though she thought she'd had the guy pinned. He had used his free arm to prop himself up to his knees with Becca still latched onto him like a pissed-off kitten. In one fluid motion, the guy flung Becca onto the floor toward Vivian. He was free, and Becca was discombobulated; however, she was able to regain her ground.

Vivian disarmed the man in the doorway.

"Here!" Vivian tossed the gun to Becca, who caught it and twisted back around to face her opponent. She aimed the weapon at his head.

"One more step," Becca warned. The man stopped his attack and put his hands in the air.

"Wait, wait, wait! Same side!" Vivian's adversary called out.

Becca looked back and saw her mother also had her attacker at gunpoint. The fight was over, and they had kicked these men's asses. Becca returned her focus to her guy and kept the gun on him. If she had to, she'd pull the trigger.

"Move," Vivian said as she and Becca motioned for the men to enter the living room. Vivian locked the front door and joined Becca, keeping both men in their line of sight.

"Code word," Vivian demanded.

"Recovery," both men replied.

"Right wrists. Now."

Both men brought their hands down and tapped their wrists. A hologram window projected from each man's flesh-colored Griffin tattoo with their photo identification and Griffin status. She hadn't realized the tattoos could be used as projections for others to see. Becca took a few steps closer to the man she had fought and read the basic information.

"Dex Rhodes, caucasian male, five feet eleven inches, stocky, two hundred pounds. Ten years with the Griffin organization, classified enforcer, tier three, Talon level."

Vivian held her cell phone with one hand and grabbed Dex's hologram with the other, bringing it to hover over her phone.

Becca continued: "At thirteen years old, he broke the nose of a bully in school, then lied to his mother, not telling her he'd been put in detention."

Vivian took over the interrogation. "What was it you told her, Mr. Rhodes?"

Dex didn't hesitate, even though he seemed taken aback by the question. "I told her I'd gone to audition for the school musical and had to sing from *Man of La Mancha*. I've never told that to anyone, not even my father. How did you find out?"

Vivian didn't answer. "Put your hands back up."

Dex did as he was told.

Becca turned to the other man's info. "Scout Amadon, African American, male, six foot, lean, one hundred and eighty pounds. Five years with the Griffin organization, classified sniper, tier two, Talon level. At ten years old, he rode his bicycle to visit a girl he'd met earlier that day. He didn't tell his parents where he was going."

"What did you tell your parents about why you were out past curfew?" Vivian asked.

Scout grinned a beautiful, wide smile. "I told them I'd gone out for ice cream and got lost in the dark. A partial truth." He sighed. "I'd forgotten all about that. They gave me hell for worrying them." Scout paused. "Our turn to verify you."

"Becca, get Scout's phone. Scout, keep your hands up," Vivian ordered.

"Right-front pocket," Scout said.

Becca reached in and pulled out his phone. Her mother tapped her tattoo, and the hologram of her information hovered over Scout's phone.

"Vivian Lake Romanov, Caucasian female, five foot seven inches, one hundred twenty-six pounds. Twenty-five years with the Griffin organization, classified attack squad, the highest-ranking woman in the organization, tier four, Claw level," Scout read. "Ms. Romanov, while married and deep undercover for the Griffins, what was your public occupation during your twenty-two-year mission?"

"Housewife."

Becca flinched. She had witnessed the beatings her mother had received from her father. But hearing it said so coldly, unemotionally, struck her deeply. Her mother was a hero to her.

"She's verified," Scout confirmed.

Becca gave Scout's phone back to him, then tapped her tattoo and gave her phone to Dex.

"Rebecca Hunter Lake Romanov," Dex read. "Caucasian female, five foot eight inches, one hundred thirty pounds. One year with the Griffin organization, classified information gatherer, tier one, Wing level."

Dex and Scout studied her with a knowing look, and Becca knew her reputation preceded her. They'd most likely heard how she'd brought down a high-ranking member of the Brotherhood using her brain and with no field experience. That was a feat the Griffins had been trying to do for decades.

"*The* Rebecca Hunter Lake Romanov?" Scout asked Dex in disbelief.

Dex continued with the protocol question. "At five years old, what did you do that angered your father and made your mother proud?"

"I read the whole *Webster's* dictionary in four days and told my father he was a tyrant, persecuting my mother and subjugating her. I didn't understand that my words would be taken out on her." Becca's heart broke at the memory. "She ended up in the hospital for two days. My mother told me how proud she was of me for standing up to my father on her behalf."

"Still am," Vivian said.

"Ms. Romanov is verified," Dex confirmed.

Becca and Vivian lowered their weapons as the tension in the room had been diffused. Vivian handed Dex back his sidearm.

"Nice move with the door," Dex acknowledged as he holstered his weapon.

Vivian smiled. "No hard feelings." She shook hands with Dex and Scout. "Are you expecting any more of us to arrive?"

"No, ma'am," Scout replied. "Dex and I escaped through exit G and lingered outside before we approached this safe house."

"We weren't sure if this location had been compromised like safe house D," Dex added. "We don't know who else is assigned to report to this location."

"Keep your guard up. We don't know if more are coming either," Vivian said.

"Now that everyone's verified, I'd love to get out of these pajamas and get cleaned up," Becca stated as she pulled a shard of broken glass out of her hair.

"There are extra clothes in one of the bedrooms upstairs. Women's clothes are usually in the bedroom on the right."

"Are you going to be okay with these guys?" Becca said under her breath.

They looked at Dex and Scout, who had moved to the windows to watch for unusual activity, as Becca and her mother had done earlier.

"It'll be interesting to learn who they are and how we get along," Vivian replied.

Ten minutes later, Becca came down in jeans, a black T-shirt, and a slightly oversized hoodie. Her hair was still damp from towel-drying. Dex kept watch as Vivian and Scout chatted about the next steps in the kitchen.

"I need a weapon," Becca said entering the kitchen. "Mine was in my go bag in the Bunkhouse, and the one I pulled off the Fox assassin was printed to his hand, so I can't use it."

Scout didn't ask any questions. He just slid a handgun down the island of the kitchen to her. Becca checked the mag clip. It was full, and she reloaded it into the handle of the gun. She concealed the gun at the back of her waistband, under her hoodie.

"You really took down a high-ranking member of the Brotherhood?" Scout asked, like a fan to a movie star.

"I didn't know who he was at the time," Becca replied.

Vivian's phone notified everyone with the holo-map of the townhouse that someone was at the door. They drew their weapons. Becca and Vivian moved to get a clearer shot as they heard the door scanner do its thing. Scout joined Dex in the living room, aiming their weapons at the door. The latch unlocked. The door opened, and Becca watched the person enter.

"Not one more step!" Dex shouted.

A young woman dressed in a wild, colorful pair of pants with a geometric design, a black, crew-necked T-shirt, and green camouflage combat boots, jumped back, terrified.

It was Cassie, from Tech Central. Her hands flew up into the air. She stammered, "I, uh, I'm Cassie Lee, ID number... oh shit, what's my ID number? G64058. I can't think. Don't shoot! Geez, my heart is pounding. Wait! Please, don't shoot! G6405851—crap." She stuck out her right arm to show her tattoo. "I'm Cassandrah Lee, tier-four Wing. I go by Cassie. I work in the tech department. My favorite show is *Powerpuff Girls*, and I love *Pokémon*. Is that the right answer to the secret question? Is that how the introductory protocol goes? Shit! Can I start again?" Cassie squeezed her eyes shut out of fear.

They watched as Cassie tried to tap her right wrist with her eyes closed and kept missing her tattoo. "Please don't shoot."

Becca hid a smile as she walked up to Cassie, aimed her phone, and scanned her tattoo. Becca was pretty sure Cassie wasn't going to be a threat, but after the fiasco that had become her evening and early morning, she wasn't willing to take any chances.

"Cassie Lee's bio, please," Vivian said in a stern voice.

Becca read the information aloud. "Cassandrah Lee, Asian American, five foot four inches, one hundred and fifteen pounds." Becca scrolled through the info. "Ten years with the Griffin organization, since she was a child. Comes from Griffin legacy. Classified as information gatherer, tier four, Wing level. Considered a profoundly gifted genius."

"Oh," Cassie said, taken aback, her hands still in the air, her body shaking. She stared at the floor, not at the guns pointed at her.

"At three years old, what did you do to have your parents test your IQ?" Vivian asked.

"Umm… Oh, that. Well, I, uh, took apart my father's laptop and left it in pieces. When he came home and saw it, he was furious. I put it back together in front of him. His mouth hung down to the floor. By the way, the fan worked better when I finished it. It was way quieter."

A smile formed across Becca's face as she turned back to Vivian and nodded.

"We're clear," Vivian said as she and the others holstered their weapons.

Cassie stayed frozen with her hands up.

"Put your hands down, Cassie," Becca said.

Cassie looked up at Becca for the first time since she'd walked in. Becca checked her pupils for any signs of tech contact lenses that could be used as a video feed. Nothing. All she saw was a poor girl scared to the bone. It was a trait Becca had recognized in herself from a year ago when she'd first met RC.

"Just breathe. You're safe for the time being," Becca said.

"How did they find us?" Cassie took deep breaths, and Becca was able to prevent Cassie from hyperventilating by cutting her off.

"We're going to find out together." Becca looked into Cassie's eyes with all the confidence she could muster and saw Cassie finally get ahold of her emotions. Cassie's tense body relaxed, and her breathing returned to normal.

"How did you get out of Tech Central?" Vivian asked, gentler than before.

Cassie removed her backpack and rubbed her shoulder. "I wasn't there when it was attacked. My shift had already ended, and I was on the way to the cafeteria when the explosions happened."

"You were luckier than many," Vivian said. She motioned to the guys. "This is—"

"Dex Rhodes and Scout Amadon," Cassie said with contained excitement. "Heroes of the Cairo mission in 2015." She faced Vivian in a shy manner. "And you're *the* Vivian Lake Romanov, the top undercover female Claw in the history of the organization. Sorry." Cassie was slightly embarrassed. "I know who all of you are. I've heard the stories of your exploits."

That piqued everyone's interest, and they all looked at each other with a newfound respect for their individual capabilities.

"It's not every day you almost get shot by four Griffin legends."

Dex turned to Scout. "Legends. I like the sound of that."

"I feel old," Scout replied and headed back to the kitchen.

Everyone's phones beeped. Becca looked at hers, and the number was a generic notification number from the Griffin network. She answered the alert, and a miniprojection of Mason appeared above her phone. The others also answered their phones and saw the same recorded projection.

"As you're all aware, three hours ago the German headquarters was attacked by the Brotherhood of the Fox. Three structures were demolished, with over two hundred and fifty confirmed casualties and seven hundred injured."

Their faces were glued to Mason's recording. An attack like this had never happened to any Griffin facility before.

"Medical protocol has been put into effect. In order to protect the League from another attack, family members will be notified of the whereabouts of their loved ones in private."

Dex and Scout stood as if ready to tackle someone. Their backs were ramrod straight, and it was clear they wanted revenge. Becca felt the same but also responsible for their rage; the sanctity of their safety had been violated. Hundreds of good men and women were now dead, and at this moment, Becca had been benched and couldn't make things right.

"This was no random attack, and it would be foolish to think otherwise. We've identified one culprit, who will remain nameless, to not alert any other possible associates. In the meantime, continue to follow your evacuation protocols until you're reassigned to a new headquarters. Honesty, loyalty, and secrecy—at all costs."

No one spoke. They had to process the news and think about the upcoming changes.

Vivian's phone rang with a video-chat notification.

"Mason," she said to everyone. She answered the phone normally and walked into the living room.

Becca and the rest moved closer to eavesdrop.

"I've never spoken to the boss man before," Dex whispered.

"Me neither," Cassie responded.

Scout shushed everyone: "Quiet."

Becca could hear bits and pieces of Vivian and Mason's conversation.

"Are you alone?" Mason asked.

"No."

"How many are with you?"

"Four." Vivian glanced around, and the four of them moved out of her line of sight.

"Is she with you?" Mason asked.

Becca wondered if Mason was talking about her.

"Yes, I got to her before they could."

"Were you followed?"

"Negative."

"Put me on hologram."

Vivian brought the phone down from her ear and tapped the hologram button. A live, full-body projection of Mason appeared in the center of the living room. Becca, Cassie, Dex, and Scout entered without being asked. They surrounded Mason's hologram, eager to listen.

"We had suspected an attack from within for the past six months," Mason informed the group. "Ever since Becca was inducted into the League, I knew the Brotherhood would do everything they could to get to her in retaliation for the death of a top member."

Mason's projection faced Becca.

"When you began your training, I assigned RC to a top-secret infiltration mission. I sent him into the shadows to find a way inside the Brotherhood to gather intel on the potential attack. Four months ago, we lost all communication with my son. Until recently, when he reappeared at the Harz Mountains, then earlier this evening with Hawk squad."

"You think he's flipped?" Scout asked.

Becca said, "The RC I know would never join the Brotherhood. It's not in him."

"You don't really know RC, Becca," Mason replied.

"Yes, I do," Becca exclaimed.

Mason held out a hand in Vivian's direction. "Did you know your mother was undercover for the past twenty-two years with the

Griffins?"

She shook her head. Mason's response put a new perspective on the situation. Becca didn't really know anybody.

"You two," Mason faced the guys. Both of them stood at full attention.

"Dex Rhodes, Claw, enforcer, sir."

"Scout Amadon, Claw, sniper, sir."

Mason pointed at Vivian. "She'll be running point. You follow her orders as if they came from me. Understood?"

"Yes, sir," they replied.

Mason looked past Becca to Cassie, who stood in the corner near the kitchen. "Who are you?"

"Cassie Lee, Mr. Carter. Tier four, Wing."

Becca saw that Cassie's name rang a bell with Mason before he turned and looked at her.

"She's the one I told you about," Becca confirmed.

"She created the app?" Mason's surprise didn't go unnoticed. "You're much younger than I expected," he said to Cassie. "Perfect it, and use it to help the team bring my son back."

"I will." Cassie nodded. "I mean, yes, sir, Mr. Carter."

"Call sign for this squad will be Falcon, and you'll report *only* to me. I don't want this operation running through the usual channels to avoid detection. Your resources will be limited. Your enemy knows you're coming. I want my son brought in for questioning, alive. Understood?"

"Yes, sir," everyone but Becca replied.

"And Becca..." Mason began.

She waited to be told her lockdown mission while the rest of the team went out to recover RC.

"Don't make me regret this."

"I'll bring him back, Mason." Becca moved away from leaning against the wall. "You have my word."

11

The blinding flash from Cassie's cell phone camera brought colored spots to Becca's eyes. Becca followed Cassie back to her laptop on the island in the kitchen. Cassie had turned the island into her own Tech Central cubical. Becca watched her portrait upload on a secondary monitor, then saw her face begin to change appearance.

"Blonde? Really?" Becca said, slightly repulsed.

"I kind of like it," Cassie admitted, "but let the program do its thing."

Becca faced the clock on the microwave: 9:17 a.m. "They've been gone a long time. You sure nothing happened to them?"

Cassie did some wizardry on her laptop and pulled up a surveillance video that showed a side-by-side feed with two windows displayed. The left side showed Vivian, Dex, and Scout as they appeared, but the right screen showed them with different faces. "Facial-alteration software is holding strong. No one would know who they were unless they had my software."

"Mom looks pretty hot, actually," Becca said. Vivian's appearance had been ever so slightly altered. "She looks like she could be my lost aunt or something. I don't know how you changed the structure of her face and still made her look like a potential relative."

"Subtlety is key. Facial-recognition software has become so advanced it can detect structures of the face, no matter if you're wearing sunglasses or a wig. The trick I developed is to program an alternatively structured face that's pinged to any Griffin ID on any camera. That way, the new face is tracked to the person and doesn't look as if anything has been doctored."

"You made Dex and Scout look more handsome, I see."

"No one said a girl can't have fun while she works," Cassie replied.

Cassie's computer dinged with a completed render of Becca's new appearance. Her hair was the same color, and her face had been altered just enough so she didn't look like herself.

"You look like you'd be called Hayley," Cassie remarked.

"I look like my unborn sister." Becca was impressed. She looked good.

Cassie's attention returned to the surveillance video of Vivian and the guys. "Okay, they made it to the cache safely. They should be back in about thirty minutes with our stuff."

Becca stared at a three-dimensional projection of the SS ring hovering above her cell phone. She twisted it around and around, hoping an idea would spawn and give her inspiration on how to find RC.

"What's with the class ring?" Cassie asked.

"It's not a class ring. It's an old Nazi SS ring that's now buried beneath the Bunkhouse at the former headquarters. RC stole my find from me before he shot me." Becca rubbed her neck, frustrated. "I've been wondering if I could find a connection between the ring and something that would lead to RC."

The hologram of the ring flickered in front of Becca and Cassie. Suddenly, it morphed from the SS ring into the emblem of the Brotherhood of the Fox. Becca froze, and Cassie stood up from her chair.

"Is that what I think it is?" Cassie asked on the edge of panic.

Becca stared at the hovering insignia and watched it disappear and return to the SS ring. "How secure are we in this safe house?"

"More secure than NORAD," Cassie reassured. She typed on her laptop, double-checking something. "There's no way the Brotherhood can trace us to this location. They have to be me in order to get past my safety protocols."

"Can we trace the signal back and see where it came from?"

"Already on it." Cassie's eyes were glued to her screen. Becca moved closer to Cassie as her computer did its thing.

"The signal came from a cell phone two miles outside the Ludwigsburg downtown area." The GPS location appeared on the secondary screen of Cassie's setup. "Running the Eye." Cassie pressed enter, and the map zoomed in to the area in real-time. "The device is still active."

Becca held her breath, full of anticipation, as she watched Cassie hack into all the video feeds around the active cell phone. RC's face appeared in different angles of videos on the screen.

"There you are, you bastard," Becca said.

"How did the Brotherhood hack into my signal?" Cassie searched through the computer code. "I don't see any trace of a breach. This is weird."

"Could they have developed a way to hide the hack?"

"They could have...but not likely on my system. Again, they'd have to be me to do it. The weird thing is, the Brotherhood-insignia message came from an out-of-date Griffin signal."

"Can you trace back to who sent the signal?"

"I did." Cassie pointed to the screen at RC. "You're looking at him."

Becca had to process this. RC deliberately sending a Brotherhood emblem to them made no sense. "He's communicating. Or he's baiting us."

"But why?" Cassie asked.

"I don't know." Becca bit the bottom of her lip as she thought about possible reasons. "Only one way to find out."

"The Eye has found RC near a building two miles from the downtown area," Cassie said.

"Send the info to Mom."

Cassie did, then said, "Based on what I'm seeing, he's moving toward downtown."

"Grab your stuff." Becca took Cassie's car keys. "I'm driving, you keep an eye on him."

"Shouldn't we wait for the others?" Cassie closed her laptop and unplugged it from the monitors.

"We don't have time, and I'm not losing this opportunity to bring him in." Becca headed out the front door.

Cassie followed while stuffing as much electronic equipment into her backpack as she could. "But Mason said Vivian's running point on this mission."

Just as Cassie said that they both received text alerts on their phones. Becca looked at it.

Surveil from the east side two blocks away from his current location. Do not engage, Vivian ordered.

"We have our orders from the boss." Becca opened the driver's side door and got in.

Cassie fumbled into the passenger seat with her open backpack on her lap and struggled to attach the seatbelt. "I'm not used to being in the field."

"There's a first time for everything." Becca ignored the Cassie-ified, tricked-out dashboard. Multiple monitors with exposed wires were all over the passenger side.

Cassie plugged her laptop into the monitors and had a mobile communications center, the same setup she'd had in the townhouse.

"I've never used my car on a mission before. This is exciting and terrifying."

"You'll get used to it," Becca said. "You still have eyes on RC?"

"Yup." Cassie hadn't once looked at Becca as her fingers flew over the keyboard following feed to feed. "RC's heading into downtown now."

They arrived at the downtown area in fifteen minutes and parked on the east side, two blocks away from RC's location. Becca put her earwig in, and when Cassie saw that she hurried to dig hers out of her backpack and did the same.

"Update," Becca said into the coms. "Cassie and I are in position on the east side. Do you read me?"

"I read you," Vivian responded. "We don't have eyes on him yet. Stand by."

Cassie frantically typed on the keyboard. Becca watched as an entire layout of the area within a three-block radius appeared across multiple screens on the dashboard. Becca saw the marked location where she and Cassie were parked. A few more colored icons appeared on the display showcasing where Vivian, Dex, and Scout were located.

Cassie added a picture of RC's face to a screen for facial recognition and let the computer do its thing. "The Eye is activated, and we should see all active devices on the screen...now."

All the screens in the car flickered as new icons appeared, showing every active device that could be hacked into. There had to be thousands. Cassie used the Eye software to hop around the area searching for RC.

"Do you think he has a face-scrambling device active like we do?" Becca asked. "If he did, it would be practically impossible to find him this way."

Cassie clicked on different pedestrian devices and street cameras, hoping to catch a glimpse of RC the way she had last time. I'm running descrambling software for that very reason. If RC does have some sort of software running to prevent his face from being detected, his head will glitch on the cameras."

Vivian chimed in over the earwigs: "Scout, I need actual eyes up above."

"On it," Scout replied.

Becca watched the marker on the screen that represented Scout's location split off from Vivian's group.

"I've linked RC's face to everyone's phones," Cassie informed the squad. "Look for a glitching head, and the software should reveal his face properly."

"I see him," Becca said.

"Where?" Cassie scoured the monitors. "I have no hits on the monitors."

"Straight ahead," Becca replied.

Becca and Cassie saw RC walking as casually as ever, a few yards ahead, crossing the street. He didn't seem to know he was being watched.

"Becca, pursue, do not engage," Vivian said over the earwig.

Becca got out of the car and walked after RC. Cassie stayed behind and scrambled to figure out how RC was able to keep himself invisible from detection by the cameras.

"Whatever tech he's using, it's new and it's good." Cassie's voice was loud and clear in Becca's ear. "The software didn't alert us to his presence. We have to follow him by actually seeing him. I'm sharing Becca's eye-cam feed with everyone."

"Copy that," Vivian replied. "We're on our way. Cassie, see if you can calculate his destination with the program."

"Already on it, Boss."

"Becca," Vivian's voice was more stern with her than the others, "this is our chance to bring him in safe and smooth. Do not lose him. Keep at it."

"Preaching to the choir, Mom." Becca followed RC around a corner onto the main street and made sure to walk behind pedestrians to avoid any chance of being spotted. With tons of windows, cars, and bus stops, there were reflections everywhere, which were practically impossible to avoid.

Becca did her best to maneuver without drawing attention. How to tail someone and avoid being spotted had been one of her favorite exercises when she'd first been inducted into the League of Griffins. It gave her an entirely new awareness about herself that she'd not had a year ago. She knew how long to hide behind someone and how to scope out where her secondary cover for hiding would be should things change in an instant. She found it fascinating.

Unfortunately, RC already knew all the tricks. He wouldn't look in the obvious areas. He would use the reflections to check behind him without turning around. He knew how to focus his hearing through the crowd of people to catch hurried footsteps approaching from behind. Because of that, Becca had to stay clear of the usual, more obvious places to stay undetected.

"I'm in position at your ten o'clock, Becca, and have eyes on you and the target," Scout said, a little out of breath. Becca figured he'd raced from rooftop to rooftop to get to his new location.

Becca did a quick glance at the buildings on her left and could barely see Scout on the roof. If you didn't know to look in that direction, you'd never see him. It's amazing how many people never look up, too busy staring at their phones.

Becca kept her focus on RC by watching his body language and using her peripheral vision to see if he was alone. She didn't notice anything unusual that suggested he was being watched. She calculated after RC crossed the next street, he'd have three ways to go. "I've got a few paths ahead of me, Cassie," Becca said. "Which one does the Eye say he's going to take?"

"It's too early to tell." Becca heard Cassie's frantic typing. "If the target continues straight or turns left at the next signal, the Eye will have to recalculate. If he turns right, there are only three places he could be going. A little restaurant, a pawnshop, or a construction site."

"Let's hope this guy turns right," Dex chimed in. "Then we can set up a small perimeter to cut off his escape."

Becca was stuck behind some pedestrians from a red light at a crosswalk. "Shit." She stayed hidden behind a man with broad shoulders and kept her eyes locked on RC. "Come on, come on, turn right. All you have to do is just turn…"

She watched RC almost bump into a pedestrian, yet smoothly

avoid contact. He then resumed his pace and turned right, heading toward the restaurant. Becca felt her heart leap. "He turned right."

"I'm sending all possible escape routes to your phones so you can block him," Cassie said, a little faster than normal.

Becca's phone dinged with the schematics.

"Becca, cover the northside alley," Vivian ordered. "I'll take the south. Dex, you get the east entrance, and Scout, I need you ready with the tranq dart from the west."

Becca hurried over the crosswalk with the crowd of people and pursued RC around the corner. She had a clear view and watched him pass the restaurant and enter the pawnshop. She rushed to find a better position from the north alleyway. Becca pulled out her phone and attempted to hack into the video feed of the pawnshop, but all she saw was snow on her screen. "Cassie, I'm blind on my end. Can you bypass this?"

"I'm working on it. He must have activated a jamming device."

"I have only two heat signatures on my scope," Scout said.

"Don't be so sure about that," Becca replied. "There could be more of them inside."

"Got the video back," Cassie said. "Still working on retrieving audio."

Becca watched the snow on her screen materialize into the image of RC and a scrawny man standing behind the pawnshop counter. The man didn't appear to be much of a threat, but you could never be sure. He lit a cigarette as RC approached. RC pulled out his phone and something else out of his pocket wrapped in a handkerchief. He placed both on the counter and unfolded the handkerchief.

"What is that?" Vivian asked, clearly able to see the video feed from wherever she was. "Cassie, zoom in."

Becca watched the screen digitally enlarge and depixelate the image. She recognized the item RC had placed on the counter.

It was another SS Totenkopf ring.

12

Becca did her best to read RC's lips as he and the other man chatted about the ring. It had been part of her training and one of the hardest things for her to learn how to do. Unfortunately, it was too difficult for her to decipher what they were saying to each other on the monitor.

"Where's the audio, Cassie?" Vivian's voice sounded stern. Becca saw her mom's location on the mini map's heads-up display at the top-right corner of her phone. The pawnshop was now surrounded by Falcon squad. RC would have a difficult time escaping.

Cassie's typing was so intense she had to speak over it. "Still working on it." Cassie couldn't hide her frantic desperation. "There's an active signal coming from that same old Griffin ID I found earlier. I'm piggybacking on it now." The technology babble was still a little over Becca's head, but it reminded her of being with Barry and his laser focus. She knew he would've loved to be friends with Cassie. They probably would've gotten married.

"Status, Dex," Vivian ordered.

"Just got my table outside the restaurant," he replied.

Becca tapped Dex's icon on the map and accessed his cam feed.

He had a good view of the front door of the pawnshop. A beautiful waitress came up to him and asked for his order in German.

"*Kaffee*," he replied in flawless German. When the waitress left, he returned to his normal mission tone. "He's not getting away if he comes out the front."

"Good. Keep an eye on him," Vivian replied. "I'm in position with the van, ready to cut him off either way."

"What about the guy he's talking to? Is he Brotherhood?" Becca asked from the alley. Luckily, there weren't any pedestrians in the area.

"I've got nothing on the pawnshop clerk," Cassie answered. "He's not part of any system. He's off the grid."

"He must be a veil," Scout said.

Becca had learned that veils were normal people who were aware of the Brotherhood and the Griffins; however, they were not part of either organization. They were a neutral party. In exchange for information, their identity was removed from all systems—no alias, no false identity. You'd never find them unless you knew of them.

"The question is, who's the veil working for?" Becca asked. Veils could thrive and make millions playing both sides against each other.

"I've got audio!" Cassie blurted, louder than intended.

Becca heard a weird buzz and some sort of synthetic zap as the audio feed from inside the pawnshop filled her earwig.

"I was wondering if I'd ever see you again." The veil spoke with a higher-pitched tone. Everything about him came off as shady, but then again, in their business, friends were hard to come by. "Things have been getting darker out there in your world. I can tell by your face."

The veil examined the ring. He bent down and looked it over with magnifying goggles, like a jeweler inspecting a diamond. He used tweezers to turn over the ring.

"I must say, I was expecting something a little more...exciting than a ring. It's not even romantic."

"I just need you to tell me what you see. It's important."

RC didn't seem responsive to the veil's attitude. Apparently, he had known this man for a long time and had become numb to his wisecracks. Becca wondered how many years RC had had this man as a veil. How many missions he'd been part of, how much he actually knew about both organizations, and how much money this weasel-looking man had in the bank.

The veil put the ring underneath a bright LED light. "It's not worth much. A skull with two sig runes, one on either side." The veil pointed to each section of the ring as he described it to RC. "A haggle rune, and, of course, a swastika. The silver is from the late nineteen thirties. I could maybe sell it for a few hundred euros. Nazi rings don't go for much unless you have them in bulk. The value goes up when you have more."

RC's demeanor was stoic, almost as if all the information wasn't anything new. "How many more to make it of decent value?"

"I don't know." The veil scratched his cheek as he thought of a number. "Maybe a thousand of these rings." He chuckled with a disapproving attitude. "If you could find that many of this quality."

"How about eleven thousand five hundred?"

The veil froze and looked up, stunned.

"Give or take a few thousand," RC added.

There was a long silence. So much went unspoken, but it was clear RC wasn't bluffing. He must have known where the rest of the rings he'd stolen were, and that knowledge fed his confidence.

The veil straightened and looked up to the ceiling. He calculated, then said, "If they're all from the same era and bear the signature of Heinrich Himmler, the value will increase dramatically."

"How much?" RC asked.

Becca heard the abruptness in RC's voice and knew he was in a rush. RC had never been patient and hated having his time wasted.

"I'd say...around sixty-five million, to the right buyer, give or take." Joy crept into the veil's voice. He examined the ring even closer, unable to contain his excitement. "A real Totenkopf SS ring."

It was strange to watch this guy get goo-goo eyed over an artifact. It was almost uncomfortable.

"The history such a tiny thing contains," the veil said. He looked up at RC. "You never disappoint, my friend." He flipped the ring around and looked inside the band. "Uh-oh."

"Problem?"

"It's a fake." The veil put down the ring and placed both arms on the edge of the counter. He hung his head, defeated. "I really didn't think you'd ever do this to me."

"You sure?"

RC knew something about the ring that this guy hadn't picked up on. Becca wasn't sure what it was yet.

"The date's wrong." The veil threw his hands up like a kid who'd just lost a soccer game when they were so close to winning. "It's written year, month, day. Germans don't write dates like that. Come on, man. You should've noticed this before you brought it to me."

Becca's mind kicked into photographic-memory mode as she pictured the ring she'd been given and unfortunately lost in the compound bombing. "Another one?" Becca said.

"What was that?" Vivian asked.

"The ring. It's not a fake."

"What do you mean?" Dex asked.

"When I researched the ring I'd been given, the date was written the same way. It can't be a coincidence." Becca smiled, as it finally dawned on her. "It's a code."

"What kind of code?" Cassie's typing was almost as loud as her voice. "I can figure it out if I know what kind of code it is."

"I don't know yet. All I know is, if RC's asking about it, that means he doesn't know what the numbers mean."

"I have a question," Scout said "If the Brotherhood already has the rings, why is RC trying to get more information about them?"

"I'm not sure. This doesn't smell right," Becca replied and returned her focus to the conversation between RC and the veil.

"I'm disappointed," RC began. "I expected more from you. The numbers are a code. I just don't know what they mean. This isn't the only ring I've come across with the date written out of order. Why would some be written in order and others not? What could that mean?"

"You're the one with all the secrets. You tell me," the veil said.

"You're the one with all the knowledge, so spill it. That's why I'm here."

"It's practically impossible to decipher a code without the key. Usually, a code like this could refer to a book; the numbers represent the page number, the line, and a word in that line. But I doubt this ring, and however many others you have, are connected to some Nazi book."

Becca's mind raced as she deduced what the numbers could mean. She agreed with the veil that the chances of the numbers referring to a book weren't very plausible. But this was more than that. Someone had buried a secret deep within these rings. How many rings had the date inscribed differently out of the thousands she had found? This new piece of information spawned too many questions. All without a concrete answer.

Becca heard some people laughing down the alley, and she moved to a different location to avoid being seen. She kept her focus on her iPhone screen watching RC and the veil.

"When are you bringing me more of these rings?" the veil asked.

"You're mistaken. I'm not here to make a sale. I just needed information," RC said as he took the ring, wrapped it back in the handkerchief, and put it into his pocket.

"You can trust me with it."

"Oh, my friend, "you have your ear to the ground like little tentacles everywhere. You know everyone and everything that goes on around here. Of course, I can't trust you."

They did a handshake that indicated they'd known each other

for years, some sort of honor-among-thieves thing that Becca was sure she'd never understand.

An alert beeped on RC's phone causing it to vibrate on the glass countertop. The noise caught both RC's and the veil's attention.

Becca couldn't tell what was on RC's phone, but his reaction was unmistakable.

"Oh," the veil said, "looks like you're not alone."

RC quickly grabbed his phone and bolted for the door.

Becca rushed through the back door of the pawnshop. She caught eyes with RC for a second. "Cut him off, Dex," Becca yelled.

"Yup," Dex replied.

RC raced out the door.

Becca hurried after RC but tripped over something and fell. She was pretty sure she'd scraped her knee as she rolled to her side. She saw she had tripped over the veil's foot, and now he was aiming a pistol at her.

"Can I interest you in some diamonds?" he asked.

She looked back to RC and saw him get tackled by Dex.

"I have no shot," Scout said over the com. "Dex, angle him toward me."

Becca motioned to get up, but the veil wouldn't let her.

"Uh-uh," he said, unfazed by the commotion. "Just wait until my friend gets clear." His lack of hostility spoke volumes. Apparently, this wasn't the first time a fight had happened at his pawnshop. "Enjoy the show," the veil said as he watched RC and Dex duke it out, even though he still kept Becca at gunpoint. Any quick motion by her, and she knew he'd fire.

"Come on, Dex, get clear," Scout said.

The grunting of the fight between Dex and RC was loud in Becca's ear. She watched the two of them, surprised by RC's skill. Dex was larger, made of sheer muscle, yet the match seemed even. Becca had witnessed RC's skills a few times and had even seen him kill a Fox assassin, but this fight could go either way. Dex was able to land a couple blows on RC, but for some reason, they didn't weaken him.

"Still have no shot," Scout reminded. "Quit dancing with this guy."

Becca realized Scout was right. RC and Dex weren't fighting. They were, in a way, dancing, sizing each other up, playing chess.

RC swung at Dex, who grabbed RC's punching arm and spun him, getting him in view for Scout to fire.

That was it. That's all they needed. Dex had done it. He had RC right where he needed him, and like a fool, he'd fallen for RC's trap. In one swift, twist of a move, RC returned the favor to Dex and flipped him around.

Scout fired and hit Dex in the back with the tranquilizer dart meant for RC.

"Crap," Scout said. Becca heard him reloading.

RC used Dex's body as a shield. Somehow, he knew exactly where Scout was and kept himself blocked from his view. Dex tried to fight back, but the tranquilizer was too strong, and his body went limp. When that happened, RC made a run for it.

Scout shot again and missed a second time. "Target's on the move," Scout reported.

Becca looked back at the veil, who kept his eyes on her. She wondered if he would keep his word now that RC had gotten away. To her surprise, the veil lowered his weapon and had a calm smile on his face.

"I hope you visit again soon. Good luck." He put the gun on the counter near the register. "Better get going. He's getting away."

Becca hurried to her feet and bolted out the front door.

13

"Which way did he go?" Becca raced down the street after RC but didn't have any idea if he'd made any turns. She was determined not to lose him this time. He had all the answers she needed, and he was going to pay for what he had done to her, so help her God.

"He's two hundred meters ahead of you," Cassie answered, "and he turned right at the first street. He didn't go for the trees."

"Copy." Becca paced her breathing as she pushed herself harder to go faster. Thankfully, her training had built up her muscles and stamina, even though her wound created a piercing stitch in her side. She wasn't going to let it impede her ability to catch up.

"It looks like he's heading for the Ludwigsburg Palace," Cassie said. "Becca, I have an alternate route for you that could help."

"You'd better." Becca raced past tourists, drawing too much attention to herself. She didn't have time to blend in. She prayed she wasn't running into a trap.

"Turn into the parking garage on your right. Run through it to the exit on the other side, then run past a white building with a red roof. More instructions will follow," Cassie said.

Becca arrived at the parking garage and turned into the entrance. A car she hadn't anticipated was exiting the garage and nearly ran into her. The driver honked at her as she leaped over the car's hood. She didn't look back, not wanting to lose her momentum. Becca thought she'd heard the driver call her a foul name in German, but she didn't care.

"I won't be able to cover you if he gets inside the palace," Scout informed.

"Then get to a place where you can cover her before she enters it," Vivian ordered. The sound of the van's door slamming shut was much louder in Becca's earwig. "I've got Dex. He's not going to be able to help until the tranq wears off. Cassie, where can I go to cut off RC?"

"It's too early to determine. There are too many exits for him, and you have the longest way to go to get ahead of him."

"Well, direct me anyway," Vivian said.

"Head toward the motorway, and make a right on the street before it."

Becca weaved in and out of people on a pathway between different buildings and raced down a path surrounded by stunning trees.

"Okay Becca, you're doing great." Cassie's encouraging voice motivated her to keep going. "Ahead is a little street. Make a left onto it, then right at the main street. That should get RC back into your view."

Becca did as instructed and turned left. Cassie's directions were brilliant. Just as Becca got onto the street, she saw RC at the far end just as he turned a corner.

"I saw him," Becca said, as she pushed herself more to catch up while ignoring the ache in her quads.

"There are only so many places he can go," Cassie said. "If he heads for the trees on the south end, visibility will be difficult. There aren't many people with phones I can use to hack into to keep eyes on him, and the basic security cameras won't pick him up."

"I won't be able to get a clear shot through all the brush," Scout told Becca.

"Cut him off," Vivian ordered. "Scout, force him to go another route."

"Getting into position," he replied.

Becca made her way around the corner with RC in her sights. He moved quickly but not at a full run, most likely trying not to draw too much attention to himself. Becca didn't care.

"Becca, you're a few meters away from him," Cassie said.

"He's heading for the trees!" Becca's voice cracked as she ran.

"Rerouting him," Scout said.

Becca watched as two sparks appeared only a few feet in front of RC. He stopped and looked back. She caught his eyes, and after a moment RC made a left toward the Ludwigsburg Palace gate entrance.

"Thank you, Scout," Becca said between breaths.

"Go get him."

Becca crossed the street, avoiding a couple of cars that she paralleled as she ran alongside them. They honked their horns and called her the equivalent of a crazy woman. She kept her focus on RC and was surprised when he ran past the gate guards without being stopped. No alarms were raised. Nothing. They let him into the palace without a whimper.

"Guys, I think I'm running into a trap." Becca didn't slow her pace. "The guards just let him in."

"Cassie, check and see if that palace is one of ours," Vivian said.

"Negative," Cassie replied. "The Ludwigsburg Palace isn't occupied by the League. It's neutral ground."

"We can't assume it's still neutral." Vivian's concern was evident. "Becca, don't enter the palace. Repeat, *do not* enter the palace."

Becca focused on her breathing, doing everything she could to maintain her speed. She hurried for the gate entrance, and to her surprise, no one tried to stop her. Instead, the guard stayed in the security box and watched her race after RC. Once she passed through the entrance, the gate closed behind her.

Yup, this is definitely a trap, Becca thought. She wasn't sure how to spring it, and usually, that's the only way to escape a trap.

"She went in," Scout said. "I have to move again."

"Becca, you need to get out of there!" Vivian's anger didn't go unnoticed.

"We have a mission to bring him in," Becca said. "That's what I'm going to do."

"Becca, for all we know there could be dozens of Brotherhood in there," Cassie said. "If there is, they won't show up on the screen."

"If there are, they'll just shoot me." Becca slowed down and caught her breath as she watched RC enter one of the palace buildings. "Come on, people. Think. This isn't a Brotherhood trap. It's an RC trap."

"You think he's doing this on his own?" Cassie asked.

"It's RC, we're talking about." Becca headed to the door of the building. "He does everything on his own."

"I don't have access to any cell phones in that building. I have no way of tracking him now, Becca," Cassie said. "You're on your own."

"Just be ready to come get me should this all go south." Becca entered the building. She wasn't exactly sure where she was, but inside looked like a fantastic art museum. Extremely well kept, loads of handcrafted sculptures and ornate designs decorated one of the long hallways in the palace. It reminded her of the Beast's castle in *Beauty and the Beast* after the spell was broken. It was beautiful, but she would never live in a place so ornate.

"Are you getting this?" Becca whispered.

"Yes. Your eye cam is still active, and I'm broadcasting your signal to all of Falcon squad," Cassie replied. "Stay on your guard."

"Cassie, I need you to direct me through these hallways. Find the exits for RC's potential routes, and give me a way to cut him off."

Becca heard Cassie's iconic sound, her typing, in her ear.

"Got it. Make a left down this hallway, then turn at your second right. That's a shortcut to the east entrance. There's the Marble Hall with a big-ass chandelier in the center of a room with vast windows. He'll have to cross through there. That's your best chance."

Becca raced through the hallways with a newfound energy fueled by hope. If she had been at this palace under other circumstances, she would've loved to study the artistry. In the back of her mind, she thought maybe one day she'd come back, that is if she made it out of this place alive.

It seemed strange that she hadn't seen a single soul in the palace. No guards, no tourists, nobody. Something was up, and she knew she was at the center of it.

She saw the Marble Hall with the chandelier ahead of her and pushed herself even more. RC wasn't in sight. She prayed she wasn't too late and hadn't missed her opportunity to capture him. She made it into the atrium of the Marble Hall, and just as she entered so did RC.

She drew her gun on him and switched to the tranquilizer setting. The Griffins had modified their guns to have the ability to shoot both bullets and tranq darts. A quick flick of the thumb and the gun toggled between the two barrels seamlessly. "Stop!"

RC came to a halt, put his hands up, and caught his breath.

Becca's emotions raced. She was thrilled to see him, as well as hurt. It suddenly became a lot harder than she realized to find words, let alone restrain herself from shooting him.

"Game hitters do fun," RC said while catching his breath.

"What the hell?"

"Game hitters do fun," he repeated.

"I'm tired of your games. Just talk to me."

He didn't say anything. Instead, he moved closer to her.

"Stay back," she said, keeping both hands on her weapon.

RC didn't listen. He continued to move closer. She countered this by walking in a circle around him while trying to maintain a decent distance.

"Tell me what's going on," Becca demanded.

"Game hitters do fun," he said again, this time moving with a more predatory demeanor.

They circled each other, playing some sort of mind game, looking for ticks or quirks that would reveal the other's next move.

"What does that mean? Why do you keep saying that?"

RC spoke a little slower as he got closer, with more intensity. "Game. Hitters. Do. Fun."

Becca picked up on a signal. At first, she thought he was being difficult, which would have been typical of RC, but there was something about the look in his eyes that told her to focus. He was communicating. Not with his words, but with his eyes. He looked scared. That was new for Becca to witness.

"You can't tell me," Becca finally realized. Of course. For all she knew, Falcon squad might not be the only people monitoring RC. The Brotherhood could be watching him somehow too. But why? He was one of them now, wasn't he?

RC moved closer. This time, Becca let him as she studied his face for any kind of subtext.

"You're frightened, and it's not because of me." She waited for a response, but none came verbally. If anything, RC's communication game worked by not answering her. If she understood RC properly, he wouldn't say the weird phrase he had been repeating. When she was right, he'd stay quiet.

"I trusted you," she said. Those words hurt more to say than she realized they would. She felt a psychosomatic pain in her stomach where he'd shot her.

He didn't respond, just kept circling her.

"You betrayed me."

Again, he didn't respond. He didn't even blink, which added to the pain in her heart. She hoped he would blink to show some sense that he was lying, but his focus was clear and true. This wasn't the RC she had known. He had changed. He had deliberately betrayed her.

"Why? You could've come to me. I could've helped."

"Game hitters do fun," he said.

So, he couldn't go to her for help. That surprised her. Becca didn't know if he'd even wanted her help. Then again, she really wasn't sure how she could've helped him. She had only been a Griffin for a year. It didn't matter to her, though. He'd saved her life last year, and she owed him for that.

"Do you know where you belong?"

No answer from RC, which worried her.

Everything he had done recently was in service to the Brotherhood, the enemy he had trained his entire life to fight.

"I won't let you do this." Becca refocused her aim on RC, ready to fire her weapon. RC stepped out of the way. Becca fired her gun, barely missing RC. He moved quickly and trapped both of Becca's arms within his. Together they fought for control of the gun. After a few quick moves, RC disarmed her and kicked the gun out of reach.

Punches and leg sweeps came at Becca with a vicious fury. A year ago, she'd be done in seconds, but her training made it manageable to block and dodge. She didn't know how long she'd be able to defend herself from the barrage. Becca had to look for an opening in RC's body language, the way he transferred his weight between attacks, something she could use to redirect his momentum and use it against him. He moved like a Fox assassin, only stronger, with a more desperate and angry intensity. Of everyone Becca had sparred with in training and fought against in the real world, RC was at the top of the list of terrifying foes. He was harder to fend off than the Fox assassin she had battled only a few hours ago at Griffin headquarters.

Becca dodged to her left and spun down to her knees, sweeping RC's legs from behind. He lost his balance and fell. It was just the break she needed. Becca punched and kicked at RC with dead-on aim. He blocked her attacks while on one knee. Their fight scenario had taken a turn. Becca was now on the assault and didn't hold back.

RC rolled backward and got to his feet, ready for round two.

They circled each other again, this time with arms at the ready. He went for the gun on the ground, which forced the fight to move closer to it. She knew that was his goal because it was hers as well.

They reengaged in hand-to-hand combat. Everything happened so quickly it was hard to plan ahead, hard to decide where to aim next. Moves and counters happened within a flash. Becca's forearms ached from the constant blocking. She trapped RC's punch and twisted behind him, shoving him away.

Becca bolted for the gun, but RC was fast and tripped her from behind. She fell to the marble floor, and they grappled, both fighting to get to the gun. RC jabbed his elbow into her rib cage and crawled toward the weapon. She mustered through the pain, grabbed his right foot, and slid him back toward her. She bent down, kneed him in the gut, and punched him in the face, forcing him to roll away.

They staggered to their feet for round three. Becca and RC kept their eyes on each other but were getting tired from all the exertion. Something had to give. Becca wasn't going to let RC win this time.

She attacked him, putting all her power and bodyweight into every strike. He didn't go down easily, and she could tell he was impressed by how far she'd come. She noticed the sweat running down his temples, which proved she was a worthy adversary. RC trapped her punching arm and twisted it behind her. She let out a yell. He had control of her now. Every way she moved could dislocate her shoulder. He twisted her arm a little more, and she screamed. Her cry of pain echoed in the atrium.

Becca gritted her teeth as her mind raced for a way to gain the upper hand. She wasn't going to be able to stay in this state much longer before her shoulder dislocated. Any second now, RC would apply more pressure, and the fight would be done. She had to do something. He pulled her arm up, which caused an excruciating amount of pain. She had to get her arm back underneath her. The only way to do that was to jump backward into him.

That's exactly what she did, and Becca felt the back of her skull impact the brow of RC's face. He let go of her arm, and they fell backward to the floor next to the gun. She was now the closest one to it.

Becca rolled away from RC, ignoring the pain in her arm, and grabbed her gun.

RC scrambled to his feet and made a run for it. The fight was over, and Becca had the upper hand.

She pulled the trigger and saw the tiny dart hit the back of his neck. RC's hand jolted to the dart and pulled it out of his neck. He did his best to keep running, but the tranquilizer had already begun working its magic. RC stumbled to the floor, fighting to stay alert. He eventually passed out halfway down the length of the room.

Becca took her time getting to her feet, keeping the gun on RC, just in case he could somehow resist the tranquilizer. He was completely out when she reached him and stood over his body, looking down.

"Becca, report!" Vivian demanded.

"I got him," she said, out of breath. "Repeat...I got him."

14

The door to the safe house flung open. Dex and Scout hauled in RC, his body still limp from the tranquilizer. They placed him in a chair in the living room and tied him down. Cassie went into the kitchen and rehooked the computer to her mobile command center.

"I'm glad you tranqued him," Vivian said to Becca as they entered the living room and stood across from RC.

"Believe me, I wanted to shoot him. For once, I didn't listen to my emotions."

RC was sound asleep, as if he hadn't rested in days. Becca picked up on a sense of doubt from her mother.

"What?" she asked.

"I don't think you should be the one to do this."

Becca wasn't going to let her mother get in the way of this opportunity. "He shot me. He wanted to kill me." She made sure that sunk in. "I'm also the only one on the team who actually brought him in."

"I could bench you…again," Vivian warned.

"Go ahead. I'll still find a way to get my questions answered." Becca looked into her mother's eyes, not willing to back down. She knew Vivian recognized her endless determination.

"If you lose control, you're off the team, indefinitely."

Vivian was the boss and polar opposite of the mother Becca had known growing up. She didn't realize how much she actually didn't know about her own mother until recently. They had yet to have a real heart-to-heart, but the thought changed as she soon realized that might not ever happen.

"Understood," Becca answered. She went into the kitchen, opened one of the cupboards under the sink, and pulled out a small kit. It was standard protocol for any Griffin safe house. Becca wasted no time as she walked past Cassie who was doing something fancy with her computers, and opened the little kit on her way back to the living room. She pulled out a syringe, added the only vial from the kit to it, cocked it, and jammed it into RC's neck.

He jolted awake. "Owww. What the hell?"

RC squirmed in the chair in the middle of the living room. Everyone watched as it dawned on him that he was tied down and unable to escape, even if he managed to free himself.

"Blue-vial injection. Ring a bell?" Becca held up the now-empty syringe gun, then returned it to its case. "It's a triple dose, as I know you've been trained to resist single doses."

"What time is it?" RC searched the room for a clock.

Becca stood tall above RC, looking down at him. "You're going to tell me everything you've done for the past six months."

"I need to know what time it is," he said, pissed.

"Doesn't matter what time it is," Becca retaliated.

"If you want me to stay alive it does."

"Seventeen thirteen," Vivian said from the corner of the room.

"Shit." Panic overcame RC, and it didn't look like he was faking. "You have to let me go."

"You're not going anywhere until you answer for what you've done." Becca was trying her best to contain her emotions.

"Oh, come on, Becca. We don't have time for this crap. I had to shoot you so you could survive. I got lucky, and here you are. Is it really that difficult to believe me? Can we move on from this, please? Life-and-death circumstances here, and I'd like to live."

Becca stared, taken aback by RC's classic blunt delivery. The truth serum was clearly working. She hadn't expected to get her answer so soon. She'd figured he'd put up more of a fight, but instead he was a chatterbox.

"The Brotherhood has all their initiates taking this new liquid tracking drug. It's coded to our DNA and makes us invisible to surveillance. Only the Brotherhood can see our whereabouts."

"So, you're saying we need to move because they'll find us?"

"No," RC said as he struggled with his restraints. "I'm saying they don't need to find us. There's a poison built into the tracker that's remotely triggered. If I miss my check-in at seventeen forty-five, they'll release the poison into my system, and bye, bye, RC."

"Why are you so special?" Becca asked.

"I'm not special," he said, tired of having to explain himself. "They do it for all initiates. It's how they keep us obedient."

Becca did her best to read the situation on RC's face. He was strong, and the truth serum was too. Something in her gut still made her not trust him.

"Uh, guys," Cassie said from the kitchen. "I just scanned his body and... he's not kidding. There's an inactive poison in his blood."

Becca didn't turn around. Her mind raced as she tried to figure out ways to make RC safe. "Can you deactivate it or scramble the signal?"

"No, the poison requires an antibody," Cassie answered.

"Which the Brotherhood already has," RC said. "Why am I repeating myself? The only way I can survive is to check in on time. I've got to go. If I'm not there five minutes after my check-in, I'm a goner." He held up his wrists, enticing them to untie him from the chair.

Becca looked to Vivian and the others. It was only for a second, but it felt like minutes.

"Tick-tock goes the clock," RC said.

"We interrogate him on the way," Vivian decided. "Get moving."

Like clockwork, all of Falcon squad packed up their gear.

Becca hurried over to RC and cut the zip ties from the armrests and chair legs. "What's the destination?"

"Meir Shipping in Stuttgart, loading bay three." RC stood.

"Got it," Cassie said. "We have to move. It's thirty-five minutes away."

The team finished grabbing everything they needed and headed out the door.

"Dex and Scout with Cassie," Vivian ordered. "RC and Becca with me."

"How much of that serum did you give me?" RC asked as he and Becca rushed into the van.

"Enough to get all my answers on the way," Becca said.

Vivian jumped into the driver's seat while Becca shoved RC into the back of the van, then got in next to him, and closed the door behind her.

"Try not to enjoy this too much," RC said.

Sweat dripped down his temples. His mouth was open as he breathed heavily, and his hands shook. This wasn't the RC she'd known for the last year. That RC had been strong, brave, and cocky. This RC looked emotionally spent and defeated.

Becca had been told in training how going undercover for long periods of time could change a person. Now she saw that firsthand. Six grueling months of constantly looking over his shoulder, always proving himself, watching his every word, and losing sleep must have warped him. RC was good at hiding his true feelings, and if she hadn't been so angry with him for shooting her, she'd feel sorry for him.

Vivian floored the accelerator and raced down the street.

"Why did you kill Hawk and Eagle squads?" Becca asked.

"They were an internal investigation I helped Dad with from within the Brotherhood. We knew we had moles inside the Griffins, and I narrowed down their options. Both squads were formed to exploit the moles. They were all traitors."

"That's why you had an old Griffin ID still activated." Becca put the pieces together. "So you could be tracked and communicate with Mason." It all made sense, even though she didn't want to accept it. She was still so mad at RC. "You cleaned house as a way to earn the Brotherhood's trust and rid the Griffins of the Brotherhood informers on the inside at the same time. You've been busy."

He nodded. "It's so easy for my father's enemies to want to use me against him. Rich boy gets annoyed with being in his daddy's shadow, decides to take matters into his own hands."

"But why?"

"Game hitters do fun," he replied.

"Why do you keep saying that?"

He glared at her like she'd forgotten her training. Then it hit her. "You have sensitive information that you won't say out loud unless we're secure."

He didn't respond, which meant yes.

"ETA fifteen minutes," Vivian notified them.

"Cutting it close, aren't you, Vivian?" RC said. "I'm all for risking my life, but this isn't what I had in mind."

Vivian skidded the van around a corner.

Becca's mind went into deduction mode. She unclipped her seatbelt and grabbed a small pad and pen from the center armrest. She returned to her seat, fastened the belt, and wrote out the phrase.

"Game hitters do fun," she repeated over and over. She felt RC's eyes on her, but she was too focused to let it annoy her.

She moved letters around and realized the phrase was an anagram.

"Found," Becca said under her breath, as she worked on another word. "Tithers? No." She scratched that out. "Grime? No." She wrote out a few more. "Sitter? No. Come on, Becca."

She braced herself as Vivian drove around another corner.

"You never could make life easy, could you?" she said to RC without looking at him.

"Well, in a few minutes you might just get your wish."

"Shut up." She scolded him but kept her attention on solving the anagram.

"You have to drop me off a block away. I need to sweat out as much of the truth serum as possible. The building will be full of Brotherhood. If they see you my cover's blown, and believe me, they're looking for you."

"Still three minutes behind," Vivian said.

Becca wrote out more words. "I found...game...mage...age." She scribbled more words.

RC looked out the front window. "You've got to let me out at that alley."

"There isn't enough time," Vivian said.

"I can run across to the loading dock, it's a small shortcut. It's my best chance." RC moved to the right-side passenger door.

"Take this." Becca pulled her earwig out and handed it to him.

"I can't," he said. "Routine check, before getting the antidote."

"Then how are we going to know you made it in time?"

"Don't lose sight of me." RC opened the door. The van came to a screeching halt, and he took off like a bat out of hell.

Becca shut the door behind RC then hopped into the passenger seat next to Vivian. They watched RC turn out of sight as he ran down the alleyway.

Vivian drove to the opposite end of the building where the loading dock was in view.

Becca did her best to not dwell on whether RC would survive. She resumed working on deciphering the anagram. The silence and nervous energy in the van was annoying. Words just wouldn't do anything to lighten the tension.

"Found..." Becca muttered while continuing to write different versions of words formed from the letters. "The...I found the..."

Becca flipped the page over the pad. "Ragtimes...no...triages...no... migrates...magister..."

"What did you say?" Vivian interrupted Becca's thought process.

"What?"

"What did you say about a magister?" Vivian asked with a shocked look on her face.

Becca showed Vivian the last sentence she'd written on the pad: "Found the magister."

Vivian's eyes widened with fear.

"What? What does 'found the magister' mean?"

"We have to get RC out of there. Now!"

15

Becca and Vivian did their best to appear like normal citizens on the street as they hurried to the warehouse. They passed the building without drawing attention to themselves and made their way to the closest door, which had two guards outside. There was an unspoken language between them. Becca and Vivian didn't need to say who they would attack and on which side. They knew to take out the closest guard to them and to do it as quickly and quietly as possible.

The guards never saw Becca and Vivian coming. Within four moves both guards were knocked out. The way they operated made it look like a dance as they infiltrated the warehouse. They used silenced tranquilizer darts as their weapons to maintain their stealth approach and didn't speak to each other for the same reason.

Falcon squad was on their game.

Dex countered Becca and Vivian by making his way into the warehouse on the opposite side. Whoever reached RC first had to help him escape.

Scout had positioned himself on a rooftop across the street from the warehouse and used his thermal scope to scan the building. He transmitted a video feed to both Becca and Vivian's eye cams. That way, they could get a wireframe layout of the building and see where everyone was positioned. The danger was that Scout had a big building to scan, and they could only get certain pieces at a time. Once it was scanned, Cassie would then interpret the scan from Scout and program a point-of-view angle for Becca, Vivian, and Dex. From Cassie's digitized version, they saw everything from the inside. They would know how many cubicles, offices, and hallways were in their path.

Cassie guided the team from within her car using all her tech wizardry. She kept the video signals clean from any interference, as the slightest glitch could cause the team to fail.

Cassie color-coded the heat signatures in the eye cam to differentiate friend from foe. Friends appeared as green, foes were red. When Scout identified RC, he would appear yellow, but he hadn't found him yet. Heat signatures appeared all over the building —a lot of red, no yellow.

Becca moved quietly next to Vivian, ready to disable any enemies they came across. She worried about RC, uncertain if he'd made it in time to avoid being poisoned.

They stopped and hid behind opposite doors in separate rooms across a hallway, as two men came around the corner heading toward them. Luckily, Becca and Vivian had moved out of the way just in time.

Becca pressed her back against the wall inside the room and controlled her breathing to not make a sound. She listened to the men's footsteps as they neared. Becca turned and faced the wall. She saw the two men's red-colored silhouettes through the wall with her eye cam. She also saw Vivian's green heat signature in the room across the way as she waited for them to pass.

Once they were clear, Vivian motioned her to keep going and moved back into the hallway. Becca joined her, their weapons at the ready. They headed farther down the hallway, passing more cubicles, staying out of the line of sight of potential threats.

A yellow arrow flickered in Becca's eye cam pointing up and toward the west side of the building. It was a guide, and as Becca tilted her head up to where the arrow pointed, she saw it led to a yellow heat signature on the fourth level.

That was RC. He was alive, but he was sinking to his knees, rocking in pain. There were three other men in the room standing above him. One wore a fox mask and held some sort of remote in his hand. The poison had been activated, and RC was running out of time. For all they knew, he only had seconds to live.

Becca and Vivian raced to the nearest stairway. They ran up the stairs, skipping two steps at a time, using the railing to hoist themselves higher. They had to climb three flights of stairs, and Becca felt panic, fearing there wasn't enough time.

Three gunshots came from upstairs. Becca looked up in RC's direction and saw his yellow heat signature holding a gun. The other three red silhouettes were on the ground, dead. The yellow image showed RC searching one of the bodies. Somehow, he had gained the upper hand, but now all the remaining red silhouettes in the building had been notified about the gunshots and were racing to find the source.

Becca and Vivian made their way to the fourth level and ran down the hallway. They fired tranquilizer darts at two enemies about to enter the room RC was in.

"RC!" Becca yelled, knowing there was no way they could stay silent now. "It's Becca. We're coming in. Don't shoot."

The eye cam showed RC's back was to them and that he'd found some sort of vial in the inner jacket pocket of one of the bodies.

Becca and Vivian entered, covering the room, and watched RC drink from the vial.

"That's disgusting," he said with a scrunched face.

Becca pressed a button on her weapon, and the light changed from blue, which meant tranquilizer, to green, meaning bullets.

"We don't have much cover here," Vivian said. "We need an exit."

RC removed the platinum-colored fox mask from one of the dead men and snapped a photo of his face on his phone. He also searched the body, but Becca had no idea what he hoped to find.

RC took the man's phone, then a photo of the other two he'd killed. After that, he confiscated the phones and put them in his pockets.

Gunfire barely missed Vivian at her door. She ducked and took cover. Becca fired back from her end, trying to keep their enemies from advancing. She shot a couple of men, then pulled back behind the wall.

"We're pinned down," Vivian shouted.

RC stumbled over to Becca's door and helped return fire down the hallway.

"I made it in time," RC said. "In case you were wondering."

"You've exchanged getting poisoned for getting shot," Becca replied. "Well done."

"At least it's more exciting." He fired two more rounds and killed two more men.

"We're not going to last long; there are too many." Vivian fired back. "We don't have enough ammo."

Three men were jolted from the side and collapsed to the floor, dead. It didn't register what had happened until she heard Scout's voice on the com.

"I can cover you after this wave. Get to the other end of the hallway after the last one goes down."

"Copy that," Vivian responded.

Becca and RC fired back at a few more of them.

The final two guys were sniped by Scout and tumbled to the floor. It was incredibly violent watching these guys get picked off.

"Go!" Scout urged.

Becca, RC, and Vivian made a run for it. They turned a corner and were startled by a barrage of bullets from the far end, forcing them to back up and hide behind the wall.

"We're cut off," Becca shouted.

RC winced, squinted, then shook his head.

Becca watched him, worried, as she saw sweat rolling down his face. Some of the poison was still in his system.

"It's working," he reassured. "The antidote is working. I just need a few more minutes, then I'll be good as new."

"You better be." Becca hunched her shoulders as debris from the bullets hitting the wall behind her sprayed around the area.

"They're getting closer," Vivian warned.

They heard shouting, felt the floor shudder, and heard the click of men reloading.

Becca used the eye cam to see through the wall: four men were just around the corner, right on their asses. She prepared for hand-to-hand combat but was surprised when all four men fell dead in front of them.

"Get a move on," Dex shouted from down the hallway. "You're clear."

Becca saw Dex's green silhouette through the wall from her eye cam. They hurried to catch up with him, keeping their weapons ready for oncoming enemies.

Dex led them to another hallway full of floor-to-ceiling windows on the left side overlooking the employee parking lot. He placed his palm against the window, and it shattered into tiny, sand-like pieces, due to his high-frequency glove.

Vivian and Becca didn't hesitate to do the same. They put on their gloves and placed their hands on the windows. The frequency was so strong, it shattered the window like an eggshell. Becca barely had to touch the glass.

Once the windows were broken, Becca, Dex, and Vivian attached a miniharpoon and cable to their guns and fired them into the floor.

Dex and Vivian jumped out the shattered window and repelled down to street level.

RC moved into Becca's space and wrapped his arms around her waist as she adjusted the cable to support their combined weight.

"Planning to drop me?" RC asked, still slightly out of it.

"I've thought about it." Becca held tightly to RC in case he couldn't support himself and used her body weight to shove them both out the window. Becca and RC descended to the parking lot below. They landed on the asphalt, and Becca pressed the retract button, which reeled in the harpoon and cable. Once the cable had fully returned, she unhooked the miniharpoon attachment from her gun and raced through the parking lot, catching up to Vivian and Dex.

"Where's my out, Cassie?" Vivian said as she kept her gun aimed at the windows they'd just repelled from.

Dex fired a few rounds when men appeared in the broken windows.

"Black Buick, four spots to your left," Cassie replied. "Your phone has the activation code uploaded already."

"Get one for Becca and RC too," Vivian ordered. "We have to split up." Vivian gave a quick glare to Becca meaning *don't kill him.*

Becca ducked behind a car to avoid being hit by oncoming fire from above.

RC shot back. Vivian and Dex entered the black Buick and started the car.

"Becca, gray Dodge Charger, two spots to the right from your current position. Specs have been uploaded," Cassie instructed.

"Two over," Becca shouted to RC amid the gunfire. They kept their heads down and practically crawled on all fours to the vehicle.

Becca made her way to the driver's side and touched the handle. The car unlocked, and she got inside, keeping her head down. RC entered through the back door on the driver's side.

"I wanted a blue one." He shut the door behind him and shuffled across the backseat, rolled the passenger window down, and continued to fire back at the men up in the building.

Becca ignored his comment as she pressed the engine button, and the car roared to life. It was truly amazing she didn't have to hotwire it. The car thought her phone was the receiver and that the owner was driving.

"I love Griffin tech," Becca said as she backed the car out of the parking spot and raced through the lot.

RC did his best to aim while Becca floored the car out of the lot.

Once clear of the building, RC climbed up to the passenger seat and got comfortable.

"Where do we go now?" Becca asked.

RC pressed the speaker button on Becca's phone and set it up so everyone with earwigs could hear through the car speakers. He also pulled out one of the cell phones he'd stolen from the men he'd killed and began searching through its notifications.

"Dex and I are picking up Scout." Vivian's voice boomed through the car speakers as the Bluetooth had already connected. "Rendezvous at—"

"No," RC said. "We have to locate the Juggernaut truck."

"The what?" Becca was so annoyed with RC she could barely see straight.

"The Brotherhood is moving the crate of rings as we speak," RC said as he scrolled through the man's phone. "It's on a Juggernaut truck. Looks like a modernized train engine."

"How do you even know that?" Becca asked, exasperated with RC for changing their plans again.

"After I borrowed the crate from you at the Harz Mountain—"

"Stole."

"Anyway, I knew they weren't going to let me stay with it, or let the rings out of their sight. They contain something the fox faces don't want out in the world."

"What is it?" Becca asked.

"A message," he said as he searched the device for more information. "The name of a magister in the Brotherhood during World War II."

"How does that help us?" Becca said.

"We get the rings. We identify the magister whose name is on the rings. We do a genealogy search with DIANA and pinpoint who's in charge of the Brotherhood now. We then end the Brotherhood for good. You can either help or get out of my way."

"How can you be sure?" Becca's heart pounded, and blood

rushed through her veins at the thought of stopping the Brotherhood from harming anyone ever again. Since they'd killed her best friend, and after what her mother had had to endure, Becca's purpose for joining the League of Griffins had been to exact revenge. To end the Brotherhood's reign of terror on the world was her highest purpose now. And, somehow, RC had a lead to doing exactly that. She could taste it.

"There seems to be a lot of security wherever the rings go," RC said, "so that, mixed with the information I extracted from multiple sources over the past six months, makes me sure."

"Why do you say Juggernaut truck?" Vivian's voice echoed throughout the car.

"Because that was the last order Mr. Fox Face, back at the warehouse, had been given on his phone before he departed for unearthly realms." RC held up the phone showing Becca the order: *Load crate onto Juggernaut.*

"His intel is solid," Becca confirmed for the rest of the team.

"Searching now," Cassie informed.

"Check within a ten-mile radius," RC added. "It can't be that far ahead of us. Depending on which way we're going."

"I should report this to Mason," Vivian said.

"He already knows," RC said. "Welcome to my mission for the past six months."

"It was all a ruse," Becca said, letting go of her anger, hurt, and confusion that had built up in the past months over RC. "Mason's panic, the concerned father…it was all an act."

"Dad and I have been doing this a long time, Becca. "We know how to deal with extreme scenarios."

Cassie's voice cut in: "I don't see any Juggernaut truck on the cameras."

"Expand the search," Vivian said.

"I did," Cassie said. "I expanded it to a hundred miles and have no hits that match RC's description."

Frustrated, RC hit the dashboard with his fist.

"I don't even know if I'm driving in the right direction," Becca said. "For all we know, we could be going the opposite way."

She saw RC's extreme frustration. It was like watching someone losing hope. After all, Becca couldn't blame him.

"Giant trucks don't just disappear," he said.

That sparked an idea in Becca's mind. "From the cameras they could."

RC looked at Becca. "What do you mean?"

"The liquid tracker in you made you invisible from all cameras," Becca began as her mind raced. "We couldn't see you unless it was with our own eyes. Did the Brotherhood figure out how to do the same for vehicles?"

"Not that I heard of," RC said. "It's possible, in theory."

"You're right. Trucks don't disappear. When was the Brotherhood order given? What's the time stamp on the email?"

RC looked back at the phone. "Seventeen thirty-five."

"We need actual eyes on the streets looking for a big truck," Becca said. "If I wanted something so important moved, I wouldn't want anyone to be able to follow it. It'd turn it invisible to cameras and count on people's laziness to not pursue."

"Cassie," Vivian said, "send out a mass alert to all Griffins within a hundred-mile radius to keep their eyes open for a Juggernaut truck that looks like a train engine. Have them take a selfie of it. If the truck doesn't appear in the photo, have them send the photo to us so you can—"

"Triangulate its route from where the photo was taken, even though it doesn't show the truck," Cassie interrupted. "Way ahead of you, Boss."

Within no time Becca received a mass text from Cassie.

"She's good," RC admitted.

"Pics are coming in," Cassie said. "Amazing."

The dashboard screen of the car displayed a map with pins in different locations. RC pressed the different pins and pulled up pictures. Multiple angles of one intersection appeared with regular cars and a giant empty space that would fit the size of a Juggernaut truck.

"Bingo," Becca said overjoyed. "Cassie, keep dropping those pins for me. We're on our way."

Becca swerved the car around, causing it to screech as it U-turned. RC braced himself in the passenger seat and gave Becca a frightened look. She ignored him, floored it, and raced down the street following the bread-crumb trail of location pins.

16

The car turned onto a busy street in Stuttgart that had many stoplights. Buildings surrounded the streets with different businesses, restaurants, and clothing stores. Becca and RC drove by as pedestrians walked the sidewalks, unaware of the dangerous game being played in their city.

Becca couldn't race among the traffic without drawing unwanted attention. She gripped the steering wheel as impatience flowed through her body while they waited at a stoplight.

"Take it easy," RC said, looking from the dashboard screen, then out the windshield. "We'll find it."

The light turned green, and Becca continued with the flow of traffic. She realized RC wasn't just looking for the Juggernaut, he was checking other cars and people on the street.

"Care to share with the class?" Becca said.

"I'm pretty sure this transportation method by the Brotherhood isn't going unsupervised," he said looking out the back window.

"Do we have a tail?" Becca asked, worried.

"No. But the Brotherhood would never move something this valuable without keeping eyes on it."

"That's like looking for a needle in a haystack," Becca said.

"Yes. Just remember the Juggernaut isn't the only thing we have to watch out for."

"Elaborate, please," Becca said.

"In my months of tracking the rings, I wasn't sure who among the movers were Brotherhood officials or just basic mercenaries working for hire. It took some clever searching, but I found a pattern. The people who were connected to the Brotherhood authority were the most basic, unassuming, ordinary-looking people you could meet." RC pointed to a few people walking on the sidewalk and someone in the car next to them. "They could be part of the supervision mission, for all we know."

Becca saw a woman dressed to get attention in high heels and a short skirt, walking along the sidewalk. As people passed her, they turned their heads to stare. "So, she wouldn't be a Brotherhood concubine."

"Concubine. Probably. Part of a top-secret mail-delivery service? Definitely not." He smiled. "But, did you notice the old couple walking in the opposite direction holding hands?"

"No."

"That's my point. You'd never suspect Uncle Bob and Aunt Louise to be carrying nine-millimeter Walther pistols. Simply because of the fact you'd never expect them to be able to run. That's how the Brotherhood delivery service likes to operate. It's basically a secret security-tracking system for your criminal FedEx packages."

The cars ahead of them came to another stop a few feet away from the corner of the next intersection. Becca noticed people on the sidewalk pulling out cell phones and taking photos of something to their right around the corner. Small crowds began to form as more people pulled out their phones and pointed them in the same direction.

"What's going on here?" Becca asked.

A massive, all-black, train-engine-looking tank, that appeared to be made from stealth-bomber-type materials, rolled up on her right and turned onto their street. When the signal went green, Becca and RC's car was only a few car lengths behind the truck.

"Um, that thing looks more like a train than a truck." The Juggernaut was a truly impressive sight. "Don't you think that's overkill for moving one crate of rings?"

"They expect someone to try to steal the rings back. Clearly, they've spared no expense."

"It looks like a minifortress." Becca stared in awe at the gargantuan vehicle. "How the hell are we supposed to get the rings out of there?"

"I can't help you answer that, Becca," Cassie said. "I'm blind here. The Juggernaut doesn't show up on any camera. Not even your eye cam. So, I'm currently useless."

"Our eye cams don't show anything either," Vivian added.

Becca saw Vivian's car appear as icons on the dashboard screen, showing that she, Dex, and Scout were two blocks away.

"What do you need to be able to see it, Cassie?" Becca asked.

Everyone heard Cassie's frustration from the tone of her voice. "I need to find the signal the Brotherhood is using to track the Juggernaut, then I can either piggyback the signal, or better yet, hijack the signal and potentially gain control of its system. Or, I have to somehow make the signal visible on all cameras to track it that way—"

"What if we were able to give it our own signal to track it?" Becca asked.

"It might work, if you're able to 3D scan it with your phones," Cassie said full of hope. "I can set your phones to scan for three-dimensional objects, but you'd have to be on opposite ends of the Juggernaut at the same time. The camera won't be able to visibly pick up the image of the truck, but it can be set to track the scan of it. Think of it like tracking a wireframe image."

"You're saying that if we get a scan of the Juggernaut, then we won't have to follow it with our own eyes," RC said.

"That's the theory."

"We'd be able to track the truck to its destination and snatch up the rings when they're being unloaded," Becca said.

"No need to infiltrate the Juggernaut en route," Vivian agreed. "Let's get that scan, people. We have a small window to pull this off. Next intersection is our best bet."

"Copy that," Becca replied.

The cars moved slowly. Becca saw on the dashboard monitor that Vivian had pulled over, and two dots appeared, indicating Dex and Scout had gotten out and were making their way to the intersection crosswalk. That put Dex and Scout at the front of the Juggernaut. Becca and RC stayed at the back behind the monster truck. They'd be perfectly positioned to scan the truck from opposite ends.

When Becca slowed, RC got out and walked casually along the sidewalk toward the Juggernaut blending into a group of people. He pulled out his phone and acted like the crowd, amazed at what he saw. Then, like the smooth walker he was, he drifted away from them and stepped into position to start scanning the Juggernaut.

The light at the next intersection turned red. Now was their chance, as they wouldn't have much time before the signal turned green. Becca watched the monitor of Dex and Scout as they entered the crosswalk. All three men started their scans.

"It's working, boys," Cassie said. "Getting a clean scan from the front and back. Still need the sides."

Becca squeezed the steering wheel tighter than before.

"I need more of the lower-right side," Cassie said.

Becca watched Dex and Scout split up to opposite sides of the Juggernaut on the screen. She checked her eye cam and watched a wireframe of the Juggernaut slowly appear in the empty space. It was extremely cool and bizarre that their plan was working.

"Wait a minute," Vivian said. "Dex, look up and to your left, twenty degrees."

Becca switched her eye cam to access Dex's point of view so she could see what he and Vivian were seeing. He was much closer to the Juggernaut, so the wireframe that formed in the empty space on the camera showed more detail.

Dex moved his camera up and to the left as instructed and focused on a wireframe outline that looked like a large oval-shaped airplane window.

"That's a gunport!" Vivian exclaimed.

"Three more on this side," Scout said under his breath, while among a small crowd of pedestrians attempting to get photos.

Then, Becca watched in horror as the gunport on Dex's side opened.

"Get out of there, that's an order!" Vivian yelled.

"The three on my side are opening too," Scout reported.

Becca tensed up as she saw a machine gun appear in the gunport.

"We're blown," Becca reported.

"Get down!" Dex shouted.

The machine gun unleashed a flurry of bullets at Dex.

Becca jolted in her seat as she watched ammunition fire out of both sides of the Juggernaut. Screams filled the air as pedestrians dropped to the ground, hurt or killed. Others ducked and cowered while trying to find cover wherever they could. Many tripped over each other as they ran away in panic.

Becca watched the dashboard screen and saw Dex had found cover behind an abandoned car. The indication dot for Scout showed him inside the corner coffee shop.

Cars and trucks drove onto the sidewalks and across the center dividing line, trying to get away from the monstrous vehicle spraying bullets into the crowd. Cars knocked over people, sandwich-board signs, tables, and chairs.

The intersection was jammed with cars attempting to flee.

Becca looked up at the Juggernaut. She saw Dex across the street, pinned down by the oncoming fire. The cars ahead of Becca crashed into each other as they frantically drove off in the distance or reversed to drive away. The car in front of her swerved in reverse onto the sidewalk, then raced across the middle of the street. Becca saw RC on the asphalt using his elbows to crawl back toward her. She couldn't tell if he was hit.

The Juggernaut fired again, forcing RC to roll out of the way toward the sidewalk. Luckily, he found cover behind an empty vehicle. Becca calculated the trajectory of the bullets and realized they were aimed at RC, Dex, and Scout. The other people were collateral damage.

"We need stronger firepower," Dex said.

"Nothing we have will even dent that armor," Scout replied.

The Juggernaut plowed through the intersection of mangled cars and sped off.

Becca jumped as her passenger-side door flung open. RC got in, out of breath.

"Please tell me we got the scan," RC said as he fastened his seatbelt.

"I only have a partial scan," Cassie said. "I can track it as long as you're within range."

"How far?" Becca asked with urgency.

"Two hundred feet."

Becca knew that meant if they followed the truck, they'd be in the line of fire and probably not last long. She looked at RC. "We lose the truck…"

"We lose the rings forever," he finished.

Becca drove around busted cars and made it to the intersection where she saw Vivian pick up Dex and Scout. As they progressed through the intersection, Vivian pulled into the lane next to them. In tandem, they raced after the Juggernaut. Cars had been plowed out of the way by the behemoth, leaving a clear path for them to follow.

"Options?" Becca asked.

"That armor is some sort of souped-up version of Chobham armor that's usually made for actual tanks. I've never heard of or seen anything like this before," Cassie said. "It sounds kind of awesome."

"How are we supposed to get in?" Vivian asked.

"Or stop it," Becca added.

"There wouldn't happen to be a bazooka hidden in this car somewhere? Like last year?" RC asked as he reloaded his weapon.

"Sure. The one car I steal is equipped with all our needs for taking on a tank," Becca said.

"Was hoping we'd be lucky." RC stared at the Juggernaut. Becca noticed his faraway expression. She almost saw the wheels turning in his mind as he tried to come up with viable options.

"Keep hoping." Becca swerved the car around a stopped vehicle that was across both lanes and continued her pursuit of the Juggernaut.

"Find where it's going, Cassie," Vivian ordered.

"I can only get an accurate calculation when you're in range of the thing. Best guess, it's heading to the highway."

"Of course," Becca said.

"We can't shoot into it," RC stated. "We can't even ram into it. That thing would just tear our cars apart. It's impenetrable from an outside attack."

"Actually, we don't need to penetrate it," Becca said.

RC looked at her funny, like she'd lost her mind.

"That thing has the rings we need to steal," Becca explained as she kept their car behind the monster truck. "Why not steal the truck itself? I'm just not sure how. We'd need something bigger than the Juggernaut. Do the Griffins have a C-130 that can land on the highway or something? Or some sort of a crane?"

"We can use a heavy-lift helicopter," Vivian mentioned. "That just might work. We'll need to stay in range of the Juggernaut in order for the helicopter to home in on our signal."

"And by staying in range, I can inform everyone which gunports are opening by seeing it on the partial scan. That should give you a better chance of survival," Cassie said.

"If you can get me close enough, I can take out the gunmen," Scout said.

"We have to time it right so we have the offensive," Dex told the team. "There's no room for error here since we don't have bulletproof vehicles."

"This is crazy," Becca said.

"I love it," RC said.

"Cassie, get me the helicopter. The rest of you, cover each other's asses. We do this as a team," Vivian said.

Both cars raced next to each other to get closer to the Juggernaut and followed it onto the highway.

"Both of you are in range," Cassie reported. "Transferring signal coordinates now."

A bigger gunport in the back of the Juggernaut opened, and two machine-gun barrels were aimed at the pursuing cars.

"Duck!" Becca yelled.

Bullets sprayed them with a vicious rhythm. The windshield shattered sending shards pouring all over her and RC. He fired back while Becca was forced to change lanes and find a blind spot from the onslaught. She felt the sting from the cuts left by the shards on her arms and forehead. Becca ignored them as she concentrated on keeping the car out of range of the guns.

The Juggernaut's firing stopped as Dex and Scout unleashed a few rounds, forcing the gunmen to duck behind the gunport.

Before the shooters could clear the opening, RC fired a shot. Becca saw a gunman jerk as if he'd been hit.

"I got one," RC said.

"Well, get the rest of them!" Becca replied from her ducked driving position.

"We need to bait them," Scout shouted after firing two rounds.

Becca switched lanes with Vivian, and together they changed formations driving in front, behind, and crisscrossing to make what was already a moving target much harder to hit. When Dex and Scout shot at the Juggernaut, Becca swerved to a side so RC could get a clearer shot. Other times she'd be the bait for Dex and Scout to do the same. They were confident they'd hit at least three of the gunmen. How many were inside the Juggernaut, that was a different story.

"Right-rear gunport is opening, Boss," Cassie reported.

Becca's car was at the left rear of the Juggernaut in its blind spot. She moved the car a lane over to the right and got RC in position to fire. Vivian moved her car one lane to the right from Becca's, which caused a random vehicle to move over a lane to his right. That allowed Becca to line up her car and give RC the best advantage to shoot into the gunport.

Becca saw the gunman aim his weapon at Vivian's car. RC fired, and the gunman dropped the machine gun out of the gunport.

The Juggernaut swerved, smashing into random vehicles, forcing Becca and Vivian to use evasive maneuvers to not get hit.

"Holy shit!" Becca had to break formation from Vivian as she jerked the car out of the way of a rolling sedan coming toward her. Another smashed vehicle slammed into the center divider, and Becca saw them struggle to recover control of their car. Becca oversteered the wheel to avoid hitting the crashed car but instead clipped it, and the next thing she knew she and RC flipped upside down and skidded to a stop in the far-left lane next to the median divider.

"Becca! Becca!" Vivian shouted. "Are you all right?"

"Yeah, yeah, I'm here." She looked over to RC who seemed a little dazed but had already managed to unbuckle his seatbelt and get upright. Apparently, he was fine. "We're alive."

"Helicopter inbound in three minutes," Cassie reported. "Do I call it off?"

"No. This is our only chance," Becca replied as RC helped her unbuckle. Becca didn't feel anything broken, but blood rushed to her head from having been upside down for a bit. RC helped her out the driver's-side window and onto her feet. He looked into her eyes like a medical examiner.

"You okay?"

She nodded and returned her attention to the highway, looking to see how far behind they were. She exhaled, more out of annoyance than exhaustion. "We need another vehicle."

A motorcyclist riding on a Ducati 999 pulled up to Becca and RC's crashed car. He opened his visor. "You two all right?" he asked in German.

Becca aimed her weapon at the motorcyclist, and he held up his hands. "Keys," she said.

He tossed the keys to her, and she handed them to RC. "You're driving," she said.

"Name?" Becca said to the motorcyclist.

"Ugh...Tobias Müller," he answered, confused.

"Did you get that, Cassie?"

"Yup. I'll put in the order, and he'll have a new Ducati by the time he gets home."

"Thank you," Becca said as they raced off after the Juggernaut with her holding onto RC as tightly as possible.

17

The wind blew through Becca's hair as RC maneuvered the motorcycle through the destroyed traffic. Smashed vehicles littered multiple lanes. Becca had to hide her head behind RC's body so she could open her eyes more. She heard a deep-base sound thudding in the sky.

"Helicopter...inbound." Cassie's voice was barely audible in Becca's ear with the sound of the motorcycle mixed with the constant howling of the wind. She looked up, and sure enough, there it was. The heavy-lift helicopter was approaching the highway.

Becca saw Vivian's car and the Juggernaut come into view. Scout and Dex were at opposite windows firing at different gunports, doing their best to conserve ammunition.

A machine gun fired back out of the right-rear port. Vivian's car was covered in bullet holes.

Becca held onto RC with her left hand and drew her pistol, aiming it at the port.

"Get us closer!" Becca yelled.

RC pulled the throttle, and they moved even faster, gaining

speed on the Juggernaut. Becca fired two rounds at the gunport. They weren't nearly as accurate as Dex and Scout's shots, but it was enough to force the gunmen inside and to stop firing for a few seconds.

"Based on...amount of gunfire...inside...Juggernaut...lack of... gunport openings...estimating...three gunmen remaining." Cassie's report was so garbled it was difficult to make out the words among the chaos. Luckily, Becca was able to hear enough to understand the message. The helicopter flew over them from the front of the Juggernaut to the back. Becca watched it begin to turn around.

The gunmen inside the huge truck aimed at the helicopter.

"Keep their attention on us!" Vivian shouted.

Becca fired two more shots, with no luck hitting her target. RC drove like a skilled pro and gave Becca as steady a shot as possible. He moved the motorcycle even closer to the Juggernaut.

Dex and Scout fired from Vivian's car, doing their best to distract the gunmen from shooting at the helicopter. Luckily, the onslaught of Falcon squad worked. The only way to keep the gunmen's attention on them was to bait them by driving their vehicles uncomfortably close. RC guided the motorcycle to the left side of the Juggernaut, while Vivian kept her car on the right. That was the distraction they needed.

The Juggernaut tried to ram the motorcycle and Vivian's car many times. RC and Vivian were entirely focused as they maneuvered to dodge the ruthless ramming attempts.

The helicopter flew a few hundred feet above the Juggernaut, staying over it as it rolled along the highway. Becca watched four cables descend from its belly.

"You need to stay as close as possible to the Juggernaut for the cable to grip and latch on," Cassie said. "The helicopter has a better chance by using your location signal."

"Easier said than done," Becca replied as she fired another shot and almost hit a gunman's arm. She fired again, but her weapon clicked out of ammunition. She holstered her pistol and grabbed RC's, ready for the next attempt from the men inside the colossal fortress.

The helicopter's cables surrounded the Juggernaut, ready to latch onto the undercarriage.

"Clear right!" Scout said.

"Clear left!" Becca added.

The cables magnetized to the Juggernaut, and the helicopter began to ascend.

"Left-middle gunport, Becca," Cassie said.

Becca fired a shot, keeping the gunman at bay.

The Juggernaut slowly lifted off the highway a foot or two, then jerked and rotated unevenly to the left. Its wheels continued to spin rapidly but had no traction. The helicopter struggled to ascend with the uneven weight.

"Becca! The left-front cable is loose," Cassie informed her.

Becca looked ahead to the driver's side of the Juggernaut; the cable was only half attached.

"If that doesn't attach properly, the helicopter will have to let go of the Juggernaut!" Cassie said.

RC sped up to the loose cable.

"We'll cover you," Vivian said, and within seconds her car was on the left side of the Juggernaut with Scout and Dex ready to fire at the gunports.

RC lined up the motorcycle next to the loose cable. Becca saw the part that was magnetized hadn't fully attached to the Juggernaut. She visualized how she would reattach the cable. It wasn't as simple as using her hands. She'd have to somehow kick it.

"Get me closer!" she shouted to RC.

Becca ducked at the sound of gunfire hitting the nearest gunport. Dex or Scout was making sure Becca was as safe as possible. Becca gripped the cable to stabilize herself. She couldn't reach the bottom magnet with her hands, so she had to kick it into place. Holding on to the cable helped steady her, so when she kicked, the recoil wouldn't unbalance RC while he was driving.

The first couple of kicks were more difficult than she'd anticipated. One time her foot slipped, another she missed entirely. She tightened her grip and angled away from the magnet in order to give her kick more power. For a second, she thought of how Bruce Lee would do his powerful karate kicks. That, mixed with her Griffin training, told her she needed more full-body power to knock the magnet into place.

"Move to the left a little, then back to the right. I need more momentum," she yelled to RC.

Bullet sparks hit the closest gunport to Becca. She did her best to focus on the motorcycle's timing as it pulled away from the Juggernaut, then moved closer to the magnet. Becca launched the most powerful kick she could and knocked the magnet into place, causing it to fully latch onto the Juggernaut.

"Got it!" Becca smiled, relieved that her plan had worked. But her happiness was short-lived as the Juggernaut began to ascend higher into the air and pulled her off the back of RC and the motorcycle.

"Becca!" RC yelled up at her.

Becca screamed as she held on to the cable for dear life.

"Oh my God!" Cassie said.

"Becca! Beccaaaa!" Vivian shouted.

Becca swung her legs around the cable to keep from dangling. "Oh shit, shit, shit!"

"Becca, climb up to the roof!" Vivian shouted.

A gunport opened, and the gunman tried to aim at her, but the angle prevented him from firing directly at her.

Becca climbed the cable as fast as she could, using her legs to steady herself and push her up, taking the full weight of her body off her arms. She was grateful for everything she'd learned from the Griffins in the past year. Without that knowledge, she wouldn't have gotten this far. She had to keep the gun in her hand, so she hooked a finger through the trigger loop and grabbed the cable. She tightened her other hand above it in a death grip and held on for dear life. Then, with slow movements, she climbed up the cable and made it to the top of the monster truck.

A top hatch opened a few feet ahead of her, and Becca knew she'd have to loosen a hand from the cable. Forcing any negative thoughts away, she grabbed RC's gun and aimed it at the gunman trying to climb out. She shot him, and he fell back inside with the top hatch closing on his head.

"What the hell am I supposed to do now?" Becca shouted. It was incredibly difficult to hear anyone's response with the sound of the rotating blades above her and the wind rushing by.

The top hatch opened again, and another gunman came up and fired at her. Becca dove across to the other side, dropping RC's gun, which slid off the Juggernaut. She wrapped her hands around the opposite cable to hold on for safety.

Luckily, the gunman ran out of bullets and couldn't continue firing. Unfortunately, he decided to tempt fate as well by climbing onto the top and doing his best to balance himself. The gunman wore fatigues with knee and elbow protection. The Brotherhood clearly had been ready to protect the crate from an attempted robbery.

Becca knew this was only going to end one way, with one of them being knocked off.

"Cassie," she said, "tell the pilot to sway."

"What?"

"Rock the Juggernaut!" Becca shouted.

Becca moved out of the way of her attacker as he lunged for her. He was crazy, but he wasn't an idiot. He grabbed the same cable she held onto and tried kicking and grabbing her.

The Juggernaut began to move side to side, causing Becca's attacker to hold on instead of attacking her.

Becca knew this couldn't last much longer, and she kicked at the man's shin to unbalance him. He moaned, and it was enough to loosen his grip. He tried to knee her in the stomach, but she saw it coming a mile away and twisted around the cable. Her foe was a big man, and she'd need to use momentum again to generate more power. Timing was everything. She had to unbalance him and loosen his hold on the cable at just the right time when the Juggernaut swayed beneath her. She imagined this was what surfing a wave might be like.

The gunman attacked, and Becca found her opening. She kicked behind his knee, avoiding his knee protector, and he lost his balance. The Juggernaut swayed, tipping downward. Becca kicked at the man's back, and he slipped over the side still holding onto the cable. He yelled as Becca kicked and kicked at his face until he lost his grip and dropped.

Becca hated being on this monstrous vehicle. The top hatch was only a few feet away from her, and she saw the handle that opened it. If she could keep her balance, she could get to it and maybe get inside. Problem was, she didn't know how many gunmen were still alive. She knew at least one wasn't injured at all: the driver.

"Cassie, have the pilot level out," she said.

A few seconds later the Juggernaut stopped swaying, which made it easier for Becca to make her way to the top hatch. She stood behind it as a precaution before she opened it. As soon as she did, bullets sparked, hitting the edges of the hatch. Becca shut the hatch and held onto the handle for stability.

"It's a stalemate," Becca reported. "I'm stuck on the top and can't go inside. There's still an active gunman."

"You're about ten minutes away from the destination," Vivian informed her. "Just ride it out if you're certain they won't go on the roof."

"I think they saw their friend fall off, so I'm hoping whoever's inside isn't willing to risk the same fate. Hopefully, they think I'm still armed."

Becca pulled out her cell phone and pressed one of her Griffin apps. "I'm jamming their communication signals. They won't be able to track where we're going."

"Good idea," Vivian said.

"And Mom...make sure there's a warm hoodie and blanket ready when this thing lands."

"Sure thing."

"And hot coffee."

18

The heavy-lift helicopter carried the Juggernaut a few miles away from the highway with Becca still holding on to the hatch's handle. It was actually quite peaceful on top of the gargantuan truck, aside from the fact that there were still ruthless gunmen trapped inside below her.

She rubbed her arms one at a time to keep herself warm from the constant blast of wind and still have a grip on the handle. Even though the flight from the highway to the destination only took about ten minutes, it felt like ages to Becca. The helicopter flew to a massive open field with a giant hangar surrounded by multiple structures, a helipad, and an airstrip. Becca figured it was some sort of private airport. At the moment, she didn't care. She just wanted to get off the damn thing and get warm.

The helicopter landed the Juggernaut between a squad of Griffins outside the main hangar. Armed Griffins surrounded the truck while others unhooked the magnets, allowing the helicopter to fly away and land elsewhere on the property.

Becca felt her body warming up as she slid down the front of the Juggernaut. As soon as her feet touched the pavement, two Griffins arrived, one with a hoodie and a warm, heavy blanket, the other with her coffee.

"Welcome back, Ms. Romanov. Job well done."

"Call me Becca, please."

The two men escorted her inside the hangar and out of the line of fire. The Griffins had their weapons at the ready for any feeble attack from the gunmen still inside.

Becca stopped to watch the squad open the Juggernaut with fancy tools.

"Ms. Romanov," one man said, "I'm instructed to take you to the briefing room."

"In a minute. I just surfed the skies to bring you this precious cargo, and I want to see my prize." Becca took another sip of coffee as she watched the Griffins open the back of the Juggernaut. Inside, only one gunman stood; the rest were on the floor, dead or severely injured.

After a strong warning in German from the Griffin squad leader to the gunman, he surrendered and was taken into custody.

Becca saw lights in the distance approaching fast and knew it was the rest of Falcon squad. Vivian, Dex, and Scout arrived first, while RC roared up on the motorcycle behind them. They parked inside the hangar next to Becca and exited their vehicles.

"Just in time, team." Becca sipped more of her coffee, enjoying the warm sensation.

RC, Vivian, Dex, and Scout watched with Becca as other Griffins wheeled the crate of Nazi rings down the ramp and toward them.

"Wait," Vivian said as the crate was almost wheeled past them. "Open it up."

No one argued. The crate top was removed by two men. Falcon squad peered inside at the thousands of Totenkopf rings that had tarnished over time.

So much fuss, Becca thought. A sense of accomplishment rushed through her as she looked at the enormous number of rings. She had found them, lost them, been shot, attacked, benched, betrayed, and taken an unexpected flight for this crate of metal. It'd better have been worth it.

"Take them to authentication," Vivian ordered.

Becca stared at the rings until the two Griffins covered them up with the wooden top. She watched the crate as it was wheeled off for authentication. Part of Becca wanted to follow them and not let the rings out of her sight, but she knew she was among friends. All the Griffins had been intensely vetted, or they wouldn't be here. She didn't deeply trust anyone in the hangar, besides Falcon squad, and RC was still on a slippery slope with her.

Dex and Scout came over to Becca. Dex put a hand on her shoulder and said, "Not bad."

Scout just nodded at what she'd done. Then he and Dex walked off, probably to find the cafeteria or something.

Vivian spoke with the two men that had given Becca the hoodie, blanket, and coffee, but Becca didn't pay much attention. Instead, she watched the crate until it was no longer in view. She looked around at the rest of the Griffin squad carrying the dead gunmen and wheeling the injured away on gurneys.

Cassie's car arrived at a rapid speed and skidded to a screeching halt in the hangar. The noise made Becca wince, but she let her annoyance go because it was energetic Cassie. She got out of the car with an enormous amount of excitement that reminded Becca of a kid about to get their first video-game system.

"You just missed the rings. They hauled them off to authentication."

"The rings?" Cassie said, perplexed. "Oh, yeah, that's your department." She turned around and faced the Juggernaut. She lit up with even more energy, if that was possible. "Come to mama!" Cassie hurried away and began studying the Juggernaut like a mad scientist.

"She's right," Vivian said walking over to Becca. "I gave Cassie clearance to study the technology used to build the Juggernaut.

Hopefully, we'll learn more about the Brotherhood's upgrades. In the meantime, the rings are our responsibility."

Becca looked at her mother for a moment. Then Vivian gave Becca one of the best hugs she'd ever remembered getting from her. It was different from how she'd been hugged back when her mother was undercover. Those were flimsy and weak, but this hug was full of a mother's proud love for her daughter, mixed with an overwhelming sense of power, confidence, and approval.

"Don't do that again," Vivian said in a quiet, calm, deeply terrified tone.

"I'll do my best," Becca replied.

"Take a few more minutes, then report to the briefing room."

Becca nodded, and her mother walked off with the two men who'd taken care of her. Becca looked back at the Juggernaut and watched an excited Cassie as she explained things to the scientists. Becca figured they were already dissecting the construction of the vehicle. Cassie nerded out, saying fancy technological words that sounded like gibberish to Becca.

A stillness caught her attention out of the corner of her eye. It was the one thing out of place: RC stood at the entrance to the hangar, not looking at the Juggernaut, not looking at her, and not showing interest in where the rings went. Instead, his attention was out toward the open field, and it appeared as if he was looking for something or someone.

"You all right?" Becca asked as she walked up to him. She was too tired to cause a fuss, and the look on his face told her he was worried about something.

"Have you ever been here before?" he asked.

Becca shook her head.

"They'll be looking for it now, and we don't know how long we have before they locate us."

"I overheard the Griffins. All signals coming from that thing have been jammed. We should be safe for now."

"For now," RC repeated, but what he meant was, not for long.

"Talk to me...please," Becca said, not realizing how much she really needed it.

"They're never far, Becca."Remember when I told you in the car about the Brotherhood and how we need to watch out for the most unassuming people?"

"Yes."

"The best way I can describe it is like a chessboard. The pawns are hired guns. The rooks are small squads that imitate security guards and escorts. The knights are deadly assassins, then you get into the upper levels, which is where the trails start to disappear. The bishops are the ones who get the orders from the Brotherhood and farm them out to the lower-tier operatives. In order for the Brotherhood to hide in ultimate secrecy, the bishops have no idea who's giving them orders, and the Brotherhood followers have no idea who the other members are."

"And no one knows who runs it," Becca said.

"That's how they stay in the shadows. You can't snitch on anyone, because you don't know who to snitch on. I'm looking for a bishop. There are only so many places you can hide a Juggernaut, so I'm looking for the most unassuming candidate nearby who could report our current location. While I was undercover, I found the bishops were the only way to find concrete information. So, in my process of tracking the rings, I had to find the person who'd received the message to pick up the stash. Turns out, that was their only task. Pick up the cargo, then deliver it to the next destination. They didn't know who would be on the receiving end. Kept things harder to track. Then I had to find the person who would take the rings to their next place, and so on." RC let out a big sigh, showing his concern and exhaustion for their situation. "Bishops follow every bit of precious cargo ordered by the Brotherhood without knowing what it is they're tracking. That's why it's so difficult to trace them. They rarely use technology, and the moment there's an inkling they've been discovered, they change their methods."

"So, you think a bishop is in the field right now?"

"There are only so many places to go after stealing a Juggernaut with a helicopter."

"And with the invisibility tech they have that hides them from cameras, they could be out there right now." Becca understood RC's concern.

"If the rings do contain the name of a magister, you can bet the Foxes won't like running around with their tails between their legs."

"There's only one way to find out," she said as she began to walk away from RC.

He didn't follow. He kept looking out at the field with concern.

"You coming?" she urged. "Six months of undercover work, tracking, shooting friends, and you're not interested in seeing if it was worth it?"

RC turned his attention away from the field and walked up to Becca. "You're not going to forgive me for shooting you, are you?"

"Would you?" she asked while walking beside him.

"I'll let you know when it happens," he replied as they moved through the hangar to the authentication room.

The room in this new miniaturized Griffin HQ reminded Becca of a high-tech car wash. They arrived at the huge viewing glass and gazed at four people dressed in protective gloves, masks, and gowns, all in the process of authenticating thousands of Totenkopf rings.

Each ring was carefully separated by one of the four people standing on opposite sides of the conveyor belt. The rings moved through a machine-operated laser scanner that digitized each ring into DIANA's system. Over one thousand three hundred and forty-three rings had already been scanned according to the projected hologram counter. Two rings had been identified with the reversed date by the counter and separated from the others.

"Within an hour or so we'll know how many rings with wrong dates we'll have to decipher," Becca said, exhausted from the chase on the highway and her flight on the Juggernaut.

RC walked away from the viewing glass, and Becca followed. They made their way to the briefing room and saw Vivian waiting for them as she stood next to Mason Carter, in the flesh, who had just loaded a plate of food.

"We've got a lot of catching up to do," Mason said as he gestured for Becca and RC to get food before the meeting began.

Everyone sat around a conference table as RC explained his six-month mission.

"I was tracking a potential mole in connection with a suspected attack on Becca and gained access to his computer while looking for evidence that would prove his betrayal of the Griffins. The evidence I found mentioned a delivery of two high-value artifacts that would be transported in an hour. High-value artifacts are only sent to actual members of the Brotherhood, not the mercenaries who work for them. It was my best chance to ID one of those members."

Becca studied RC's body language as he elaborated. She didn't see any sign of deception.

"I intercepted the package before it arrived at the drop point and was disappointed. No Foxes were waiting for it. Just another bishop. I opened the package, and inside were two Nazi rings and a piece of an old letter from Heinrich Himmler."

RC pulled out his phone and uploaded a photo to the hologram that hovered in the middle of the table. It projected the piece of the letter for everyone to see. The German words of the partial letter glowed with a light-blueish hue. DIANA translated German into English:

With this newfound knowledge, I have permanently etched your name on my rings to expose your false rule as the self-proclaimed "magister" of your organization of Foxes. Only I know which rings contain your secret and where they are hidden. If I am killed to ensure my silence for knowing of your existence, instructions have been given to publicly release this information you're so desperate to keep hidden.

Your delusions will end, and my Reich will prevail. Once the Allies are defeated, my Reich will hunt down all your Foxes, and you will be replaced by God's rightfully chosen.

Me.

   Heinrich Himmler

"I didn't know how to decode the rings and could have used the help of DIANA, but I couldn't access her without blowing my cover. So, I took a photo of the message, returned the message to the empty package, and sent it on its way in order to buy some time. I kept one ring for myself and sent the other one to Becca through Antonio Herrero. I knew she wouldn't be able to resist another treasure hunt. Whenever I got a sense that the Brotherhood was closing in on Becca, I sent the fox logo as a warning so she could escape in time. You know the rest."

"It was all you?" Becca's heart filled with relief. The entire time she'd thought RC had betrayed her, but he'd been protecting her from afar. Becca wasn't going to let him off that easy, though. "That message would've saved me so much trouble, RC!" She gritted her teeth. Becca couldn't believe he'd had that kind of valuable information on him this entire time.

"Where's the fun in that?" he said.

His attitude always made Becca's blood flow with anger. It made it easier to be mad at him, no matter how good-looking he was.

"Is there any other evidence I can use to ID a new member of the Brotherhood?" Mason asked.

RC shook his head. "All the information I found stated the rings and letter supposedly contained the name of a magister from World War II. I couldn't find any more info, as a bishop almost blew my cover, and I had to lay low for a while."

"Almost?" Vivian asked.

"He disappeared after I had words with him."

"You killed him," Becca stated.

RC didn't answer, but it was clearly a yes. What bugged Becca the most wasn't the fact that RC had killed someone to keep his cover intact, it was that she'd gotten used to killing to survive. It made her uneasy how casual she'd become when talking about killing. A year ago, she would have flipped out. She didn't recognize herself anymore.

"You did a good job identifying all the moles you could, son." Mason was very good at hiding his thoughts. "It's even more dangerous for you now that we have the rings. That goes for all of you," he said, looking at Becca and Vivian.

"With all due respect," Becca began, expecting to be cast aside, "Falcon squad actually recovered the rings, sir."

"And a job well done," Mason said. "But the targets on your backs are even bigger now."

"So, you just want us to sit back and do nothing?"

"Becca," her mother warned.

"On the contrary," Mason stated. "I'm going to use Falcon squad as bait."

19

Becca sat still, surprised at Mason's attitude toward the current situation with Falcon squad. She had become accustomed to his always benching her and giving the "fun" missions to more qualified operatives within the League of Griffins. She had expected to be cast aside because of her continued punishment for her previous failures.

"Exactly how do you plan to use my squad as bait?" Vivian asked, while casually leaning against one of the walls of the room with one foot on the floor and one against the wall.

Becca was surprised Vivian questioned Mason.

"If the rings contain what that part of the letter says, then we've finally gained the upper hand against the Brotherhood," Mason said with more joy than Becca had ever seen in him. "This will be the first solid lead we've had at discovering a magister for over a hundred years. You can bet they're nervous."

The surprise wore off, and Becca found her voice. "And where do we come in?"

"Draw them out," Mason said.

Becca's mind raced to find the real meaning behind that

statement. Questions scrolled through her brain so fast she was unable to verbalize them.

Mason's nonchalant attitude matched RC's, which Becca had become all too familiar with. It was the first time she truly saw a resemblance between father and son.

RC and Vivian didn't speak up, although it was clear they wanted to. Everyone was just as surprised as Becca.

Mason walked around the conference table. "You've angered the Brotherhood, and they're going to be looking to kill you any chance they get. I want you to let them," Mason said with complete confidence in his new plan. He stopped walking.

It took Becca a few moments to really comprehend what Mason had suggested.

"You're talking about staging something," RC said.

"Yes."

RC sat back in his chair with his hands clasped behind his head. "I love staged killings. I'm in."

"They'll know we're baiting them," Vivian said, arms crossed. "They'll know it's a trap."

Mason showed no sign of frustration. "Of course, they'll know. But they won't risk missing the opportunity to spring the trap."

Becca tried to understand Mason's strategy. If they were going to set a trap, they'd have to create some kind of bread-crumb trail to actually get the correct people to show up. That meant the bait had to be something the Brotherhood really wanted or needed, something they'd have no choice but to come out of their damn foxholes for.

"We draw them out by auctioning off the rings," Becca suggested. "After we decode them, of course."

Everyone stared at her. What she suggested was bonkers. They'd just risked their lives to retrieve the crate of rings, and now she was suggesting they give them back to the enemy.

"We set it up as an auction," she explained, "and we use my charity, partnered with Brittany Hewes." Becca looked around and saw the group was intrigued. "I'll post about it on social media, then let the rest of the media platforms publicize it. The Brotherhood would know about the auction instantly."

"Do it," Mason said. He looked at Vivian. "Nest-protection protocol."

"Yes, Boss." Vivian nodded.

Nest-protection protocol was one of the most expensive strategies the Griffins had. Becca had heard about it in her basic training but had never been part of it. A nest was any location where Griffin operatives were being kept safe—a hotel, a restaurant, and in this case, the auction venue, filled with undercover Griffin operatives. Everyone working the event would be a Griffin. The waiters, the MC, the coat checker, the valet, and the caterer. So, if the Brotherhood tried anything, there was little chance the thieves would get out alive. The problem was getting the right bad guys to show up to the party.

"Good hunting," Mason said.

RC stretched his arms in his chair and let out a groan. Then he slapped his palms on the conference table. "This'll be fun."

A ding notification and a red blinking light appeared in the middle of the conference table. Mason pressed the button, and a hologram projection of one of the authentication workers appeared.

"Yes?" Mason said.

"We've completed scanning the rings. All the information has been sent to you through DIANA."

"Thank you. Good work."

Becca watched the information appear, hovering in different windows above the conference table.

"Isolate the rings with the misprinted dates," Mason said.

The hologram rearranged and showed nine specific rings, each with the date printed the same way.

"We might still be missing some rings," the authenticator said. "Unfortunately, sir, if we don't have all the rings, we won't be able to fully decode the message."

Mason leaned on the conference table with his fists. "We have the most advanced supercomputers to date, and we're still unable to decode the message. So much for making things easier."

Becca went into decode mode, considering she'd been yearning to solve the mystery of the rings for what felt like ages.

"I know a missing ring's date. The year, nineteen thirty-eight, the month, July, and the day, the twenty-third." Becca was unable to contain her excitement. The hologram added the new date to the rest, and 38.07.23 hovered in the air above the conference table. Everyone stared at her, startled by her energy. "Those are the numbers on the ring I had. Photographic memory, remember? DIANA, plug in all the dates, and run the decode programs."

Processing, DIANA said.

The hologram lined up the ten dates in order and produced multiple possibilities for what they could mean. Different algorithms did their mathematical decoding, but the results weren't helpful.

"Something's not right," Vivian said, talking to the hologram of the authenticator. "Doesn't look like we have the full code."

"That's everything that came in the crate, Ms. Romanov."

"All right, thank you." Mason pressed a button, and the authenticator disappeared.

"We only have a piece of the puzzle," RC said. "Himmler was clearly no dummy if he knew how to hide these rings without anyone finding them." He leaned back in his chair and closed his eyes after letting out a disappointed sigh.

Becca continued to look at the hologram algorithms, watching the different types of decoding processes it was running. Anagrams, cryptos, the Enigma-device algorithm, and the Caesar cipher. Nothing produced any result that made a remote bit of sense.

"What I don't understand is," Mason said, "if I was Heinrich Himmler, why would I want to hide the rings in the first place?" Mason scratched the white hairs on his chin as he thought about potential answers.

"He knew World War II was ending," Vivian said. "He didn't want the Allies to obtain them. Maybe he was covering for the Brotherhood? Ensuring their secret would never be found."

RC rocked back and forth. "Yeah, but if he wanted to do that, why not just give the rings to the Brotherhood and let them hide it?" RC spun around in his chair.

Becca searched through the decoded meanings of the rings. There were so many results.

"Becca," Vivian said. "What do you see?"

"Gibberish." She waved her hands, rearranging the numbers, letters, and meanings. "The year of the date on the rings are all the same and don't appear to mean anything other than when the rings were made. Same thing for the months. But the last numbers on the rings don't make any sense, no similarities. They could be the day they were manufactured, but it just...it doesn't feel right."

Becca reset the dates to their original way and started over.

"DIANA, translate the last number of each date into the German alphabet."

Translating.

It was done in a second.

"DIANA, rearrange the letters into word possibilities," Becca said.

DIANA did her thing, and different words, like *bing, ewe,* and *win* appeared on the screen, but none of the words or letters lined up to reveal a full name.

RC moaned. "We're going to be here a while."

Becca didn't care. Yes, she was tired and sore, but solving this puzzle was something she could stay up all night doing. She enjoyed it, and it somehow gave her boundless energy. Or, her coffee had finally kicked in.

"Keep at it," Mason said as he walked to the door of the conference room. "Report to me when you've cracked it. Becca, I'll inform your superior you're no longer suspended."

Becca inhaled with relief, feeling a heavy weight lift off her shoulders.

Mason nodded, then left the conference room.

RC went over to the food table and grabbed a croissant. "Congratulations. All it took was you surfing a Juggernaut to get back on the team."

"Who said you were even on the team?" Becca replied.

RC shrugged and looked around. "I'm here and not behind Griffin bars." He slumped back down in his chair, took a bite of the croissant, and put his feet on the table. "So, what the hell are we supposed to do with this?" He gestured to the hologram of the rings' dates.

"We're still missing a piece," Becca said.

"That's obvious," RC said with a mouthful of croissant. "But what piece?"

Becca didn't look at RC. She was too focused on the puzzle. "Some sort of key cipher or something that will tell us the proper way to arrange these letters or words."

Becca began her own deduction process out loud. "What was it Mason asked. If I was Heinrich Himmler, why would I hide the rings in the first place?"

"Yes," Vivian said. "Becca, what are you on to?"

Becca continued rearranging letters and words. "I think that's the wrong question." She felt Vivian's curious look. "Not *why* would I hide the rings, but *who* am I hiding them from?"

"The Allies. Obviously," RC said.

"Or the Brotherhood," Becca said. "Think about it." She used World War II images of Himmler in the holograms to explain her theory to Vivian and RC.

"I'm Heinrich Himmler. I'm an egomaniac. I'm in charge. I give orders. I want to hide some rings, they get hidden, but only I know where they'll be hidden." Becca took a breath. "Maybe the men who buried the rings were killed so they couldn't leak the secret."

Vivian sat down in a chair, intrigued by Becca's out-of-the-box thinking.

"Once the war ended, maybe it was a financial insurance policy for him if he wasn't executed," Vivian suggested.

"Or he didn't like reporting to a superior," Becca said. "What if Heinrich Himmler was one of those," Becca gestured to RC, "bishop guys back then?"

RC sat up and listened.

"What if he didn't know who he was taking orders from?" Becca said.

"I hated that for the past six months," RC said.

"Exactly." Becca pointed at RC. "And history tells us Himmler was a massive diva. He wanted control. Especially of his own destiny. DIANA, pull up everything we have on Heinrich Himmler and the Totenkopf rings."

The holographic browser windows appeared, and Becca moved everything around as she narrated her theory. "Himmler had men at his disposal. If he wanted to conduct a secret investigation, he would have men do it on his behalf without them knowing why. If they didn't follow his orders, they'd be eliminated. He'd start by following the mail, so to speak. Where did his mysterious orders come from?"

"Follow the messenger. Like I did," RC said. "Maybe he traced it back to its source."

"A member of the Brotherhood," Vivian chimed in as she began to understand where Becca was going with her theory. She leaned on the table watching the holograms. "If Himmler actually did trace the message back to the source, he might've discovered the man's identity."

"And discovered that this man was in charge of a secret organization known as the Brotherhood of the Fox," RC said. "I don't know, Becca, that's a big stretch."

Becca stopped rearranging the hologram windows and looked through them at RC. "During the war, the Brotherhood didn't have the technology to stay as hidden in the shadows as they do today. Considering they sent orders on paper, it's possible Himmler found the magister."

RC said, "So...Himmler discovers there's a magister, identifies him, then secretly inscribes his name on the inside of the rings? Why?"

"Leverage," Vivian said. "Himmler wanted ultimate power, even more than Hitler, and what better way to stay in power than to be able to blackmail those trying to control you?"

RC bobbed his head from side to side as he thought about the possibility. "The Brotherhood wouldn't like that. They'd kill him."

"Precisely," Becca agreed. "So, Himmler decides to hide the secret name on some of the rings and send the Brotherhood on a massive scavenger hunt."

"To keep himself valuable," Vivian added. "Only he knows where the rings are, and if they kill him, they lose the rings forever."

RC continued to state the chain of events. "But, when the war ends, the Brotherhood decides to cut all loose ends and allow the secret to stay hidden forever."

"Yet, Himmler has the last laugh, because the secret of the rings is still out there."

"That could be anywhere in the world," RC said. "We need some sort of clue to help us narrow down where to look."

"I've missed something. I know it." Becca thought about it for a while. "DIANA, pull up the rings that have the weird dates."

Each ring appeared across the conference table.

"Scan them for any defects or similarities, something that's different from the rest of the rings in the crate, besides the dates."

Scanning, DIANA said.

The rings were scanned at the same time, and certain sections of each ring were highlighted in different colors. Pieces of the sig runes were all highlighted on each ring.

"Isolate the runes," Becca said.

The rest of the rings disappeared, leaving only the highlighted portions of the runes. They each looked like a lightning bolt or a spider's leg when not part of the rest of the ring.

"I've seen this somewhere," Becca said. "But where?"

Becca twisted one of the floating runes around in midair, hoping to trigger her memory.

"Just looks like a bad drawing of the SS logo to me," RC said.

"Ohhhh!" Becca said. "DIANA, put the runes in a radial formation, then search all the Heinrich Himmler records for similar symbols."

Processing.

The sig runes hovered in a circle. They looked like legs, but two were missing. DIANA searched through known Himmler and Nazi symbols, then bleeped with a match.

"Holy shit," RC exclaimed as he stood and looked at the newly formed hologram matching an old picture.

The symbol matches the Nazi sigil known as the Black Sun, DIANA said.

"And where is a known Black Sun sigil? In Wewelsburg Castle," Becca said.

The hologram pulled up a photograph of an atrium with the Black Sun logo as a dark-green mosaic in the center of the white marble floor.

"The SS Generals' Hall in the North Tower," Becca said.

"Pack up," Vivian ordered. "We leave in an hour."

20

Becca and RC arrived around eleven thirty in the morning at Wewelsburg Castle, a triangular Renaissance castle that had been built between 1603 and 1609. The castle, situated on a hilltop, had three round towers at the corners and was surrounded by massive walls and nearly hidden by beautiful landscaping. On this gloomy day, the exterior seemed shrouded in an aura of despair.

Becca looked around, marveling at the architecture. Her knowledge of the castle came from the research she had done and overflowed in her mind. "Did you know Himmler planned for the castle to be the spiritual center of the world once the war had ended?"

"Fascinating," RC replied, not interested.

They crossed the entrance bridge that had been built over a former moat and was now filled with grass and a walkway. After passing through a stone archway, Becca and RC continued into the castle. They played tourists as they passed a small group of students there to learn the history of Himmler's time in the fortress. Not far in the distance, Becca saw Vivian by herself, at a safe distance from her. Dex and Scout were across the way, being as casual as ever, not drawing attention to themselves.

If you didn't know any of Falcon squad, you'd never suspect they were working undercover together. They methodically progressed from one area to the next. First Dex and Scout would enter, then Vivian, and then Becca and RC would follow. This made it so they could cover all exits in case of an attack from the Brotherhood. They were securing each room.

"I wasn't expecting to be outside so soon with targets on our backs," RC said. "Are you sure Cassie's invisibility camouflage will do the trick?"

"I didn't understand what she said, other than she stayed up all night adapting the technology from the Juggernaut to create her own version of it for us," Becca replied. "She seemed really excited about it." Becca held her phone to RC. The left side of a split screen showed an image of where she and RC, as well as the rest of the team, were. None of Falcon squad appeared on the right screen. "Seems to be working just fine."

Becca and RC passed Himmler's wine cellar, then went up the stairs to the North Tower and into the SS Generals' Hall. The Generals' Hall was thought to have been the inner sanctum of the Nazi-SS upper echelon. The circular room had beanbags for guests to sit on, and there, in the center of the room, was the green Black Sun symbol etched into the marble floor with twelve sig runes symbolizing the twelve spokes of the sun. The hall was surrounded by twelve pillars and had twelve windows in alcoves around the room that clearly showed Himmler's obsession with a cult significance for the number twelve.

Using DIANA, Becca scanned the Black Sun logo with her cell phone. The X-ray appeared on her screen, and she saw what looked like faded mechanics way beneath their feet.

"Something's hidden under the floor in the room beneath us," she said.

Falcon squad casually made their way below to what turned out to be the crypt. Vivian did a hand motion that told Dex and Scout to guard the entrance and exit, preventing bystanders from entering while they inspected the room.

The crypt was directly below the General's Hall. It had twelve pedestals near the walls underneath twelve descriptive, disturbing paintings depicting what life had been like under Nazi rule. In the center appeared to be an old firepit.

"This is where the Nazis made s'mores, right?" RC asked with a grin.

Becca couldn't help but smile. "According to history, this chamber housed an eternal flame to honor officers who'd died, but no one knows for sure."

"History usually has it wrong, from my experience," RC said.

Becca scanned everything in the crypt with her phone. It showed there was indeed a room or chamber below them. What appeared in the X-ray was a bunch of mechanical arms leading from the pedestals to the firepit.

"There's definitely a secret room under us." Becca pointed to the pedestal next to Vivian. "Those stone things are all connected to the center somehow. Looks like a lock of some kind. We need to open it in order to proceed."

RC walked over to another pedestal and pushed down on it. He struggled a bit, but eventually, the top receded downward. "Ha! It's a big-ass button." He let go, and the stone lever returned to its original position.

Becca looked around at all twelve pedestals, searching for hints on what to do next.

"There must be a specific sequence to press in order to unlock the mechanism in the middle," Vivian said.

Becca's mind spun with possibilities. She looked at the room and the paintings on the walls, but nothing contained a hint of what the combination was to unlock the mechanism.

Vivian aimed her phone at the firepit. "DIANA, scan the lock mechanisms, and identify the unlock sequence."

Scanning, DIANA replied. Within seconds, DIANA sent a diagram that highlighted the order to press the twelve pedestals to everyone's cell phones.

Vivian was closest to the first one. "I've got it," she said as she stood on top of the stone and let her bodyweight press it down until it clicked into place. "Becca, you're next."

To the left, behind Becca, were the second and third pedestals in the sequence. Becca followed her mother's lead. She stood on the second pedestal and waited for it to click into place, then moved to the third one. RC had to press the fourth, Becca the fifth, and RC the sixth. Vivian stepped on the seventh and waited. Once it clicked, she got off the pedestal, and it snapped loose and returned to its original position.

"Crap," she said.

"It broke?" Becca asked.

"Of course," RC said.

Vivian got back up on the seventh pedestal, and everyone heard the mechanism unlatch. "Looks like I have to stay here. You two continue without me."

Becca moved to the eighth pedestal and stood on it. After the click, RC did the same for the ninth and tenth. Becca stood on the eleventh, and RC finished by standing on the twelfth.

A fire flared up from the center of the pit. The crypt began to echo with rusty mechanical noises from beneath them. The cement rim that encompassed the firepit moved clockwise, revealing steps that surrounded the fire. Once the rim completed its orbit, the flame descended down the center of the floor, revealing a large spiral staircase that led to the secret room.

"Don't take too long," Vivian said.

Becca and RC hurried down the spiral staircase for three stories. The fire illuminated the middle section of the large square room but didn't reach the dark corners. Becca and RC used the flashlights on their cell phones to illuminate the darker areas of the room.

"I love secret rooms," RC said. "Look at all this stuff."

Becca shared RC's excitement as she aimed her flashlight around, illuminating old stolen treasures. Paintings were stacked up against walls, and different kinds of jewelry mixed with loose rubies, diamonds, sapphires, and jade-colored emeralds were hidden in chests with gold coins.

"Oh, shit." Becca stopped in her tracks.

"What is it?" RC asked aiming his flashlight in the same direction as Becca's.

Toward the back of the room, their flashlights illuminated a desk full of papers next to a row of filing cabinets. Becca lowered her flashlight to the floor, and her eyes widened as it highlighted the bones of a man dressed in black, wearing a gray-and-white fox mask, only it wasn't the same as the one worn by Becca's attacker. Instead, it looked dated. Clearly, the Brotherhood had upgraded their assassin gear since the forties.

"Well…we're definitely in the right place," RC said.

Becca walked over to the body and removed the mask. It was brittle to the touch and broke apart as it revealed the skull underneath.

"Looks like your theory was pretty accurate. The Brotherhood was after Himmler."

Becca inspected the body and found a hole in the chest.

"Think he's been here seventy years, give or take a few?" RC asked.

"We'd need an actual expert to verify it." Becca took a screenshot of the skull and mouth. "DIANA, run a dental scan, and search for any matching records from the end of World War II."

Processing, Diana said.

"Maybe we could get lucky with this guy's identity," Becca said.

Her phone beeped. *No records are available*, DIANA reported.

Becca sighed.

"Well, he's definitely Brotherhood," RC said. "Identifying Fox assassins is damn near impossible without more leads. Even with our tech."

Becca opened filing cabinets that lined the walls and saw papers from the 1930s and '40s. She went to the desk while RC wandered around.

Being extremely careful looking at the papers on the desk, not wanting to contaminate any precious piece of information, Becca gently moved the papers around. She opened the desk drawers and found a journal.

"RC!" she said.

He hurried over. "What'd you find?"

She held up the leather journal with the Nazi eagle and swastika on the cover. They cleared an area of the desk for them to search through the journal. RC held his cell phone flashlight so Becca could flip through the pages.

"There are dates and times of schedules with orders Himmler had given to the SS," Becca said. "Thefts of Jewish art, execution orders, and secret transportation orders for the Führer's movements throughout Germany. Also, his architectural plans for this castle."

"Spooky stuff," RC said. "It's like it was supposed to be a Nazi Temple of Doom."

She flipped to the back of the journal and saw a somewhat blurry photo of an Asian man in a crowd of people. She held up the photo to RC. "Any ideas?"

RC shrugged.

"Last entry is dated May 21, 1945. That's two days before Himmler supposedly died from cyanide poisoning."

"Again, I have the feeling history got it wrong, but that's probably because of the dead Fox assassin to my right." RC returned his attention to the journal. "There's a page missing."

"So, his last entry is gone," Becca said, getting more bummed by the second.

"Or is it?" RC aimed his phone at the blank page behind the

ripped one and took a photo. "DIANA, isolate the imprinted letters in this photo."

Processing.

RC turned his phone to hologram mode, and the letters floated in front of them.

Complete, DIANA said.

There, hovering in front of Becca and RC, was a digitized version of the impressions on the last page of Heinrich Himmler's final entry, translated into English.

"Oh, wow," Becca said.

RC smiled. "It's the other piece of the note I intercepted with the two rings."

False Magister,

I have discovered your secret organization foolishly operating under the flag of a fox. To partake in any organization, let alone be a leader of said organization, is an abominable crime against the Nazi party. My Reich will never do the bidding of the Chinese.

With this newfound knowledge, I have permanently etched your name on my rings to expose your false rule as the self-proclaimed "Magister" of your organization of foxes. Only I know which rings contain your secret and where they are hidden. If I am killed to ensure my silence for knowing of your existence, instructions have been given to publicly release this information you're so desperate to keep hidden.

Your delusions will end, and my Reich will prevail. Once the Allies are defeated, my Reich will hunt down all of your foxes, and you will be replaced by God's rightfully chosen.

Me.

Heinrich Himmler

Becca felt an extra surge of energy flow through her body. She looked back at the photo of the Asian man in the crowd.

"This must be the magister." She looked at RC, who showed the same excitement on his face. She could tell he was thinking the same thing as her. "No wonder DIANA couldn't decode the name on the rings."

"She wasn't looking for the correct ethnicity."

Becca looked back at the hologram. "DIANA, pull up the letters from the decoded rings."

The ten letters appeared, hovering next to the full note left behind by Himmler.

"Arrange the letters to form names of Chinese descent," Becca said.

The letters floated in the air, swirled, and moved around as they formed a multitude of names in different variations. The hologram listed each name, one after the other.

RC watched with anticipation. "There are quite a few names here, Becca. Might still be a while before we can narrow it down."

Becca took that comment to heart. "Cross-reference all names during the year 1945, emphasizing any possible association with the Nazis."

Processing.

One name was highlighted.

"Wei Bingwen," RC said, staring at the hologram.

Becca's heart skipped as she stared at the name. Time appeared to have come to a standstill as she reveled in knowing she'd solved the mystery of the rings. Granted, she'd had a super computer's help, but even then, she'd used her own mind to complete the puzzle.

"Who the hell is that?" RC blurted out.

"Not a clue," Becca said as she hurried up the spiral staircase out of the secret chamber.

"Oh, I guess we're leaving now." RC grabbed a handful of coins and hurried after Becca.

They reconvened with Vivian, Dex, and Scout at the van outside of Wewelsburg Castle. Vivian drove while Becca sat in the passenger seat and the rest sat in the back.

"Souvenirs from your museum visit, gentlemen?" RC asked as he handed a coin to Dex and Scout.

"Should be able to get a few beers with this," Dex replied as he admired the coins.

"That's right," Becca said into the phone. "W-E-I, Bing, like *ding* with a *B*, W-E-N. Bingwen appeared as one word."

Mason's hologram replied. There's a Wei Shipping Company that deals out of China, owned by a Chen Wei."

"I'm having DIANA cross-reference Chen Wei's facial similarities with the photo I found from the journal with Wei Bingwen." Becca pulled up the hologram processing from her phone and held it in the center of the seats for all to see. "Let's hope it's a match."

Everyone but Vivian watched the progress bar with immense anticipation. Vivian glanced back for a second, as it was too difficult for her to resist.

Seventy-four percent... Seventy-nine percent... DIANA said as the progress bar kept moving.

"Come on," RC said. "Don't make my past six months turn out to be for nothing."

Becca agreed with RC's sentiment but didn't say anything. The amount of hope building up inside her as she watched the progress bar was enough to have tears forming in her eyes.

The progress bar finished and flickered. *Ninety-four percent probability match.*

"Yes!" RC sank in his seat, relieved.

"Well done, Falcon squad," Mason's hologram said.

A few tears fell down Becca's cheeks as her heart filled with hope, knowing she was even closer to keeping the promise she'd made to Barry to bring an end to the Brotherhood. She wiped away her tears, not wanting the rest of the team to see her vulnerability.

"Nice work, Becca," her mother said with a smile and a quick glance, before returning her attention to the road ahead.

"Now it's time to set a trap for Chen Wei," Mason said.

21

The InterContinental Hotel in Frankfurt was the ideal place to stage the gargantuan auction event. With Rebecca Lake Romanov and Brittany Hewes as the hosts, this was an occasion all media outlets would cover. The more publicity, the better. On the surface, it appeared to the public to be just another peek into the glamorous lifestyle of the wealthy, but in reality, the more eyes on the event, the more difficult it would be for the Brotherhood to attack.

News outlets from all over the world had been invited to cover everything, the ancient items being donated for auction, celebrities, social-media influencer's, fashion, even the food being served. This charity event rivaled the yearly Metropolitan Gala in New York City.

Becca made her way through the ballroom in an incredibly comfortable, yet stylish and classy, dark-blue dress. She wore one strap across her right shoulder. The dress had a tight waist, and a skirt draped from her waist to form what looked like a small pool on the floor. The blue color changed from a deep-colored bodice down to her knees, where it turned into a medium blue, reminding one of stunning waterfalls in Bora Bora.

Vivian, dressed to the nines in a floor-length purple dress, walked close to Becca. Dex and Scout, dressed in tuxedos, walked behind them, acting as security guards. The Romanov persona was in full effect, as was the Griffin nest-protection protocol.

The building was under the control of the Griffins.

Cassie's voice sounded strained in the earpieces. "Don't take this the wrong way," she said, "I'm glad I'm on the computer. Everybody I've scanned that has entered the building has concealed weapons. Must be 3D printed, which explains why they're all getting past security undetected."

"Keep calm," Vivian responded. "Stick to the plan. Let's not provoke anyone into using them."

As Becca looked around, she thought there was no way Chen Wei would be leaving without giving her and Falcon squad the information they needed. The only problem was, the auction had already begun, and Chen Wei hadn't arrived yet.

A gavel hit the mallet. "Sold!" the deep-voiced and enthusiastic auctioneer said. "Three million dollars to bidder number two-five-seven. Thank you, madam, for your generous contribution. Next up, lot number fourteen, an archaic jade dragon from the Shang dynasty."

Becca and company made their way out of the auction room to the press room where many celebrities and icons were reveling in the glamorous attention. Brittany Hewes, Becca's friend, and cohost for the event was dressed in a black, slightly outlandish and revealing dress. A tight, sheer bodice with appliquéd swirls that looked like octopus tentacles stopped just below her waist. The skirt had three different puffy layers. Each layer changed from a light shade of black to darker shades. As the layers fell from her hips to the floor, they became bigger and bolder. Brittany finished her interview as she stood next to the step and repeat banner and reached out to Becca, inviting her to join.

Vivian spoke in Becca's ear: "There are only three more items before the rings, and our guest of honor hasn't shown his face."

"Understood," she said before heading over to Brittany. They shared a big best-friend hug and smiled at each other.

"I still can't believe how quickly this event was put together," Brittany said in Becca's ear while still hugging her. "You're getting a knack for this."

"It's only because I learned from the best," Becca replied. She wasn't going to tell Brittany she had nothing to do with setting up the event. It was all the Griffins' handiwork.

They looked at each other while holding each other's arms.

"I hope nothing tragic happens this time," Brittany said, referring to the attack at her grandfather's funeral. "As awful as it was, it was an exciting experience."

Becca's eyes widened with surprise. "Brittany, I didn't know you had such a dark side."

"The dark is where things are more interesting," she replied.

"Depends on the level of darkness." Becca concluded Brittany was tired of her good-girl image the world had come to know. She wished she could share the full truth with Brittany, but it was too dangerous.

The photographers made a lot of noise, shouting directions at them for photo opportunities.

"Ms. Romanov, Ms. Hewes, let's get some more photos of the hosts," a reporter shouted in German. Camera shutters clicked rapidly. Becca and Brittany posed as besties for the photographers, while Vivian, Dex, and Scout waited off to the side, keeping their eyes open for the target and any other potential threats.

The constant flashes that went off in Becca's eyes made it difficult for her to see. Brittany was a natural in front of the cameras and made it appear so easy as she struck different poses. Becca had to really fake it and find the right kind of modeling stance. This sort of crap reminded her that she required more social training.

"Oh my...look at *him*," Brittany said glancing to her right.

Becca saw RC, handsomely dressed in an all-black tux, coming toward them. He was also a natural in front of the cameras. Add that to the list of things that annoyed Becca about him. His natural charisma, his good looks, and the ease with which he lived in high society were all part of a growing list Becca kept to herself. She was pretty sure she saw a bit of drool in the corner of Brittany's mouth as she gawked at him.

RC waved at the cameras. "I haven't missed my item's auction yet, have I?"

"One more before yours, RC," Becca replied with a put-on sense of respect for him, hoping to mask her jealous feelings. "RC, this is one of my best friends and the cohost, Brittany Hewes. Brittany, this is—"

"Reed Alexander Carter," Brittany said, unable to contain her excitement. "I can't believe it's taken Becca this long to introduce us."

RC, Becca noticed, enjoyed pissing her off with his reaction and the flirtatious gazes he gave Brittany.

"Becca told me she was making waves with you in the charity world but neglected to mention that photographers were unable to capture your true beauty." He kissed the top of her hand. Brittany was all for it.

"Thank you," Becca blurted out, trying to break up the flirting, "for your...generous donation." She was surprised by the amount of jealousy that flowed through her as she watched RC and Brittany flirt. She had to keep reminding herself that RC was putting on an act, but it was way more difficult to accept than she'd anticipated.

"Yes." Brittany's eyes continued to shower sparks all over RC. "The statue of the Egyptian goddess, Isis, your family donated is an incredible artifact and one I'm sure wasn't easy to part with."

"My family became tired of it collecting dust somewhere." RC smiled at Becca. "They decided to put it to good use."

Becca forced a smile back, knowing he was enjoying this exchange.

Brittany said, "I'd love to know the story of how your family acquired it."

RC glanced at Becca. She knew he was ready to move on. He kindly held out his arm to Becca. "Some stories are best kept secret," he said as Becca looped her arm through his.

The photographers had become louder and were now aiming their cameras at a white Hummer limo that pulled up to the sidewalk. An Asian man, about five foot ten, stepped out and didn't acknowledge the crowd. He wore a top-of-the-line custom black velvet tux with deep-red velvet lapels. He seemed to glide along the red carpet in his perfectly polished Louboutin black-leather and red-soled shoes. A dark-red satin scarf draped around his neck completed his attire.

"Target has arrived," Vivian said in Becca's earwig.

"Eye cam has a positive-identity match," Cassie said from her operations van. "It's him, it's Chen Wei."

Chen Wei was a good-looking man, Becca thought, but something seemed off about him. Something sinister. Probably because he had thousands of dark secrets he didn't want out in public. What did she expect from a person who ran the most terrifying secret organization in the world? What really bothered Becca was that she couldn't get a solid read on Chen's personality. He didn't carry himself like a thug or Fox assassin, nor did he carry himself like a trust-fund baby. He was definitely a businessman, but Becca deciphered from his appearance that he wasn't an honest one. She could tell he knew how to manipulate situations, and Becca made a mental note to be extra cautious when trying to trap him.

Chen Wei didn't stop to answer questions and had his three bodyguards open a path for him to finish his entrance without being disturbed.

"Is it me, or does he look...bored?" RC asked.

RC's instincts were right on the money. Chen Wei looked underwhelmed by the event. His demeanor exuded boredom. That seemed odd to her. For someone who was supposed to be in charge of such a dangerous organization, boredom shouldn't come with the territory.

"Be ready for anything," Vivian cautioned.

Wei approached, and Becca stepped forward, putting on the Romanov charm.

"Welcome, Mr. Wei. Thank you for coming to our little auction."

Wei didn't even look at Becca. Instead, he focused his attention on Brittany. "An invitation to an event hosted by Ms. Hewes is never a wasted opportunity." He kept his gaze on Brittany in an almost robotic way. It was extremely unnerving. "It's an honor to be in your presence again."

Brittany, with her effortless professionalism, acknowledged Becca and RC. "I didn't do this all by myself," she said. "Let me introduce you to my cohost, Ms. Rebecca Lake Romanov, and I believe you might've heard of Mr. Reed Alexander Carter, whose family has made a favorable donation to our charity."

Chen seemed resistant to look at Becca and RC, but he finally obliged.

"Yes," he said with no expression of interest, "I have heard of Mr. Carter. You recently returned from a six-month...what was it? Vacation? Excursion?"

RC froze, and his eyes narrowed. Only Mason and Falcon squad knew he had been off-grid for the past six months. The only way Chen Wei would have known of RC's absence was by being Brotherhood. That, mixed with his ancestral name being on the rings, added to the confirmation that they had verified their target.

Chen didn't give RC a chance to respond as he turned his calm, eerie attention toward Becca. "And the recently newfound descendant of the Romanovs. Quite a find you discovered. Thousands of Nazi Totenkopf rings lost since World War II. You should be careful. There are many who would kill for such a prize."

"Nothing compares to the financial killing these rings will earn at auction." Becca didn't blink. "I'm honored these historical artifacts will finally be used for a...positive cause." She wasn't afraid of him. She didn't care if he was the magister of the Brotherhood. He was going down, and she wasn't going to be underestimated.

Chen Wei nodded.

Vivian interrupted the staring contest. "Mr. Carter, if you'd like to join everyone inside, your donation is about to go up for auction." Vivian gestured for everyone to go back into the ballroom.

"That's what I'm here for," RC said. He motioned for Wei to go first. "After you."

Wei didn't hesitate. He entered the ballroom and took a glass of champagne from one of the waiters' trays. His bodyguards followed him, keeping their eyes on Dex and Scout. Becca glanced at RC, and they shared a quick exchange of *here we go*.

"Next up is lot number sixteen," the auctioneer said. "Donated by the esteemed Carter family, an authentic Egyptian statue of Isis. Starting bid is one million dollars."

A woman raised her paddle. Another man in the back of the room raised his and another at a table taking phone bids raised his hand, driving up the price.

Chen Wei let out a sigh of boredom, like a child seeking attention.

"Are you not enjoying yourself, Mr. Wei?" RC asked.

"Although the venue is exquisite and the cause of our...lovely hosts is noble, I find the function of auctions to be a bit dull."

"In what way?" Becca asked.

"I find the artifacts not nearly as valuable as the stories they represent. Take the story of you finding your crate of rings in the mine, Ms. Romanov."

Becca froze, as it wasn't public knowledge that she'd found the rings in a mine.

"I believe your information is mistaken," Brittany said. "Becca found the rings beneath Wewelsburg Castle. The facts were confirmed in her press release."

That had been, indeed, the false statement that had been released by the Griffins to protect Becca's cover.

Wei didn't seem fazed. "You and I both know, Ms. Hewes, that the best sources of information are from our own network and not the public eye." Chen looked at Becca with an unnerving amount of confidence. "It makes things more...enjoyable."

Another person raised their paddle for RC's artifact.

"Five million, five hundred thousand. Thank you, sir. Do I have five million six?"

Becca saw Vivian a few paces behind Chen keeping her eyes on him and his bodyguards. Dex and Scout were ready to pounce. Becca also noticed that Brittany had become more intrigued by Chen Wei's point of view about the auction.

"And what might we do to help you enjoy yourself more?" Brittany asked.

"Raise the stakes to be of more value," Chen said.

Chen's attitude finally made sense to Becca. He wasn't interested in anything at the auction. How could he be? Since he was the head of the Brotherhood, a mere auction was nothing to him. He valued the secret of the rings.

"Sold!" the auctioneer said with a bang of his gavel. "Seven million, five hundred thousand to bidder six-four-zero."

The crowd clapped.

"Main-event time," Cassie said in Falcon squad's ears.

Two security men wheeled the crate of Totenkopf rings onto the stage. They removed the top, and a camera guy zoomed in on the thousands of rings.

"Lot number seventeen," the auctioneer read. "Discovered by one of our hosts, Ms. Rebecca Lake Romanov, deep within a secret chamber of Heinrich Himmler's Wewelsburg Castle. Here we have 11,500 Nazi Totenkopf rings, lost since World War II. Starting bid, ladies and gentlemen, is sixty million dollars."

People raised their paddles as the price climbed. Becca realized Chen wasn't bidding, and that wasn't good for Falcon squad. If he didn't bid on the rings, then their plan to trap him was shot. Part one of the plan was to draw him into the limelight, and part two was to separate him from his bodyguards. The best way to do so was to get him in the winner's room backstage after he won the bid on the rings.

"Come on, make him bid," Vivian said in Becca's earwig.

More people raised their paddles as Becca frantically thought of something that would urge Chen to participate.

"Seventy-five million," the auctioneer said. "Do we have eighty million?"

Chen took a sip of champagne and showed no sign of interest in bidding.

"If you win the bid," Becca said, feeling their window of opportunity slipping away, "I'd be willing to share the true secrets of how I recovered the rings."

RC looked at Becca with alarm. She knew he didn't like this dangerous game she was playing. To tell the truth of how she'd found the rings would mean exposing the secrets of the Griffins. If the magister of the Brotherhood knew all their secrets, they'd be destroyed. There was extreme value on the table now.

"Ninety million," the auctioneer said. "Do I hear ninety-five?"

Chen Wei looked at Becca, and for the first time, it felt like she actually had his full attention. "It is not your secrets I'm interested in, Ms. Romanov." Chen turned his attention to Brittany. "It's yours, Ms. Hewes."

"Excuse me?" Brittany said, taken by surprise.

"I've never been so intrigued to know someone's secrets as I am to know yours. Would you honor me by sharing time with me one evening?"

Becca couldn't believe what was happening. At first, she thought she'd misheard Chen, but by the look on Brittany's face, she'd heard him perfectly.

Brittany seemed startled and flattered. "You want me to go on a date with you?"

Chen and Brittany had locked eyes. Becca saw Brittany's confusion and felt the attraction between them.

"Is this really happening?" RC asked.

Becca was just as shocked as everyone else.

Chen held out his hand to one of his bodyguards who placed his bidding paddle in his palm. "Does this raise the stakes for you, Ms. Hewes?"

"I'm game," she said, unable to resist the intrigue. "If you win the bid, I'll honor a date with you where I share some of my secrets. Not all, mind you. But you have to win."

"Of course. A woman must maintain some of her secrets. I find the stakes agreeable."

Becca couldn't believe this outcome. She would never have suspected the magister of the Brotherhood would genuinely want to go on a date with her friend. In a way, it was so petty it actually made sense. Becca didn't even have to look at RC, as she could see the shock in his body language. Becca caught Vivian smiling in the distance at the randomness of the events.

Chen Wei raised his paddle. "Two hundred million."

The room went silent.

"Two hundred million dollars," the auctioneer announced. "Do I have two hundred ten?"

Becca looked around the room, as did the rest of the crowd, and wondered if someone would partake. Brittany enjoyed the attention she continued to receive from Chen Wei, who didn't even face the crowd or the podium.

"Two hundred once? Two hundred twice..."

No one raised a paddle to challenge Chen Wei. The auctioneer slammed the gavel.

"Sold!"

22

A room backstage had been designated as the signatory area for all winning bidders to sign and make their purchases official. There was a man at the desk who oversaw all money transfers for the auction. He was also a Griffin. Chen Wei's bodyguards examined the room before allowing Becca, Brittany, or anyone else inside. They frisked the agent to see if he had any concealed weapons on him, checked the main desk, chair, and other potential areas that might conceal threats. Once everything was cleared, they allowed Chen, Becca, and Brittany to enter.

RC stayed behind, interacting with patrons at the auction. Dex and Scout entered the room with Becca as her bodyguards. Becca and Brittany went behind the main desk next to the agent and proceeded to have Chen sign the necessary documents. It wasn't on paper. The signing was all done digitally, with hand scans and voice recognition. Two hundred million dollars was not an amount to transfer lightly.

Vivian entered the room. "I'm sorry to disturb you, Ms. Hewes, but you're being asked for by a Jennifer Waters."

Brittany sighed with annoyance at the name.

"Forgive me, Mr. Wei," Brittany said. "If I don't deal with Ms.

Waters now, she'll call every day for the next month asking me to host her annual fundraiser for Procter and Gamble."

Chen nodded and watched her leave with a possessive eye. Vivian escorted Brittany out of the room. Once they were no longer in view, Chen returned his attention to digitally signing the necessary documents. He placed his palm on the last document and had it scanned.

"One would think you'd have a simpler way to sign all the documents. My hand is cramping."

Four suppressed shots were heard, and Chen's bodyguards fell to the floor, limp with tranquilizer darts in their necks. Chen didn't have time to react as Becca, Dex, Scout, and the sales agent all held tranquilizer guns aimed at him.

"I knew tonight was going to be fun," Chen said.

Dex and Scout relieved the fallen bodyguards of their weapons, then frisked Chen. He didn't have any weapons on him.

"I suggest you take a seat, Mr. Wei," Becca said.

He sat down with the biggest smile on his face. He was enjoying all the excitement.

RC entered and drew his weapon. "This one's loaded with live rounds, Mr. Wei."

Becca flicked the switch on her gun from tranquilizer to bullets.

Wei sat comfortably and crossed his legs. "To what do I owe such grand attention? Ask me anything. I expect my champagne was spiked with truth serum. That would explain why I feel so relaxed."

"You're going to identify and disband all members of the Brotherhood of the Fox or, so help me God, you will not leave this room alive," Becca said with a burning fire in her eyes. She felt Barry's spirit behind her, waiting to witness justice for his death.

"And then what happens to me after I do what you ask, Ms. Romanov?"

"Against my better judgment, you'll be handed over to the Griffins, and your fate will be decided by them. If I had my way, I'd pull the trigger right now."

Chen smiled again. "I believe you, Ms. Romanov. Well, this all sounds quite adventurous. Unfortunately, there's a major flaw in your plan."

"What's that, Mr. Magister?" Becca asked, ready to shoot.

A knowing smile appeared on Chen's face. "I'm not the magister."

"Bullshit," RC said. "We have hard evidence that proves you're in charge of them."

"No. My sources tell me you have hard evidence that points to me being a *potential* magister of the Brotherhood of the Fox. Not *the* magister." Chen tapped his hands on his chair's armrests and looked around the room at everyone. "Awkward."

"Your grandfather's name is on the inside of ten of the Totenkopf rings," Becca said, frustrated, knowing he wasn't lying. There was no way he could be resisting the truth serum.

"That means *he* was once the magister," Chen said patronizing Becca. "I say, good for Granddad." Chen's attitude showed he really didn't care.

RC shared Becca's frustration. "Brotherhood tradition keeps leadership in the bloodline."

"Traditions change," Chen said. "Besides, why would I run the Brotherhood of the Fox? Think about it."

Chen's words forced Becca to imagine different scenarios about why he wouldn't actually be the magister. For all she knew, his grandfather was forced out of leadership at the end of World War II, and Chen didn't seem like a responsible leader. The options were endless, and she didn't have time to guess the answer.

"When did the tradition change?" Becca was pissed. "Who's running the Brotherhood?"

Chen shrugged. "Your guess is as good as mine."

"How did you know all that stuff about us when you arrived?" RC asked. "Only people in the Brotherhood know that information."

"Wrong again, Mr. Carter. You don't get to be me without having your feet in both puddles."

It hit Becca like a brick in the back of the head. "You're a veil," she said, more frustrated than ever. "You play both sides."

"Exactly, Ms. Romanov. I knew you'd get there, eventually."

"If he's a veil, then this entire op is a bust," RC said. "We need to leave."

"But we're just getting to know each other," Chen said with a childish whine.

RC kept his weapon aimed at Chen but moved closer to Becca. "We'll find another way."

Becca shook her head. "No. He knows more than he's telling." She saw it in Chen's eyes. Becca lowered her weapon and moved closer to Chen, putting her face in his. "You just dropped two hundred million dollars for a date. You like to play games. You like to play both sides. Now you expect me to believe you have no idea who the magister is?"

"It's one of life's great mysteries. The Brotherhood is extremely thorough. Much like the side you fight for. You have my condolences about your friend Barry."

He was trying to push her buttons. It worked. Becca lunged toward Chen but was pulled back by RC. Dex and Scout moved forward as they kept their guns on Chen.

"Don't, Becca," RC said. "We'll get him later."

Chen laughed. "I hardly think so."

Becca realized he was a master at playing deadly games, but she was going to win, and she vowed he wouldn't see it coming.

"You don't care who the magister is." She saw from his eyes that he didn't. "Nor should you. As long as the money comes in, you don't care which side it's from. You get what you need, and that's all that matters."

"It's paradise, Ms. Romanov," he said.

"No, it's boring." The moment the words left her lips, she knew she'd found Chen's true pressure point. To someone who has everything—money, power, and a well-established machine—the one thing money and power couldn't overcome was flat-out boredom.

"What are you going to do with the rings?" RC asked.

"Store them in my collection," Chen replied. "It's a good insurance policy. You never know when you might need one."

"You won't last long with the Brotherhood knowing you have the rings that contain the secret of their magister," RC said.

"They need me."

"For what, exactly?" Becca asked.

"Everything."

"Every veil has an expiration date," RC said.

"You're not wrong, Mr. Carter. That's why I've managed to make myself indispensable."

"No one is indispensable," Becca said.

"Incorrect, Ms. Romanov. In order to be indispensable, I knew I had to be different from any other contact who worked each side, and you know what? It was incredibly easy."

"What did you do?"

"I played along. The worst thing anyone could have in this business is a conscience. Morals impede one's ability to be effective. Eliminate your morals, and you can achieve anything."

"Except how to overcome boredom," Becca said, which wiped away Chen's smug smile.

"True. When you get to my level, it is extremely difficult to keep your mind motivated. It's all too easy to fall into the mental abyss of dull living. Fancy events, terrorist attacks, drugs, murder, going to the mall, it's all dull, dull, dull!"

"How sad for you," RC said.

"But now I'm making new friends. Life is on the up," Chen said.

"We're not your friends," Becca replied.

"Ohhh. That's harsh. I just gave your organization two hundred million dollars for a box of rings. I deserve more of your attention. Think of what we could achieve together."

"He's trying to mess with us, Becca," RC said. "Don't listen to this weasel."

"There's no need for name-calling, Mr. Carter. I believe Ms. Romanov is capable of thinking for herself. Something you're spectacularly failing at this year."

RC moved to punch Chen, but Dex held him back. "Keep your wits about you, man."

"Such a fragile, tiny ego," Chen said. "Believe me, we can resolve all of this without the need for violence. Do you have any more of that truth serum? I'm afraid it might be wearing off, and I'm having too much fun."

"Who's your contact in the Brotherhood?" Becca asked. "If you're playing both sides, you're communicating with both sides. Who's your contact?"

Chen shrugged and threw up his hands. "I repeat: your guess is as good as mine. The process is very old-fashioned. I receive notes many different ways, with instructions and drop points. That's it. It's all very mysterious." He smiled, intrigued by the process.

"You've never tried to learn the identity of your contact?" Becca asked.

"I never want a good mystery to end."

Becca wasn't getting anywhere with Chen. This entire setup had been a bust. The decoding of the rings had led her to a dead end. Becca's blood boiled with frustration knowing they were back to square one. The smirk on Chen's face made her want to scratch it off like an angry cat, but that wouldn't help the situation. Instead, Becca decided to abort the mission. Somehow, they had to find another way of discovering the real magister.

"We're done here," she said to RC and the rest of Falcon squad. She returned her attention to Chen. Becca didn't want to leave him feeling superior in the situation. "I'm bored."

That broke through Chen's armored confidence. His eyes narrowed at her. Apparently, no one had insulted his presence so simply and with such effect.

Becca smiled and nodded for the team to exit. Like clockwork, Falcon squad left the back room without drawing attention to themselves. Becca and RC were the last to leave. RC kept his gun on Chen so he'd stay in his chair.

"Let's move," Becca said after concealing her weapon underneath her dress.

Becca and RC returned to the ballroom and headed for the front to make their exit.

"One day, I hope I get to shoot him," RC said.

"Not if I shoot him first," Becca replied.

They made it halfway to the ballroom entrance when a spotlight shined on her and RC, causing them to stop.

"Leaving so soon?" Chen's voice carried throughout the ballroom, causing people to hush and look at him. "We were just getting acquainted."

Becca and RC watched Chen emerge from the back room with a newfound sense of control. He didn't even need a microphone.

"You know, I find the cure for boredom to be surprisingly simple at times. When you find yourself drained of enjoyment, just spice things up."

He snapped his fingers.

In an instant, the cameramen, the reporters, and the bidders all drew weapons and aimed them at Becca, RC, Dex, and Scout.

"The Brotherhood has a hefty bounty on both Mr. Carter's head and your own, Ms. Romanov. I can't help but feel I'd be missing out on an opportunity by letting you go." He put his hands in his pockets and rocked back on his heels. "And I can't resist a good opportunity."

23

Becca had hoped everything would go smoothly with the auction, but who was she kidding? The worst part of all was these people weren't even Brotherhood. They just worked for Chen Wei.

"That's what we get for rushing to organize this auction." Becca kept her cool and focused on Chen as he approached.

"So, what do you say?" Chen began. "Shall we go for a ride and dump you both into a foxhole?"

Becca smiled. "Not today."

RC and the rest of the waiters and staff in the room drew their weapons on Chen and his goons. Dex and Scout joined in the standoff by aiming their weapons at the enemy. The entire ballroom was full of guns pointing at one another. The only two people who faced each other in the room that weren't looking down the barrel were Chen and Becca.

"I can't remember the last time I was in a standoff," Chen said, overjoyed. "I'm starting to like you, Ms. Romanov."

"I can't say the feeling is mutual, Chen," Becca replied.

Chen took a tiny step closer. Becca wasn't intimidated. RC and a few others fidgeted, ready to pull their triggers.

Chen spoke softly. "You and your security were well equipped, but I was unable to get a clear read of Ms. Hewes. Is she…aware of our affiliations?"

He wanted to know if Brittany knew of the war between the Griffins and the Brotherhood. It had been in Becca's best interest to keep Brittany in the dark.

"Not at the moment," she said.

"I would like to keep it that way, if you don't mind. I don't want to blow two hundred million on a date that doesn't happen, now, do I?"

"Falcon one. Did you copy that?" Becca asked into her com. She didn't care if Chen heard her.

"I did," Vivian replied. "She's safe. Working on an extraction for you."

"Negative. There's no need for extraction. I have the situation under control," Becca said.

Chen looked around the room at the standoff and smiled, not believing Becca's statement. "You have the situation under control? Funny way of showing it."

"Let's face it. You're not going to turn us over to the Brotherhood." Becca had learned from Chen's personality that he loved to gameplay, and she wanted him to know she knew it.

"And why would I not do that?" Chen asked.

His enjoyment of the game and absolute confidence in his control helped Becca maneuver the situation. She decided to throw him off by tantalizing him with something he'd never have dreamed of. "Because you'd be throwing away an extra valuable asset."

"I already do business with your organization from time to time, Ms. Romanov."

"Not business with *my* organization," Becca said with a slow smile. "Business with me."

"Becca, what are you doing?" RC asked with Chen still in his sights.

Becca held up a hand for RC to calm down and let her do her thing. Something she knew was very difficult for him.

The room was eerily quiet as the fate of everyone rested on this conversation.

"What could you, a nineteen-year-old girl, possibly have that'd be of value to me?" Chen asked, intrigued by Becca's implication.

"You're too well known among our affiliates. That's why you're stuck. Forced to operate at a distance. I, on the other hand, am able to play in the field."

"And you're willing to double-cross your organization just so I don't turn you over to your enemy?"

"No," Becca said with an unwavering strength fueled by her deep code of honor, "I'd never double-cross my organization, but I am willing to do a side deal for you using their resources."

"Becca, don't do this," RC warned.

"Oh, Ms. Romanov, you are naughty." Chen's face lit up. He paced in front of them, giving thought to her proposal. "To have you and Mr. Carter in my back pocket...oh, the thrill."

"So, we have a deal?" Becca asked.

"No. Not yet. I need proof you'll honor our agreement and not just fly back to your nest the moment I call off my men."

"Then what do you suggest?" Becca wasn't looking forward to what Chen's devious mind would come up with.

"A trial of trust."

Becca and RC glanced at each other with concern, knowing they might be leading themselves down a dangerous road.

"Trust goes both ways, Chen," she said.

"Should your trial prove fruitful, it may spark a partnership between us." Chen put his hands in his pockets, relaxed with all the guns still pointing at him.

"You'd have to have something I really want to truly partner with me, Chen," Becca said.

"I can help you find the magister. The *real* one."

That unexpected offer made Becca's heart race. RC wasn't as convinced.

"You don't even know who your own contact is. How could you possibly be able to help us find the magister?" RC asked.

"I haven't taken the time to look, Mr. Carter. My arrangement with your enemy has been incredibly beneficial to me over the years. I've seen no reason to look a gift horse in the mouth."

"So why risk ruining your arrangement now?" Becca asked.

"Ruin my arrangement? No, no, no." Chen smirked as he paced. "There's nothing I could do to ruin my relationship with them. They need me. I insured my survival with them long ago. Worse thing they could do is spank me."

"So, what is this trial then?" Becca asked, ready for him to get to the point.

"I've heard from my sources that you and Mr. Carter have encountered an actual Fox assassin and lived to tell the tale. I find that fascinating. Grown men in costume, wearing masks to instill terror in their victims before they kill them. Except, when it comes to you two, they failed. Looks like the Brotherhood is slipping, or you have unparalleled skills. Skills that could prove useful to me."

"What do you want, Chen?" RC asked, annoyed.

"I want you to acquire one of these alleged Fox-assassin masks for me to see with my own eyes and keep in my collection."

Becca was taken aback. The irony of it all. She had numerous opportunities to collect a Fox-assassin mask. If only she'd known one would be needed. She felt a smile form. "That's it? That's what you want?"

Chen spread his hands wide to show the simplicity of his request. "Problem?"

"No one knows who a Fox assassin is, Chen. You know that." RC was rapidly losing control. "What you're asking for is lunacy—"

"We'll find one," Becca said.

"Becca...*how*? We never kept the mask we found on our last mission, and the mask from your attacker the other night was broken in the fight." RC's frustration indicated he thought the plan was preposterous.

"I'm intrigued," Chen said.

Becca gave him a withering glance, then turned to look into RC's eyes with the strongest determination she'd ever felt. "We'll find one," she repeated. Then she faced Chen again. "We have an agreement."

"Excellent," Chen said, overjoyed. He snapped his fingers, and his people lowered their weapons and resumed socializing as if nothing had happened. It was terrifying. Even Dex and Scout blended with the crowd by holstering their weapons, although they were still ready for anything. RC was the last person to put away his weapon. He wasn't happy at all.

"I do look forward to watching the great Reed Alexander Carter and the famous Ms. Rebecca Lake Romanov in action, the two kids who have caused the Brotherhood such trouble."

"One day, Chen, I'm going to punch that smile right off your face," RC threatened.

"Perhaps you'll make it an improvement. Oh, I forgot to mention. I'm giving your team forty-eight hours to retrieve my mask; otherwise, I report you to the Brotherhood.

RC lunged at Chen, but Dex and Scout held him back.

"We don't have time for this, RC," Becca cautioned.

RC pulled himself together but didn't hide his anger.

"We're coming back to you now," Vivian said in Becca's earwig.

Becca looked toward the entrance to the ballroom and watched Brittany and Vivian walk in. Vivian's face read that she'd heard everything that had gone on during Brittany's absence; however, Brittany's face radiated she didn't have a clue.

"Such a beautiful creature," Chen said gawking at Brittany.

"I swear, if you hurt Brittany, I'll kill you, Chen." Becca knew her threat carried much more weight than anything RC had said.

"Hurt her? No, Ms. Romanov. My intentions with your bestie are far more sinister."

Becca didn't like the sound of that.

"I intend to marry her."

24

Becca and company arrived at the penthouse suite of the Villa Kennedy in Frankfurt, originally a family villa that had been turned into a five-star hotel. It was only a couple of miles away from the auction. As soon as they entered, they saw Cassie with her portable command center all set up on the dining room table. Multiple computer screens surveilled the auction after-party, which was still in full swing.

"What's our status with Chen?" Vivian asked as she entered the suite.

Cassie clicked a few buttons on her keyboard, and the screen switched to radar tracking, and Cassie's Eye application.

"He's on the move. Tracking signal from the rings is strong," Cassie replied, dialed in to what she was doing.

"Good," Vivian said. "Let me know when they stop."

"You got it, Boss."

RC was the last of the team to arrive and shut the door behind him. "You know, next time we do nest-protection protocol, could we not allow *so* many people inside with guns? I mean, even though we pretended to be surprised, seeing all the weapons was unnerving, even for me."

"I have to agree with the rich kid," Dex said, undoing his bow tie and removing his jacket. "Let's not do that again. I broke a sweat just standing there. That hasn't happened in years."

"It got the job done," Becca said as she sat on the sofa and kicked off her heels. "Kind of."

"We trapped the wrong guy," Scout said. "Now we're on a scavenger hunt for a wacko with no guarantee he can deliver his end of the bargain."

A door from the kitchen sprung open, and everyone looked to see who else was in the suite. To Becca's delight, out came Winston, the Carter's butler, and a long-time Griffin, wheeling a large food trolly filled with multiple perfectly polished, dome-covered dinner plates.

"That sounds up to par with your adventures, Mr. Amadon," Winston said as he walked past everyone and placed the trolly next to the coffee table.

"Winston!" Becca was overjoyed to see him. Once he removed the top of one of the dishes and finished showing the filet mignon to everyone, Becca threw her arms around him. She'd never forget the kindness he'd shown her a year ago when they'd first met. To her, his calm demeanor, dry wit, and generosity helped keep her grounded during the chaos she'd endured when she'd first met RC and the Carter family.

Winston was a little startled by Becca's embrace, but she didn't let that stop her from showing her affection. She didn't care if it wasn't very professional of her.

"It's a pleasure to see you again, Lady Romanov." Winston patted her on her back, grateful for the embrace.

"Winston, call me Becca, please. I'm sick of the Romanov formalities."

"Of course, my dear." He placed his gloved hands on her forearms and gave a confident squeeze of affection before resuming his duties. "I've taken the liberty of preparing the team's clothes for your next assignment. The men's clothes are in the left bedroom, and the women's are in the right. Don't forget your sustenance."

Mason Carter surprised everyone when he came out of the kitchen. "You all have a long forty-eight hours ahead of you," he said.

Dex and Scout were shocked to see the head of the League of Griffins there, in person. They stood at attention like soldiers to their general. "Sir!" they said at the same time.

"Take it easy, guys." Mason waved a hand for them to relax as he turned to Winston. "Thank you, Winston."

Winston nodded and headed back into the kitchen.

"Chen Wei's connections inside the Brotherhood are deep," Mason said. "Getting on his good side was a brilliant move, Becca." Mason walked around the sofa and stood in front of Falcon squad. "However, you're aware that you're dancing with a devil now." He looked at Becca.

"I am," she replied.

"Yet, this is the perfect opportunity to ensure Chen's loyalty to the Griffins." Mason continued the meeting while Dex and Scout changed from their fancy garb into tactical clothing. RC went for the food that Winston had brought.

"The guy is a psychotic, top-level veil," RC commented. "There's no way we can sway his loyalty to us, let alone trust him."

"RC's right," Becca said. "He's in love with the game, and he only plays by his rules."

"So we change the game," Mason said.

No one spoke as they waited for Mason to explain.

"I've known about Chen Wei for years," Mason said as he paced the room. "He's managed to acquire a contact list along with incriminating leverage on each contact to ensure his own survival. That's his lifeline and why no one will touch him. If he feels the hint of a double-cross coming, he releases the information destroying his contact's life, professionally and personally, just for fun. After you acquire the mask for him, I want you to steal, in any way possible, that contact list. Understood?"

The team nodded as they continued changing into tactical clothing and eating the exquisite dinner.

"Once we get him what he desires, there's no way of knowing what kind of favor Chen is going to ask from Becca," Vivian said. "He could make her do something that betrays the Griffins entirely."

"Acquire the mask and the list, and she won't have to deliver on the favor," Mason replied. "Right now, the priority is delivering the mask."

"Why can't we just give Chen the mask RC was given when he killed the moles?" Vivian asked.

"That was a pure-white follower mask," RC informed. "Not an assassin mask. The assassin masks are gray and white."

Becca remembered seeing the Fox-assassin mask that had belonged to the dead man in Himmler's secret room in Wewelsburg Castle. If only it hadn't been so fragile, that would have made everyone's lives so much simpler. She even regretted bashing her assailant's mask to pieces back at Griffin headquarters.

"Falcon squad is the only team I have that has ever been this close to uncovering the magister of our enemy. We cannot screw this up." Mason turned to Becca. "Becca, I'm promoting you to tier one, Claw level, so you'll have full access to our resources. You will no longer have to report to Brady Washington."

Becca nodded but hid her excitement at the promotion.

"Sir, I don't think Becca is ready for that," Vivian said.

"We don't have time for her to be ready," Mason said, moving on from Vivian's concern. "Besides, the best way to learn to swim is to dive into the deep end."

"That's what I told her last year," RC said.

"How do we even find a Fox assassin?" Scout asked. He'd finished getting dressed and grabbed his dinner.

"All the stories say *they* find you," Dex answered. "The last face you're meant to see before you die is that fox mask."

"Someone forgot to tell that to the assassin who attacked Becca and me last year," RC said, speaking from personal experience.

Becca nodded, not mentioning her recent bout with the Griffin-turned-Fox-assassin she'd recently fought back at the old German headquarters.

"You have less than forty-eight hours to find a ghost," Mason said. "Otherwise, we can kiss any leads to the magister goodbye." His words made the squad's task seem impossible. The stakes were high, and there was no promise they'd prevail. "Good luck," he said and left out the front door where two Griffin security men waited for him.

"Has the crate of rings stopped moving?" Vivian asked Cassie.

"Nope, they're still en route, and there are too many possible destinations to determine where they'll end up."

"And what about that crazy Chen?" Dex asked.

"He's still in the car behind the truck with the crate," Cassie said, not looking away from her monitors.

"Could he have given us the slip?" Scout asked.

"Not likely," Cassie replied. "The liquid tracker is still active in his system from the champagne he drank at the auction."

"Keep watching," Vivian said.

"Can we use DIANA to locate a potential Fox assassin?" Becca asked. "That's a place to start looking."

"DIANA needs more information on an individual before she can produce an accurate result," Cassie said. "We don't have enough info to have her identify an assassin at this time.

"You spent six months inside the Brotherhood, RC. What do you know that can help us?" Becca asked.

"Correction. I spent six months trying to identify members of the Brotherhood. I was never officially one of them. There's a big difference. I never really got close enough. The only ones I was able to identify were the—"

"Bishops." Becca finished his sentence as an idea popped into her head. "Would they have any connections to a Fox assassin?"

"Possibly," RC said. "We'd have to find one to be sure. Bishops usually just oversee shipments of high-value artifacts."

"I've got nothing useful on the Eye to identify a potential bishop," Cassie said as she looked at her designated monitor. "It'll be easier once Chen and the crate arrive at their destination to do a scan of the area."

"And if that doesn't work, what are our other options?" Vivian asked.

No one answered. Vivian headed over to the trolly and ate a French fry out of frustration.

RC continued to eat his steak as Becca changed out of her dress into comfortable jeans, a tank top, and a leather jacket. She caught RC sneaking a peek and did her best not to blush. She usually would've been shy, but there wasn't time to worry about it now.

"The rings have stopped," Cassie said. "Looks like an Indian restaurant."

Becca pulled up DIANA. "Bring up everything in the database on Chen Wei and any connection with that restaurant."

Requires Claw access level, DIANA responded.

"Romanov, Rebecca Hunter Lake, tier one, Claw," Becca said. A red light scanned Becca's retina.

Access allowed, DIANA said, and all the files appeared in hovering windows.

"The restaurant is a front for Chen's black-market smuggling," Vivian said.

"Stinger missiles, drugs, he's smuggled everything through that restaurant," Dex said. "I'm actually impressed. I wonder if the food is any good."

"Chen is out of the vehicle. I have audio," Cassie said.

"Take it to the estate, and add them to my collection," Chen ordered.

"Yes sir," the truck driver said, then barked some orders to the other men in Chinese. Falcon squad watched Cassie's monitors as

Chen's goons unloaded the crate of rings and took them from one truck to another.

"Scan the area now, Cassie," RC said through a mouthful of food. "If there's a bishop around, he's nearby." RC got to his feet and moved over to the monitor using the Eye app.

Cassie typed frantically on her keyboard, sending multiple commands to the program.

"Becca," Vivian said, "make sure you eat something."

Becca loaded her handgun and holstered it, then walked over to the trolly and took a few bites, waiting for Cassie and RC to do their thing.

Vivian watched Becca, which annoyed her.

"What, Mom?"

"You're being too reckless with your life."

"It's getting us closer to the goal." Becca took another bite.

"This is a bishop you're hunting now. It's not going to be easy."

"It never is." Becca drank some water. "At least this time, we'll have the element of surprise on our side."

"You need to stop creating situations like this. You're obsessed, Becca. You think you can bring down an ancient organization that has lasted for nearly a thousand years because they killed Barry, and you don't care about your own life anymore."

"My life ended last year."

Vivian's eyes narrowed. "You need to be more realistic about this. You have a new life ahead of you."

"And I plan to be around for a long time."

"You won't be if you keep acting this way."

"Believe me, Mom, I'm open to other options, but so far we don't have any."

"It's our job to create other options. That's what we do. There's never just one way to complete a mission."

Becca knew her mother was right; however, she felt incapable of finding alternatives that would lead to success. She'd backed herself into a dangerous corner making the deal with Chen.

"There!" RC pointed to Cassie's screen. "Looks like a bishop."

Becca and Vivian joined the rest of the squad at Cassie's mini headquarters. Cassie had zoomed in on the person in question and filled all her screens for the rest of the squad to see.

The man looked anonymous. Average height, plain features, wearing jogging attire. He blended in with the pedestrians across the street from the Indian restaurant. The perfect person to be overlooked by everyone who passed by him.

"Can you access his phone?" RC asked.

"Duh," Cassie said as she tapped the screen and used the Eye to hack his phone.

"Oh, I need this program," RC said.

"Well, you can't have it...yet. Mason's orders," Cassie said.

"Put everything on the hologram," Vivian said.

A few clicks later and all of the man's information appeared in the middle of the room with Falcon squad surrounding it.

"DIANA, cross-check all emails, texts, and contacts with words associated with *fox, asset,* and *drop point.* Anything that could potentially be used to order an execution," RC said.

Searching.

The hologram flickered and scrolled as it categorized anything related to the words.

"Nothing's hitting," Vivian said. "That's odd for DIANA."

Becca looked at the screen of pop-ups that showed the man's text messages. The majority of texts were to Sarah and Reynard.

"I don't see any common patterns that look suspicious," Cassie reported. "Nothing out of the ordinary in his emails or texts. Just basic stuff. Grocery-list order from his wife and sports chatter with his son. Weird name for a kid."

"Wait a minute." Becca stared at one of the texts. "His son's name isn't spelled the usual way, Renard. It's spelled with a *Y.* The son's name isn't Renard, it's Reynard."

"I still think it's a weird name for a kid," Cassie said.

"A reynard is a doglike, wild animal with a pointed nose. Another word to describe an animal like that is…"

"Fox," Scout, Dex, Vivian, and RC said at the same time.

"Getting an ID trace on the number." Cassie typed on her keyboard. It was so loud, Becca wondered if Cassie's fingers ever got bruised.

"Got it," Cassie said. "Address sent to your phones."

When their phones buzzed, they all looked at the address.

"Frankfurt am Main," Dex remarked. "That's a big financial district for Germany."

"The guy certainly lives in an expensive place for looking so incognito," Scout said.

"That's our Fox assassin," RC said.

"Plenty of people live like that, but we have to be absolutely sure," Vivian replied.

"Do a multiscan of apartment three-five-zero-six," RC told DIANA.

A 3D model of the complex appeared in the center of Falcon squad, while different beams scanned the hologram model.

"There!" Scout said. "A secret compartment in the closet of the master bedroom. Zoom in on that."

The hologram adjusted and continued to scan. First, a wireframe scan, then a thermal, then an X-ray.

An object appeared on a stand.

"Enhance," Vivian said.

Becca would recognize the object anywhere, having come face-to-face with it twice before.

There, on the stand, perfectly displayed and in pristine condition, was the mask of a Brotherhood of the Fox assassin.

25

Clouds diffused the full moonlit sky as most of Germany's cities slept. The Griffin King Air jump plane flew high above the skyscrapers at thirteen thousand feet. Becca, dressed in parachute gear, sat nervously in her seat. The air from the open door hit her face as goggles protected her eyes. RC stood across from her by the door holding on to a safety strap as calm as ever. He'd probably done hundreds of jumps from a perfectly good airplane.

In a couple minutes, this would be her first time jumping out of a plane. She hadn't even gotten to this point in her Griffin training. Her palms were sweating within her gloves, and her heart beat louder than the twin engines. She tried to calm herself by controlling her breathing and ignoring the copper taste in her mouth.

"Hook up," RC said.

Becca skipped a breath. She blushed at the thought of being with him, but then realized he wasn't talking about romance, he was talking about a standard tandem jump. She hoped his focus on the task at hand would blind him to her embarrassment as she went up to him and waited while he linked their harnesses together.

"One minute," Vivian said in Becca's earwig, which didn't do anything for her nerves. "Run the plan out loud again, Becca." That was her mother's way of helping Becca calm down.

"We jump to the rooftop of the apartment building. Infiltrate down the stairs to apartment 3506. Decode the lock, enter the premises, make our way to the master-bedroom closet, open the secret door, and obtain the mask."

"Thirty seconds," RC said.

They moved together, closer to the open door. Becca's eye cam contact lens flickered to life with a heads-up display, showing the path RC would need to follow to make a successful landing on the rooftop.

The red light on the display changed to green.

"Good luck," Cassie said in the earwig.

"Oh my," Becca said breathlessly.

RC leaned forward, nudging them out of the plane. She didn't scream but instead yelled profanities for ten seconds with her eyes closed before opening them and screaming with delight.

Becca and RC fell for forty-seconds. She took in the stunning sights of the city lights below and marveled at the freeing feeling, finally understanding why so many people enjoyed skydiving. For a moment she forgot all her worries, her fears, and why they were even doing this in the first place, allowing herself to fully enjoy the rush of the moment.

RC pulled the chute, and reality sank back in as the force jolted her back to awareness. She made a mental note that once this debacle was over, she would definitely do another jump.

Becca watched the roof of their destination get closer on her eye cam, impressed by how smoothly RC stayed on course. They touched down on the roof and scurried their feet beneath them to regain balance. Once in control, Becca and RC detached themselves from each other, got out of their harnesses, and stripped off their jumpsuits. RC reeled in the parachute, and Becca ditched the jump clothes they'd worn over dark jeans and T-shirts in a trash bin before heading to the stairway door.

"Deposit has been made," Becca said into her earwig.

"Copy that," Vivian said. "Retrieval team is on standby after you complete the objective."

"You're all so efficient." Chen's voice sounded just as annoying through the earwig as it was in person. "I'd give you a seven-point-five on the landing though, Ms. Romanov."

Becca rolled her eyes as she waited for RC to hack the lock to the stairway. It bugged her that Chen had a direct feed to their current assignment. He sat at home watching all their movements on a monitor. Of course, it made sense, considering she had to prove how useful she could be to him, but it was incredibly intrusive, and something didn't feel right about it.

The stairway door unlatched, and they descended the stairs to the thirty-fifth floor as quickly and quietly as possible.

"I've got control of the cameras," Cassie said. "You're clear."

Becca and RC entered the hallway and made their way to the door of apartment 3506.

"I'm not picking up any heat signatures inside," Cassie said.

"Nobody's home," Vivian commented. "Stay alert."

RC placed a master key in the lock, and after a few seconds, the door beeped and unlocked. They entered the apartment and shut the door behind them.

The space was vast, with dark-wood flooring, marble countertops, expensive furniture, and floor-to-ceiling windows that overlooked the city. Not a speck of dust was in sight. Clearly, this assassin was a stickler for a pristine environment. The place would've been beautiful, if it hadn't housed a monster.

"Tick-tock, Ms. Romanov," Chen said, clearly enjoying being a fly on the wall.

Becca and RC hurried to the master bedroom and opened the closet, careful to leave no trace of their presence. They moved clothes to the side and found the false wall that contained their objective. On it was an ID camera. RC looked at Becca, worried.

"Oh, dear me," Chen said. "Looks like you need facial recognition to open the wall."

Panic crept into Becca's body, but her training helped her ignore its effects. She focused her eye cam on the facial-ID camera, hoping Cassie would have a way to bypass it.

"Why wasn't this on the schematic?" Vivian asked, pissed.

"The scan didn't pick it up, Boss," Cassie said. "Must be cloaked by the same kind of technology that hid the Juggernaut."

Becca watched RC motion to Cassie to cut the camera feed and see if that would help, even though he seemed sure it wouldn't.

"I'm trying to bypass it. Need a moment," Cassie said.

"You've got a bigger problem," Chen chimed in, pleased. "Looks like someone is home."

Becca and RC looked at each other, confused.

"Oh shit!" Cassie said and clicked a few keys to share the security feed of the front door to Becca and RC's eye cams. There, just outside the apartment, was a man and a young boy. The man used his electronic key to open the door.

Becca and RC stared at each other. The probability of getting out of the apartment clean was reduced to zilch.

"Cassie, you'd better hack that wall cam right now!" Vivian shouted. "Falcon three, Falcon four, stand by to engage."

"Copy that, standing by," Dex and Scout responded.

"This is better than reality TV," Chen said. "A Fox assassin with a child. What a twist."

Becca and RC stayed in the closet, controlling their breathing and listening to the man and his son enter the apartment. Lights went on, and the sound of pocketed items hitting the countertop echoed throughout the apartment. From what Becca could understand, the son was tired but had enjoyed some movie they'd seen.

"I've got it," Cassie said, speaking at a rapid pace. "I can't wirelessly hack into the wall cam, but we can fake it." She spoke while she typed. "Falcon six, I'm sending you a digital facial scan. Just a moment."

RC pulled out his phone and waited for the scan to appear.

They heard footsteps in the hallway and hoped the man was helping his son to bed in the room next door.

"Yes! Scan complete. You should have it now," Cassie said.

RC's phone received a silent notification with a file attachment.

"Use your phone hologram, and project the file onto your face in front of the wall cam."

RC turned on the hologram and aimed it at his face. Becca watched his face change into the assassin's. RC stood in front of the wall cam, but nothing happened.

"Are you sure this will work?" Vivian asked, concerned.

"In theory, it should," Cassie said. "Facial projection just needs to be projected onto the proper gender face. The scan should do the rest."

Becca didn't know what to do. She overheard the man telling his son to go to bed, while RC kept trying to get the facial projection to work.

"Uh-oh," Chen said and chuckled. "Time for plan B, Ms. Romanov."

"It has to be perfectly aligned!" Cassie said.

Becca heard the man flip off the light to his son's room, and his footsteps came closer. Becca grabbed RC's phone from him, crouched down between RC and the wall cam, and projected the holographic face onto his. It worked, and the wall opened behind her. Becca fell backward, but RC caught her. They froze, waiting to see if they'd been too loud, and listened for a change in the pace of the footsteps. They were lucky, sort of. The man was now in the master bedroom and had gone into the bathroom. If they played their cards right, all RC and Becca had to do was wait for the man to go to sleep and sneak past him to get out of the apartment.

The secret pocket door closed behind RC and Becca. RC made sure Becca had her feet firmly beneath her and was fully stabilized before letting go of her. She let out a quiet sigh of relief and turned around, only to see the Fox assassin's wardrobe with weapons racked on the wall and an empty mask display stand.

"Oh, dear," Chen said. "What to do? Only forty-four hours left." He giggled.

Becca and RC heard footsteps coming closer and hid on opposite sides of the pocket door. It wasn't much of a hiding spot, as the moment the man stepped foot in the hidden room, the jig would be up. All they could do was try to keep the element of surprise as long as possible.

Time seemed to slow as each footstep came closer.

"Tranquilizer only," Vivian said. "I'd rather not be responsible for the death of someone's father tonight."

Becca and RC switched their handguns from real bullets to tranquilizer darts. Thank God for Griffin tech. They didn't have to say anything to each other. They knew they would fire the moment the door opened. Becca took a deep breath. The pocket door slid open, and she and RC aimed their guns at the man, fired...and missed.

The assassin's defenses were lightning fast. Becca and RC had an extremely difficult time getting a clear shot. Before Becca knew it, she was in a chokehold from behind while being used as a human shield. RC couldn't get a shot. Becca was able to get out of the chokehold by pinching and twisting the flesh under the assassin's triceps. He let go and shoved her toward RC, who avoided Becca's body and reengaged in close-quarters combat. RC forced the man back out of the closet, and Becca joined in the fight. It was two against one, and this time Becca was just as much of a threat as RC.

The man gave them a run for their money. Every time Becca thought she had a shot, he was able to move out of the way. Becca kicked him onto the bed, and he evaded as she fired a tranq dart at him, barely missing. He tossed a pillow at her as a distraction and attacked. Becca blocked his blows feeling her forearms and legs begin to weaken after each impact. RC grappled the man from behind and trapped his arms and legs. Becca fired a tranquilizer bullet into his neck, and after a few seconds, the man went limp.

Becca and RC picked up the assassin, put him on the bed, and threw the sheets over him to make it look as if he'd fallen asleep in his clothes.

Becca searched through a duffle bag in the bedroom and found the desired fox mask to complete their objective.

"Target acquired," Vivian said. "Nice work. Get to the rendezvous point."

"Daddy?" The little boy's voice called in German from the hallway.

Becca and RC hid behind the bed just before the door opened and waited to see what the kid would do. For a moment he just stood at the doorway. RC had the tranquilizer gun aimed at him, ready to knock him out. Becca watched, praying the kid wouldn't take one more step. If he did, she knew RC would take him out. Luckily, the kid went back to his room.

They let out a sigh.

"Bring the mask to my estate here in Germany," Chen demanded.

26

The gates that guarded the massive three-story estate opened as the SUV with Becca, RC, Vivian, Dex, and Scout drove down the gorgeous road past a lake with a beautifully sculpted fountain spraying sparkling multicolored water. Chen Wei wasn't one for subtlety, and his surroundings amplified that.

Two of his guards carrying automatic rifles opened the doors of the SUV as it pulled up to the round driveway. His manservant opened the polished mahogany front-entrance double doors, inset with stained glass, and let Falcon squad inside. Chen's entryway consisted of beautiful Italian Travertine tile squares angled point to point, which created a stunning pattern. A gleaming mahogany staircase rose to the second floor, then split off to the left and right.

It would have been more impressive to Becca if her visit had been under different circumstances. Chen's estate was probably one of the most beautiful places she'd ever seen, right up there with the Carter mansion, but she was in work mode and knew any second things could go wrong and they might have to fight their way out. Chen was someone she'd use, not trust.

Falcon squad was escorted through the enormous home and

brought to what appeared to be a miniature museum of highly valuable artifacts. The room was full of ancient relics in multiple display cases, everything from jade tea sets to Egyptian statues, oriental vases, weapons, and lost paintings by Van Gogh, Rembrandt, and Raphael. The list went on and on.

Clapping came from the opposite end of the room. Becca winced when she saw the annoying glee Chen displayed as he emerged and walked toward them.

"Not bad...not bad...and with only..." he looked at the time on his cell phone, "eighteen hours left."

Becca's eye cam scanned Chen's body for concealed weapons. Nothing appeared.

"He's clean," Cassie said in her earwig. Cassie operated remotely from the Griffin protected hotel so she could use its full resources.

"We did what you asked, Chen," RC said. "Now it's time for your end of the bargain."

Chen held up a hand. "Why rush a momentous occasion, Mr. Carter?" He focused on the messenger bag slung around Becca's body. His eyes glimmered. "Is that it? Is that my lethal foxy mask-y?" He waved his fingers for Becca to bring him the mask. "Let me see, let me see."

"I'm scanning the room, and there's a hidden entrance in the west wall that leads to an exit by the garden, but it's unoccupied," Cassie informed the team. "If Chen plans to give you the slip, that's where he'd escape."

Becca saw the hidden entrance door flicker a light blue in her eye cam notifying her of its location. Dex and Scout casually moved in between Chen and the wall with the hidden entrance to block any attempted escape.

"Why rush a momentous occasion?" Becca repeated to Chen, standing her ground with no intention of showing him the mask until he showed his end of the bargain.

"You're a quick learner, Ms. Romanov." He smiled. "I'm liking you more and more." He held up his phone and projected multiple stakeout images in the air behind him. Some were of street corners, events, restaurants, all everyday activities, each full of people.

"Behold…your magister." He faced Becca and pointed to the messenger bag. "My mask, if you please."

Becca and the rest of Falcon squad gazed at all the hovering photos of people.

"What the hell is this?" RC asked. "This is junk. Just a bunch of crowds."

"No," Scout said, enthralled by some of the photos, pointing at one as he moved closer. "I know that street, it's in Paris. That's the Champs-Elysees. But it doesn't look that way anymore. I remember a clothing store exploded due to a gas leak. Only it was a Brotherhood attack on a CEO of a private bank. He went shopping with his daughter. I was tasked with protecting them. I didn't make it in time."

Dex stepped forward and studied a photo of protestors. "This one is the Passeig de Gràcia in Barcelona, moments before protestors shot innocent bystanders and wiped out over a hundred people. It was reported to be a terrorist attack, but I was part of a Griffin team to prevent the attempted theft of a coded Leonardo da Vinci painting that contained information about the Brotherhood. Someone betrayed us. The attack was staged by the Brotherhood, and we lost the painting."

A photo caught Vivian's attention. "Oxford Street, London. The Brotherhood poisoned a Parliament official before he could vote against changing trade policies with China. The vote was a cover-up to allow private companies electronic-monitoring privileges of financial exchanges. The official contacted the Griffins to warn us, but the Brotherhood got to him before we could."

Becca's heart raced, and she did her best not to let tears form in her eyes as she stared at a photo of a café in New York City. She would know that café anywhere. She couldn't bring herself to say anything.

"That café," RC said pointing to the photo Becca had been staring at. "That's—" RC faced Becca and didn't finish the sentence.

Becca mustered the strength to say one word without bursting into tears: "Barry."

"I heard about this café," Dex remarked. "Last year. The reports said a suicide bomber cracked and tried to kill a recently discovered living descendant of the Romanovs." Dex looked at Becca realizing it was an attempt on her life. "You."

All the photos changed, showing the destruction of the buildings and the devastation caused by the Brotherhood's attacks in each city.

"He was murdered," Becca said. "They trapped him, killed his family, and put him in a vest because he was my best friend. It wasn't suicide."

"Yes, this is all very tragic sounding." Chen's impatience reminded them of a seven-year-old. "My mask, Ms. Romanov."

Becca pulled the mask out of the messenger bag and held it up to taunt Chen. He reached for it, but she pulled it away. "These photos don't show the magister."

Chen sighed, frustrated, his impatience getting the better of him. "Look closer," he said, keeping his hand out for Becca to hand him the mask.

The photos all zoomed in to different quadrants of each picture and showed a blurry rendering of an individual in the background.

"While you and your team were hunting for my mask, I did some digging. It always baffles me when people are able to disappear into thin air. So, in order to find someone who doesn't exist, you have to take a simpler approach. You have to uncomplicate things."

Each picture began to depixelate and clear up the image of the individual.

"You start by looking at the known whereabouts of important attacks. Assassinations are my favorite subject to research. Especially high-value targets to the Brotherhood. If I was in charge, which I have no desire to be, what better way to misdirect someone than by playing the victim?"

The pictures became clearer and clearer, showing the individual in different clothes, from different angles.

"Looks like a woman," Dex said, confused. "The Brotherhood doesn't allow women in their organization."

"You're right," Chen agreed. "What better way to hide within a secret organization? A woman who operates at the highest level, controlling an organization that doesn't allow women. The perfect hiding spot."

No wonder the magister was so hard to find. No one would have ever considered a woman to be the leader of the Brotherhood.

Becca kept the mask away from Chen, even though his theory made sense.

He shrugged and stopped reaching toward her. "Very well, Ms. Romanov. The computer should be done depixelating soon. I always enjoy a dramatic reveal."

"You could just tell us," RC said.

Chen held up a finger. "I haven't seen who it is yet, Mr. Carter." He turned around and faced the photos. "This is a historic moment, and I wanted us to share in it together." He spread his arms out for dramatic effect.

The pictures became clearer, and Becca's mind raced, trying to remember where she'd seen this person before. The hair, the posture. In a few moments, she knew she would have enough to finally uncover the identity of the magister.

"Wait," RC said. "That looks like…"

The photos disappeared. The lights turned off.

"I've lost visual!" Cassie said with alarm. "Repeat. I've lost visual. That's not possible from—" Cassie's signal went dead.

Becca's eye-cam signal died as well, making it practically impossible to see in the dark. Her eyes would have to adjust.

Sounds of garbled pain came from doorways. Dex and Scout drew their weapons but were unable to see anything. RC stayed close to Becca, back-to-back. She knew there were multiple people in the room with them now. She felt their deadly presence all around them.

"What the hell is this, Chen?" Vivian said in the dark.

"Looks like I have uninvited guests," Chen said, uncertain.

"We're surrounded." Dex aimed his weapon all around.

Becca felt movement in the darkness.

The hologram projected back to life, but this time, instead of it being the photos, it was a large bust of a man in an ancient ceremonial robe, wearing the most ornate porcelain, red-and-black headpiece of a fox head.

The light projecting from the hologram illuminated multiple figures who emerged from shadowed corners of the room. Each was a Fox assassin, all wearing white-and-gray masks, and there were twelve of them. Becca flashed back to Wewelsburg Castle and Himmler's infatuation with the number twelve.

Falcon squad was outnumbered. They may have stood a chance against two or three assassins, but twelve, no way.

"I don't believe we've ever been introduced," Chen said to the hologram, intrigued.

The hologram raised its hand, and half of the assassins stood next to Falcon squad making sure they didn't try to escape.

Two Fox assassins went up to Becca. One stood in front of her, ready to restrain her if she made any attempt to resist. The other held out his hand, wanting her to give him something. She knew what it was. The assassin pulled out her earwig, threw it on the floor, and smashed it under his combat boot. The remaining assassins did the same to the rest of Falcon squad.

Once all the earwigs were destroyed, half the assassins trashed the antique display cases, while the other half made sure Falcon squad didn't try to stop the destruction.

"Wait, wait, wait!" Chen said. "I exposed a flaw in your operation."

The hologram appeared to have no interest in what Chen had to say. He raised his hand again, and more antiques were destroyed. The assassins knocked over life-sized statues, armor, and tore down tapestries.

Chen winced at the destruction of the priceless pieces of art and pleaded with the hologram. "You should be thanking me. If I could find you..." he motioned to Falcon squad. "It was only a matter of time before they did. I figured, why wait?"

RC aimed his gun at Chen, right between his eyes. "You son of a bitch!" He was immediately disarmed and put into a chokehold by the nearest assassin.

"Control yourself!" Vivian ordered RC. "There's no use in putting up a fight. They're trapping us to make our deaths look like an accident."

RC calmed down, and the assassin released him from the chokehold.

Some assassins began pouring liquid all around the room, making sure they doused everything they could. Becca smelled the foul aroma of gasoline. They had barricaded Falcon squad inside a ring of destroyed artifacts. One assassin wrapped a piece of ripped medieval tapestry around a splintered piece of wood from a picture frame and doused it with the gasoline. Another assassin opened a cigarette lighter, ignited the flame, and lit the tapestry on fire, turning it into a torch. They stood at attention waiting for their next order from their leader.

The assassins were going to burn them all alive inside Chen's estate.

Dex shook his head, angered. "I'm not dying without a fight." He launched at the assassin closest to him, throwing punches and kicks with lethal power.

"Stand down!" Vivian ordered, but Dex continued his assault, ignoring the order.

The assassin evaded Dex's attacks with ease, almost like a fluid dancer, taunting Dex.

"Stop it!" Scout yelled. "There's no use. They've got us. He's toying with you."

Dex continued his attack. In three swift moves, the assassin broke Dex's right leg and left forearm, then shoved Dex to the floor, forcing him to slide backward.

Dex howled in pain and tried to get back to his feet. He couldn't. He was done.

Scout hurried to Dex and did his best to help him up. He ripped his clothes and began creating splints for Dex out of whatever he could find.

The hologram moved its hand, and all the assassins next to Falcon squad backed out of the ring of broken artifacts and joined the circle the rest of the assassins had already formed. They waited for the order to light the fire.

RC moved to take a step, but a throwing knife lodged itself in the floor, half an inch away from his foot, stopping him in his tracks.

"If you've got any ideas, I'm all ears," RC said.

"I delivered them to you!" Chen continued to plead his case with the hologram. "I'm still of use. Call off your men."

The man behind the mask didn't respond. He continued to stare through his mask at them with every intention of watching them burn alive.

"Say something!" Chen fell to his knees begging. "We can make a new deal."

Becca's photographic mind went into overdrive. With all the destruction caused by the assassins, their exits were blocked. Any attempt at resisting was futile, and they'd all end up like Dex, severely injured and with no way out. Becca needed to solve the mystery of who wore the mask. If she could do that, maybe she'd be able to get a response from the hologram and use that information to spare their lives. It was a long shot, but it was worth a try.

Becca remembered clear as day all the photos that had been projected. Each one flashed, and she focused on the different images of the woman who was being depixelated. She mentally cross-referenced every known woman she'd encountered with the image of the woman from the pictures. All she could compare was the woman's posture, and she had to deduce the potential walk pattern from the still images. Luckily, there were enough images to create a mental picture of the woman's gait, which would be just as good as a fingerprint. She pictured the woman's pace and felt the sensation of recollection, knowing she had seen this person before. She compared different flashes of different women to the walk pattern, eliminating options as quickly as she could.

The hologram raised his hand again, authorizing the assassins to proceed. One assassin tossed the torch into the rubble and watched as the flames erupted from the floor to the ceiling racing closer to the circle the assassins had created around Falcon squad.

"Are you all just going to burn with us?" Vivian shouted at the assassins as they stood their ground, the flames surrounding them, unafraid of the danger.

Becca tuned out all the distractions and focused on who the woman in the photos could be. She felt her mind getting closer to a result. Then she remembered something. It wasn't a walk. It was the hand motion. Her mind jumped back to a year ago, when she'd had dinner with RC and his family, the very first time she'd ever met them. She saw Sherylynn Carter, RC's mother, raise her hand for Winston, the family butler, to come over and refill her drink. It was something she'd paid no attention to at the time, but the hologram's repeated arm motion from ordering the assassins around sparked the memory. It was thin, but it was the only lead she had.

Her mind raced through all potential possibilities comparing Sherylynn's mannerisms to the woman in the photos. Her ramrod-straight posture, her authoritative presence, and her walk pattern appeared identical to what was portrayed in the photos. There were hundreds of reasons why this theory would be incorrect; however, Becca didn't have the time to hash it out.

She stepped forward in front of the giant hologram and stood nose to nose with the fox mask.

"You killed my best friend." Becca's eyes narrowed. She wasn't going to allow the smoke and the heat from the flames to impede her ability to be clearheaded. A burning beam fell from the ceiling behind Becca. She stood her ground and stared with rage at the magister.

"When I get out of here, I'm coming for you...Sherylynn Carter."

27

The flames had grown much larger and closer to Falcon squad. The smoke felt like it burned the inside of Becca's lungs as she tried to breathe. She did her best not to show weakness while standing face-to-face with the magister. Becca knew she'd get some sort of a reaction from her silent adversary. She saw the magister's body language change after her accusation. The giant ornate fox mask moved closer to Becca's face.

"You won't escape." A perfectly clear, deep, male voice responded and vibrated throughout the room. The hologram disappeared, and the magister was gone.

Becca wiped the sweat from her temples as she returned her attention to the rest of Falcon squad. Scout had finished creating splints for Dex's leg and forearm and helped him to his feet.

Becca peered through the flames at the Fox assassins leaving through the hidden door in the wall paneling. The last assassin fired a grappling hook at another loose beam just above the exit and yanked it free from the ceiling. The beam and part of the ornate ceiling smashed to the floor, blocking the only exit Falcon squad could use to escape. They were trapped with only minutes left before they would pass out from suffocation.

When Becca looked at RC's face, she saw confusion. She knew it was from her statement that his mother was the magister. The moment was short-lived as Chen hurried in front of her.

"I thought they'd never leave," he said. "Move." Chen gently shoved Becca out of his way and headed to one of the wooden display cabinets that had started to burn. He opened one of the double doors, then hurried to a fallen marble statue of Aphrodite that stood near Vivian.

"You can all just stand there, or you can help me with this if you want to get out alive!" Chen yelled over the roaring flames.

Vivian, RC, and Becca hurried over and helped Chen raise the statue to an upright position. It was extremely heavy, but the four of them were able to manage it. RC coughed and backed away.

Chen put his hands on either side of Aphrodite's head. "Sorry, my beauty." He turned her head left, then right.

The fire grew larger at one end of the circle as it devoured the majority of the piled relics. Chen raced to the opposite end of the circle with the least amount of destroyed antiques, jumped through the wavering flames, and disappeared.

"What the hell's he doing?" RC asked, covering his mouth as he tried to mask out the smoke. "Dex can't make that jump."

"He abandoned us," Scout said. "He's saving his own ass."

The wood floor began to move beneath their feet. Becca stepped back as an opening to a staircase down to an underground passageway appeared. RC wasn't quick enough to get out of the way of the sliding floor and fell down a few steps.

Chen leaped back through the inferno and fell to the ground, rolling on his back to put out parts of his clothing that had caught fire. Becca helped him to his feet.

"After you, Lady Romanov," he said.

They hurried down the stairway, one after another. Scout and Becca helped Dex go sideways down the stairs. He yelped and winced with every step. Once they were clear of the stairs and in a wider passageway, Chen pulled a latch on the wall and closed the floor opening above them. They coughed, gasping for air as they tried to clear their lungs.

"I've always wanted to use this tunnel." Chen smiled. "Never had the need, until now. It's exciting!" He hurried down the corridor. "Don't tell anyone, or I'll kill you all."

Becca helped Scout carry Dex down the long walkway, grateful to be away from the inferno. At the end of the corridor was a small set of stairs that led up to a trapdoor. Chen and RC shoved open the door, and sweet, fresh air filled everyone's lungs for the first time in what felt like ages. The dawn light illuminated the foliage as they climbed out of the tunnel.

Scout laid Dex on the ground.

Becca walked to an area where the bushes thinned out and stared across Chen's lake at the flames engulfing his mansion.

Chen walked up next to Becca and sighed at the sight of his burning estate. "In all honesty, it wasn't my favorite, but now I have a thrilling story to go with this place."

"Dex needs medical attention, now," Scout said behind them. He pulled out his phone and went to dial but stopped and appeared to lose hope.

"What is it?" Vivian asked.

Scout held up his phone showing the emblem of the Brotherhood of the Fox that filled the screen. "The phone's hacked. It's useless."

RC pulled out his phone. "Same here." He tossed his phone into the lake, pissed.

Becca looked at hers, and sure enough, the fox symbol had corrupted her phone too. She couldn't bypass it or turn it off.

Vivian and Chen checked their phones with the same result.

"I'm going to frame this," Chen said.

Vivian grabbed Chen's phone from him and smashed it on a nearby rock. "They can still track it," Vivian growled, having had enough of Chen and his attitude. She chucked the phone into the lake as did the rest of Falcon squad with their own phones.

They watched Chen's estate burn in the distance. They had no transportation, no communication, and Dex was in extreme pain and couldn't walk.

Becca felt helpless. She had no idea what to do next. It appeared their only option was to walk up to the nearest road and flag down a passing car, but Dex wouldn't be able to make it unless he was carried, and that risked further injury. No one spoke as they tried to figure out the next steps. Chen was the only one who didn't appear bothered by everything that had happened.

The thumping of helicopter blades sounded in the distance. As the helicopter began its descent, everyone took cover behind bushes, tree trunks, and boulders. RC and Scout dragged Dex behind the nearest bush. The helicopter flew low over them toward the burning estate.

Scout and RC ran to the edge of the lake and jumped up and down, trying to get the helicopter's attention.

"What the hell are you doing?" Vivian shouted.

"Dex passed out," Scout said. "He's lost a lot of blood."

Becca emerged from the bushes. "N33GFN." She read the helicopter tail number. "That's one of ours."

"We don't know if it's been hijacked," Vivian said.

"We'll know if they start shooting us," Scout replied. "For now, we don't have a choice. Dex is going to die unless we get him medical attention." He resumed jumping and waving his arms, doing whatever he could to get the helicopter's attention.

Becca joined in the attempt, but the helicopter was busy circling the burning estate.

Vivian walked up next to Becca. "If they do start attacking, Becca and RC, you take cover in the left bushes. Scout, Chen, and I will hide to the right behind the boulder." She waved her arms for the helicopter as it circled the estate and faced their direction.

Chen also joined in the fun, flailing his arms and shouting. It was embarrassing to be next to him but nonetheless necessary. Becca prayed they weren't setting themselves up to be slaughtered. They wouldn't last long hiding in the brush if the helicopter strafed them

"Here we go," Chen said.

Becca stopped waving her arms and waited for any sign of hostile intent. The helicopter grew larger as it approached. Her knees shook.

"Getting closer," RC said, not helping Becca's nerves.

The helicopter flew low over their heads, and Becca clearly saw Cassie sitting in the passenger seat of the cockpit.

"It's Falcon Five!" Becca shouted over the loud rumble of the helicopter blades.

"Thank God," Scout said as he and RC hurried to the bush that concealed Dex. RC helped Scout hoist Dex across Scout's back and shoulders so he could carry him over.

Once the helicopter landed, Cassie hopped out and ran to Becca and Vivian while RC and Scout loaded Dex.

"What the hell happened to the signal?" Vivian shouted over the loud helicopter blades.

"All Griffins worldwide are under attack," Cassie said.

28

Dex was in bad shape, and with all the Griffins under attack, there wasn't a safe hospital to take him to, given the circumstances. They had to go off-grid and, of course, the only person who had the nearest underground medical facility was Chen Wei.

The hospital was an old converted German-military underground installation that had been built during World War II. High walls with curved stone ceilings were lit by ultrabright lights. The room was modern, with all the comforts Chen could steal.

This medical facility was one of many entities in Chen's off-grid empire. The place had more state-of-the-art equipment than any hospital Becca had ever been in. It even had newer equipment than some Griffin facilities. You'd never suspect it from its out-of-date surroundings.

While Dex was in surgery, the rest of Falcon squad had gathered in the waiting area. There were only a few chairs at one end of the room, with the rest of the room occupied by multiple beds surrounded by curtains that sectioned off the recovering patients. There wasn't a need for a visitor's waiting room because this establishment was a hospital for black-market criminals. Falcon squad would have to be cautious with their conversations, even though they knew they were on neutral ground. Yet, if any of the recovering patients were Brotherhood, their plans would be compromised.

Cassie worked frantically on her laptop as she sat in one of the chairs, while Vivian stood with the rest of the team and brainstormed a plan of action.

"We've now lost HQs in Cairo, Lesotho in South Africa, Algeria, Oulu in Finland, and Nepal since Cassie informed us of the attack," Vivian said with her arms folded.

"Any word from my father?" RC asked Cassie.

"Don't talk to me right now," Cassie said as she continued looking at her screen.

"We can't just sit here and wait," RC said.

"We don't know which HQs they're targeting next," Becca mentioned. "Cassie said the pattern was too random to calculate, remember? And we've lost the use of DIANA."

"How the hell did the Brotherhood do that?" RC asked. "DIANA's supposed to be unhackable."

"Nothing's unhackable. No matter how well protected," Cassie said.

"Then why don't you hack them while they're hacking us?" RC snapped.

"What do you think I'm doing right now? Shut your face, and let me work."

Vivian took RC to the side so Cassie could focus. "Take it easy."

Scout sat in a chair next to Cassie and didn't say a word.

"Next one over," Cassie said to him.

Scout moved to the next chair.

Becca joined Vivian and RC, not wanting to interrupt Cassie.

RC wasn't calming down.

"You need to pull yourself together. You're about to compromise our right to be in this place." Vivian wasn't messing around. She stood in RC's face as a true team leader would when making a critically important point.

Becca knew her mother was right. If RC didn't get a hold of himself and caused a worse scene, their rights to medical assistance would be revoked, as would every other member of the Griffins. This was something that couldn't be allowed to happen.

Becca grabbed RC's hand. The gesture was so subtle and unexpected, it distracted him from his anger and made him take a deep breath.

"What did you mean?" RC asked Becca between breaths. "Back at Chen's place. What did you mean when you said *Sherylynn?*"

Becca looked into RC's eyes and felt she could see the conflict going on inside him. He had risked his life for the League of Griffins, saved countless lives, recovered thousands of priceless lost treasures, and the past six months had been the most dangerous he'd ever faced. Now the reveal that his mother could be the head of the organization he'd hated for so long might break him mentally. Becca needed to respond carefully.

"I'm sorry, RC." She squeezed his hand a little harder. "If you follow her trail…it'll match."

"You don't have proof." He squeezed her hand back, not wanting to believe her theory. "It doesn't make sense. She's a woman. No woman has ever been in the Brotherhood."

"And the magister spoke to us in a male voice," Vivian added. "It's a real stretch, Becca."

Becca didn't take offense at the doubt from RC and her mother. They were right, she needed proof, and the history of the Brotherhood was clear. No women had ever been part of that organization; however, Chen's research made perfect sense.

"Best place to hide is in plain sight," Becca said. "I know there's not enough proof yet, but I bet when you cross-reference the photos with her schedule, you'll find matching destinations. Two places that have attacks could be a coincidence. But all of them?"

"The Brotherhood could've been hunting my mother," RC said.

"Even Dex and Scout had other reasons for being in those places when the attacks happened," Becca replied. "If the endgame was to attack Sherylynn, the wife of the head of the Griffins, they would have easily gotten to her."

Becca saw her logic resonated with RC and pressed her point. "There were no security details with her in any of the pictures. That wasn't normal for her when she traveled. Also, it goes against Griffin protocol for high-valued members."

"You still don't have any proof," RC said. "We need solid proof."

"I'm in!" Cassie said. "They shouldn't be able to detect me, as I'm using their server, but I'll stay cautious. I'm backing up all my files to my private server. Pray they don't have any of my designs already."

"Do you have any recordings from Chen's estate after our signal went out?" Becca asked.

"Yes. I still have the recordings. Only the broadcast signal had been cut so we couldn't see or hear each other."

"Do you have a recording of when the magister spoke to me?"

"I should." Cassie pulled up the audio, got out of her seat, and joined Becca, RC, and Vivian. Scout stayed seated, more concerned about Dex. Cassie played the audio.

"You won't escape," a perfectly clear male voice said.

"It's a guy, Becca," RC reiterated.

Becca looked at the audio waveform on Cassie's laptop. "Anything look out of the ordinary to you?"

"No," Cassie replied. "It's a perfect audio file."

Becca thought for a moment, certain of her deduction. She just needed proof. "Play it again, Cassie."

Cassie pressed play on her laptop. "You won't escape."

"It's a male voice," Vivian said. "There's no vocal distortion to suggest otherwise. It's a clear man's voice."

"Perfect...clear..." Becca said thinking out loud. "When was the last time you made a transmission that had a perfectly clear signal? No interference."

"Hardly ever," Cassie said catching on. "You think it's an altered voice?"

"That male voice is too perfect, like it wants us to know it's a man," Becca said.

"Running a voice-decryption program now," Cassie said. "Pray this doesn't get traced."

They waited for the decryption software to render the audio file. The only sound Becca heard was the faint breathing of the other patients in their beds in tune with the rhythm of the medical machinery.

"You won't escape." The file completed its render, and the looped audio track changed from a clear male voice to a female voice.

Becca watched RC's eyes widen in shock, then his face changed to anger.

"It is her," Vivian said in disbelief.

RC's voice dropped to a whisper, as it was too much for him to process. "How?"

He squeezed Becca's hand tighter. "I don't know." She stared into his eyes, giving him all the comfort and confidence she could.

"Where is she now?" Vivian asked.

"One moment." Cassie typed on the keyboard and pulled up Sherylynn's whereabouts. "She's in the Carter mansion. "

"We need to get a message to Mason, now!" Vivian said.

"I can't contact him. All known forms of Griffin communication are disabled. If I reactivate his phone, the Brotherhood will trace the signal and know where we are."

"We need to stay dead and somehow get back home," RC said.

"Ask and you shall receive," Chen said from behind. No one had heard him enter.

Becca let go of RC's hand, and all of Falcon squad tried to hide their emotions.

"You'd best get going. The world is becoming one big fox den without the public noticing. I will let you borrow one of my supersonic jets. You'll be across the pond in three hours. There will be a car waiting for you outside with new burner phones for you to use and sidearms for your squad."

"What do you gain from helping us?" Vivian asked.

"Oh, I'm not helping you," Chen corrected with a sinister tone. "I'm helping myself. You're all part of my plan."

Becca wasn't having any more of Chen's schemes. "We can find our own way."

"Ms. Romanov, you don't have a choice. At this very moment, your organization is dying. Your enemy doesn't know you've survived. You owe me for saving your lives from the fire, and you owe me for getting you back in the game unnoticed."

He moved uncomfortably close to Becca's face. "I will be calling in my favor, Ms. Romanov, when the time is right." Chen walked away and without looking back said, "Tick-tock, Ms. Romanov, tick-tock."

Becca looked around at the rest of Falcon squad. Chen was right. They didn't have a choice, and they wouldn't be effective at foiling any plots while waiting in the medical bay. The Griffins were under attack, all communication had been cut off, and they were the only ones who could inform Mason that his wife was the leader of their enemy.

Becca watched RC suck up his anger and carry on like the soldier he'd always been.

"Let's move," RC said.

Cassie grabbed her bag from the chair, and everyone headed for the exit, except Scout.

Becca turned to him. "Scout, you coming?"

"We'll rendezvous with you later," he said referring to Dex and himself.

Becca faced Vivian, surprised at Scout's disobedience. Vivian held up a hand. "It's best one of us stays behind to protect Dex while he recovers. We don't need any more surprise attacks.

Especially in here. Who better to protect him than his best friend?"

Becca looked back at Scout who sat in the chair with perfect posture. She realized he wasn't waiting for Dex to recover, he was guarding him.

Becca nodded and hurried after her mother, RC, and Cassie, joining them outside.

29

Cassie had tracked Mason's whereabouts to one of the Griffin authentication laboratories in New York City. He was at the lab where Becca had discovered she and her mother were descendants of Anastasia Romanov. Chen's supersonic airplane would get them to Mason in about three hours. That was a dangerously long time not to be able to warn him about Sherylynn. They flew at sixty thousand feet giving Becca a bird's-eye view of the curvature of the horizon. She knew only the Concorde had flown at that level, though some military planes flew higher.

The phones Chen had provided were just that, phones. They didn't have the capabilities of Griffin tech and couldn't run Griffin software. Cassie could've done some wizardry to the phones, but she was too busy tracking Sherylynn and Mason on her laptop.

"There's been another attack on the Griffin HQs in London and Bodo, Norway," Cassie informed the team. "There's still no pattern to pinpoint where the next attack will be."

"There's always a pattern," Becca said. "I just can't see it, yet."

"Do we have a way to contact Mason?" Vivian asked, trying to stay focused.

"All Griffin phones are still disabled from the Brotherhood

hack," Cassie said. "If I enable any of them, they could track the signal back, and we'll lose the element of surprise."

"There has to be another way," Vivian said.

"Morse code? Contact a trusted veil?" RC went down the list.

"You said yourself veils can't be trusted," Becca commented, "if Chen is any indication."

"They can't be trusted, but they can be used. That's what they're there for," RC snapped.

"So, call someone in New York," Becca said, irritated by RC's short temper.

"I don't know the numbers off the top of my head. They were in my old phone."

"Veils are too sketchy to trust with this information. We need someone more personal who will help us and has no connection to the Griffins." Vivian paced the aisle, biting her knuckle while deep in thought. "There has to be someone we can contact who isn't being tracked by the Brotherhood and can get to Mason."

"It doesn't matter," Becca said. "Without an active phone in his possession, the only way we can warn him is verbally or somehow give him a note."

"We give him a phone!" Cassie practically jumped out of her seat.

RC pointed at Cassie's laptop. "Maybe you've been staring at that screen too long. We still have two hours before we land. How the hell are we supposed to get a new phone to my dad when all phones are disabled?"

"Someone has to plant one on him," Becca said.

It finally dawned on RC, and he punched in a phone number he did know off the top of his head. "You two are brilliant," he said as he put the phone to his ear.

"I have an immediate switch-and-bait request. Top dog, eastside antiques, deep pocket, string and cups." RC waited for a second. "Confirmed." He hung up the phone.

The code RC used wasn't difficult for Becca to decipher. Switch and bait, instead of the usual bait and switch, meant for the person to plant an item on someone. Top dog had to be code for Mason. Eastside antiques referred to Mason's location, not the name of a shop. Deep pocket and string and cups meant to plant a cell phone in his pocket. Child's play.

"How long until the phone is planted on Mason?" Vivian asked RC.

"Fifteen minutes. So we need to keep a sharp eye out. He'll call me when it's done."

Cassie continued to monitor Mason and Sherylynn's locations while trying to discover a way to send cryptic messages to other members of the Griffins. Vivian and Becca looked for attack patterns by the Brotherhood on the remaining Griffin headquarters still standing.

"Still nothing, beyond the obvious," Vivian said, frustrated.

Becca faced Cassie. "How much time elapsed between the attacks?"

"There's no pattern. Cairo was five hours ago, Nepal two hours, Angola three hours—"

"You think there's a hidden code in the time between attacks?" RC asked.

"We're fighting a secret society. There are codes in everything," Becca replied. She plugged in the coordinates of each attack on an iPad Chen had left for them on the plane. The iPad's screen was shared on the big conference monitor for all to see.

Becca had already marked all the known attacks on the map. At first, the attacks in Africa appeared to show a pattern, but with the attacks in the UK and Norway, it threw any of Becca's theories out the window.

"Guys," Cassie said, "they've just sent out another order notification. They've activated attacks on Yuman, in China, The New Siberian Islands in the Laptev Sea north of Russia, Serov in Russia, Dublin, Zambia, Toronto, and Yellowknife in Canada's Northwest Territories."

Becca added each new attack to the map.

"Why all these random HQs?" RC stared at the wall screen, confused. "If the Brotherhood wanted to hit us where it hurts, why choose these locations? The one in Yellowknife is small and rarely used." RC's phone buzzed with a text message. "He's planting the phone now."

Cassie put the feed on the airplane's monitor so everyone could watch the footage. "I've hacked a street cam just outside the New York antique store where Mason's located."

They watched as Mason exited the antique shop and walked toward a parked black SUV. As Mason got closer, a random New Yorker in a beanie, dancing to music in his headphones, crossed in front of Mason, nearly bumping into him. Mason had to dodge the dancer and didn't put up a fuss as the dancer motioned an apology, then continued down the street, bobbing his head to the tunes.

"That was it," RC said. "The phone has been planted." As soon as he said it, his phone rang. RC listened for a few seconds then said, "Good job," and hung up.

"Contact him now," Vivian ordered.

Cassie's fingers flew over the keys.

Sherylynn responsible 4 attacks! – Cassie.

She pressed enter. "Text has been sent, Boss."

"Can you access the camera in Mason's car?" Vivian asked. "So we can make sure he gets the message."

Cassie pulled up the camera angle using the Brotherhood signal she'd hacked.

They watched Mason pull the phone out of his pocket. He looked around, confused for a moment, before he read the text. His expression changed from confusion to doubt, then to a boiling fury. They watched him instruct his driver to take him to the mansion. There was no audio, but it was clear from reading his lips and seeing his body language.

"Good work, team," Vivian said. "Now we just keep an eye on Sherylynn until we land and can aid Mason."

"What about warning Mason about all the other attacks?" Becca asked.

"The burner phone was a one-time use," RC explained.

"The text was encrypted with a software wipe that activates once the text is opened and read," Cassie added. "That way the Brotherhood can't trace the text back to us."

"My father's on his own until we can get to him," RC said. He headed to the galley where he poured himself a drink. Becca went over to him, knowing RC was on edge.

She poured herself some coffee and leaned against the counter, waiting for RC to talk.

He took big gulps of bourbon. "Twenty-one years. She was right next to us for twenty-one years, and we never suspected her. Not once."

"You don't know if she's been with the Brotherhood for that long."

"That's our job, Becca. That's what we do. Griffins are supposed to know this stuff. We're supposed to protect the world from being infiltrated and stolen from." He took another swig. "Some protectors we turned out to be."

"You can't blame yourself," Becca said.

"Yes, I can, and I can blame my father too. This is our mistake. She was right there in front of us this entire time, and who knows for how long? Every time I ate dinner. Every morning I woke up. The source of all evil was two doors down the hall from me the entire time."

"Usually, when children call their parents the source of all evil, it's a metaphor," Becca said, attempting to lighten the moment, even though her deceased father fit the description.

RC didn't laugh.

"I know it probably won't amount to much, but believe me when I say that I understand how you feel."

RC swallowed the rest of his bourbon. "I know you do," he said, then turned around and leaned against the counter, just like Becca.

"Still sucks." He put down his glass. "She was right under our noses while we were too busy looking in the wrong place."

Becca's mind kicked into gear again. "Wait. What did you just say?"

RC faced her, confused. "I just said that it sucks because she was right under our noses the entire time."

"No, no. After that."

"We were too busy looking in the wrong place."

"Misdirection," Becca murmured, then hurried back into the cabin and grabbed the iPad. "Sly Foxes." She started connecting the dots on the map of known attack locations.

RC followed Becca and focused on the video screen at the front of the cabin. The rest of Falcon squad watched as Becca drew the lines from location to location.

"What's going on?" Vivian asked.

"Not now, Mom."

Cassie's laptop dinged with a notification. "They just issued the order to commence the attack on Algeria," Cassie reported.

"Algeria. Got it." Becca marked it on the map and redrew more lines.

"How far away from home is my father?" RC asked Cassie.

She checked the GPS. "Thirty minutes away."

"And Sherylynn?" Vivian added.

"She's still in the mansion."

Becca continued to draw and erase connection lines between attacked locations.

"Cassie, I need you to tell me the order in which the Griffin headquarters were attacked."

"Okay." Cassie pulled up the times of the attacks. "Zambia, then Libya."

Becca drew the line from Zambia to Libya.

"Libya to Cairo. Cairo to Yuman, China," Cassie said.

Becca followed Cassie's instructions. "Next."

"Yuman all the way across Russia to the New Siberian Islands in the Laptev Sea."

Becca drew a long line crossing the map. "The next one is Serov, Russia, correct?"

"Correct. How'd you know?" Cassie asked.

"I'm seeing a pattern. Next headquarters hit was the one in Finland?"

"Yes. It's Oulu," Cassie said. "Then Bodo, Norway, to London."

Becca drew another line connecting the dots.

Vivian joined in. "London to Dublin. Then Dublin to Yellowknife."

"Then the attacks move south," Becca realized from the location of the unconnected dots. "Toronto has to be next."

"Correct," Cassie confirmed.

Becca saw the rest of the pattern in her head and drew the last few lines. "Toronto to Lesotho, South Africa. Connect that to Nepal."

"Oh my God," Vivian said as Becca finished the somewhat diamond-looking shape.

Becca drew the last two lines of the most recent attacks connecting them to each other. "Angola to Algeria."

Becca sat back and looked at the drawing she'd made on the bulkhead monitor. "There's going to be one more attack, and I know where it's going to be."

Becca drew the final line from Algeria to New York City and felt anger fill her as she and the team stared at the final line, which completed the fox-head insignia of the Brotherhood.

"Mason is heading into a trap, and we just sent him into the foxes' den."

30

"Call him back. Call him back right now!"

Becca turned and faced RC who grabbed his phone. "We have to stop Dad from going there."

"It won't work," Vivian explained. "We planted a burner phone on him. It only allows one message to be sent and read, then the phone's useless, remember?"

RC tried every number he could think of to contact more people in order to get a new message to Mason. "No one's close enough to tell him he's going into a trap."

Becca looked at Cassie. "Activate Mason's phone, and call him directly."

"Absolutely not," Vivian said. "We will *not* compromise our advantage."

RC stood up to Vivian. "He's my father and the leader of the Griffins!" he shouted.

Vivian kept a clear head, not allowing emotions to drive decisions. "We are of no use to him if we give away both of our positions."

She shut down RC's protest in a heartbeat. Everyone knew she was right. Falcon squad was presumed dead by the Brotherhood, and that was the only advantage they had.

"We don't even know what the trap is," Vivian stated. "Cassie, anything on the laptop that can tell us about the coming attack?"

"I'm looking, Boss. Nothing so far. Just the random activation notifications that are sent to Brotherhood pawns. I can see what they see, but I don't have access to their plans. I'm sorry."

"Damn it," Vivian said as she pushed hair out of her face. "Keep looking."

Becca studied the map with the fox emblem she'd drawn. The attacks were a massive, coordinated distraction, but for what purpose? To take over Griffin headquarters throughout the world? There were still hundreds of headquarters that weren't being attacked. So that couldn't be it. How were these attacks related to trapping Mason? Becca shook her head.

"Ohhh," Becca blurted, as the obvious answer presented itself. "Thinning the herd."

"What are you talking about?" RC asked, defeated. "Will you translate for the rest of us?"

"What are the basic protocols all Griffins do when under attack?" Becca asked.

"Relocate to the designated safe house," Vivian answered.

"Exactly. Just like what happened to us when the compound was bombed. We all rendezvoused at our designated safe houses."

"Where are you going with this?" RC asked.

"What is Mason's protocol during an attack?"

Becca waited for someone to answer. For a moment, no one did.

"I don't know," RC said. "That information is private, in order to guarantee the individual's safety. That goes for all Griffins."

"Correct," Becca said. "The only way to know someone's movements is to study them. In this case, do a test attack, like with the German headquarters. Make it look like an assassination attempt on my life and blow up the compound, when in reality the Brotherhood was watching Mason's movements the entire time."

"How does watching Dad's movements relate to the New York headquarters? His movements would be completely different."

"I don't know," Becca said, "but they'd be looking for a pattern, and maybe they found it."

"So, bombing the German compound was practice, and this is the main event?" RC asked.

"Becca's right," Cassie said. "I just found a study of Mason's known movements recorded by the Brotherhood. It looks like he went back to the main headquarters beneath the Carter mansion from his office in the city and..." Cassie read more info on the screen.

"And what?" Becca asked.

"Oh my God." Cassie's eyes widened.

"Cassie!" Vivian snapped her out of her distracted reading.

"Target's protocol has been confirmed to rendezvous at secure headquarters under Carter mansion in the event of any attack worldwide." Cassie read the report on her screen. "All Zyklon D chemical agents have been installed. Reported twelve hours ago."

"Zyklon D?" RC said. "A bomb in my house?"

"No," Becca corrected. "Zyklon is a form of cyanide gas. Famous for its use as Zyklon B in the concentration camps."

"Zyklon D must be a more advanced version," Vivian stated.

"I've pulled it up," Cassie said. "Zyklon D is a delayed form of Zyklon B. Ultimately causing the victim to suffer longer before death."

"Sherylynn is going to gas everyone inside the mansion and the underground HQ when Mason arrives!" Becca said.

RC seemed to shut down as the horror of the coming attack sunk in. "We're still an hour away from landing."

Becca realized they'd lost. "And an hour's drive from the airport to the mansion."

RC moved in front of Vivian. "Activate his phone!" he ordered.

"No." Vivian stood her ground, knowing how high the stakes were.

"He's my father and your boss!" He raised his voice, not hiding his rage. "Activate his phone, *now*! Save him!"

"No," Vivian said. "We can't risk it. You know that."

"He's going to die! You can save him! Do it!"

Becca watched tears form in RC's eyes as rage and pain exuded from his face. They were all helpless. RC had endless loyalty to the Griffins, and now it was clear how much he loved and respected his father. He was trapped in the plane, just like the rest of them.

"I'm sorry," Vivian said as a tear fell down her cheek.

RC quieted down knowing Vivian wasn't going to make an exception. "Please." Tears poured down his face.

Becca felt a tightness in her chest, and tears formed in her eyes as she watched RC's pain.

"He's at the mansion," Cassie said.

RC collapsed into one of the seats. He texted on the phone, but no hope radiated from his body language. Vivian looked over Cassie's shoulder and watched the screen. Becca joined RC at the chair and held his hand again.

Cassie hit two keys and put the video on the bulkhead screen so Becca and RC could see it. They all watched Mason's car pull up the driveway and stop in front of the mansion. Then they held their breaths as he made his way to the front door. Nothing could be heard.

"Give me a scan of the entire mansion and headquarters below," Vivian said.

Cassie had it up in no time, next to the live video feed of Mason walking through the mansion to Sherylynn's room.

"Locate the gas," Vivian said.

Cassie typed in the necessary commands, and eight objects appeared in the wireframe. "Four canisters above ground level hidden in the mansion and four canisters in the underground HQ. I calculate the gas, when activated, will fill both areas in five minutes."

"How did they even get the canisters inside?" Becca asked.

"It doesn't matter. Somehow, they did," RC said.

"What is that on the canister?" Vivian pointed to one of them on the screen, and Cassie zoomed in.

"The transmitter," Cassie said, getting excited with unexpected hope.

"Hack it. Hack it right now," RC said.

"I'm trying," Cassie replied, feeling the pressure.

"If you can hack the transmitter, can you jam the signal so the gas won't activate?" Becca asked.

"That's the idea," Cassie said trying to work her magic on the computer.

"We have to be cautious," Vivian said. "There's only one chance to play this right."

"He's at her bedroom door," RC said.

Becca and RC watched Mason enter Sherylynn's master bedroom. He looked around, but she was nowhere to be found.

"Where the hell is she?" RC asked, glued to the screen.

Becca watched as Mason shouted Sherylynn's name, but the audio feed wasn't on.

"Where's the audio, Cassie?" RC said, about to lose his temper.

"The audio signal can be traced back to us. Audio has to stay off."

RC regained some control. "Save him, Cassie, please," RC begged.

"I'm working on it! Don't talk to me."

They watched Mason head toward the master bathroom. He shouted Sherylynn's name one more time. The bathroom door flung open, and there stood Sherylynn with a gas mask covering her face and pointing a gun at Mason.

"Oh shit!" Vivian said.

Mason didn't have time to react. The gun fired. Mason twisted and fell to the floor clutching his side.

Becca jolted, startled by what had just happened.

"Dad!" RC jumped to his feet watching his father struggle on the screen. "No!"

Sherylynn walked closer to Mason and towered over him. She didn't say anything, but everyone knew she enjoyed watching him struggle in agony. She raised the gun and aimed the barrel at his head.

"Do something!" RC roared.

Becca stared at the screen in horror as she prepared to watch Mason be executed. Her heart skipped a beat, and she lost all sense of time as she held her breath.

Sherylynn began to pull the trigger but was tackled to the floor by Winston, the family butler. He and Sherylynn rolled, kicked, and punched at each other as they fought for control of the gun. They both grabbed hold of the gun and fired shot after shot, trying to aim at each other, narrowly missing Mason. Winston had strength over Sherylynn, but she had speed. She was able to regain control of the pistol and fire a shot in Winston's chest.

"No!" Becca yelled at the screen.

RC's hands flew to his head, and his mouth dropped open in shock. No words were spoken. All anybody could do was watch the two men struggle for their lives against Sherylynn.

Mason struggled to get up but was stopped when the gun was aimed in his face. Sherylynn pulled the trigger. No bullet fired.

"She's empty," Becca said as she let out a breath she hadn't realized she'd been holding. Winston had purposefully fired as many rounds as he could before he lost the struggle. The painful strategy had paid off.

Sherylynn threw the gun at Mason, but he ducked and fell to the floor due to the pain from his wound. He wouldn't last much longer. Sherylynn had the upper hand, and she knew it. She pulled out a remote-trigger device and pressed a button.

"Cassie! Cassie!" Vivian shouted.

"I see it, Boss."

"She activated the gas," RC said, his tone subdued, his body hunched.

The wireframe model of the mansion showed the poisonous

substance as a red cloud on the monitor. The gas began to fill different rooms throughout the Griffin facility.

Sherylynn tossed the remote on the floor between Mason and Winston. She blew them a kiss, walked over both of them, and exited the master bedroom.

"I've got something, I've got something," Cassie said. "I've locked onto the transmitter, but I can only deactivate one. There's not enough time to deactivate all the gas canisters, as each is on a different wavelength."

"Deactivate the one nearest them!" RC demanded.

"I can't yet. Mason's moving somewhere. If I deactivate the one nearest him, he could move into a different zone, then we're screwed."

"Wait to see where he ends up," Vivian ordered.

Mason mustered the strength to stand, grabbed both of Winston's feet, and dragged him out of Sherylynn's bedroom, doing his best to hold his breath.

"Where's he going?" Becca asked.

"He's heading to his bedroom," RC said. "There's a secret high-speed elevator that goes down to his office in the headquarters."

"His office is next to the medical bay, and there are gas masks in there," Vivian added.

"Come on, Dad," RC said.

Mason dragged Winston through his bedroom to a wall panel on the north side. He coughed and placed his hand on the wall, and it opened revealing the elevator. Mason painfully pulled Winston inside the elevator. Winston was unresponsive. The elevator doors closed, and Falcon squad lost sight of them.

"What happened?" Vivian asked.

"There are no cameras in the elevator. We have to wait for them to get into his office," Cassie replied. "I've located the gas canister nearest his office and the medical bay."

"Deactivate it!" RC said.

"She can't," Becca said. "Not yet."

"Why?" RC's emotions clouded his judgment.

"I'm going to suck the air out of that zone like a vacuum," Cassie explained without looking away from the screens. "If I do that before they're wearing oxygen masks, I'd kill them."

"Shit," RC said.

"I see them." Becca pointed to a new camera angle, and Cassie adjusted the screen position to feature it as the main feed. Mason dragged a limp Winston out of the elevator. He was coughing more intensely and stumbling from his bullet wound. Mason fumbled as he used every ounce of energy he had left to get to the medical bay and find two gas masks, each with its own reserve air tank built in. He found them and turned them on. He put the first one on Winston and the second over his own head, then collapsed to the floor, unconscious.

"Do it now!" Vivian shouted.

Cassie pressed the enter key, and they watched the red cloud on the monitor be sucked out of the underground medical bay.

"Refilling the room with clean air...now." Cassie hit a few more keys, and a green cloud appeared on the wireframe model of the mansion.

"How much air is left in the auxiliary canister for those masks?" Becca asked, referring to the mask Mason had put on before he passed out.

"One hour," Vivian explained. "He'll bleed out from his injury before then."

"We don't even know if Winston is going to make it either," Becca said.

"There's no one left alive in the mansion and underground," Cassie said with a cracked voice. Different camera angles appeared on the screen and showed bodies of men and women in rooms and hallways, slumped over, lifeless.

"Jesus," Becca said, stunned and horrified. Hundreds of people were horrifically murdered by Sherylynn. Becca's knees gave out underneath her, forcing her to sit down after having witnessed the unspeakable brutality of the attack on the Griffins. No one spoke as they stared at all of the dead people on the screen. No words of comfort would have had any effect. The cunning of Sherylynn was staggering.

RC's phone buzzed with a text message.

Becca looked over. His body language changed from despair to hope.

"What is it?" Becca asked.

"They're there." RC could barely say the words.

"Who's where?" Vivian asked.

"Veils." RC got out of his seat and headed to Cassie.

"I don't see anybody on the cameras," Cassie said.

"That's because I told them to stay in a blind spot. I used to use it all the time to sneak out of the mansion when I was fifteen. Can you loop the current footage so the Brotherhood won't see them go in?"

"Sure," Cassie said.

"Won't that give away our position?" Becca asked.

"Not if I do it carefully," Cassie replied as she looped all the cameras covering the Carter mansion. "Done."

RC called the veil and put it on speaker. "You're clear." His voice cracked as he tried to contain his hope. "You're looking for two survivors in the basement, both severely injured."

"Entering now," a male voice responded.

They watched the screen and didn't see anything change, which was a good thing, considering Cassie had hacked the Brotherhood feed.

"We're in. Heading down now."

"Copy that," RC said.

They waited on pins and needles, their attention fixed on the monitor.

"Loop is still good," Cassie said.

Becca folded her hands together praying the veils would get to Mason and Winston in time. They waited and waited.

"We found them," the male voice said. "They're alive. Extracting now."

31

Falcon squad arrived at the unmarked private medical quarters for Mason Carter. The room had highly advanced medical technology. Unlike the equipment Becca had seen in Chen's underground medical bay, this place looked like it was out of a science-fiction movie. There was no way any of the technology inside wasn't experimental.

Mason had been administered a sedative and lay in the most luxurious hospital bed Becca had ever seen. He wore an oxygen mask and was connected to a spider web of wires that monitored all of his vitals and more.

Becca, RC, and Vivian stood by the clear plexiglass room as they watched two Griffin doctors conduct a new type of procedure on Mason's bullet wound. The video of the surgery was projected on the plexiglass so they could see what the doctors saw. One doctor held some sort of medical wand that was about a foot long. Two prongs protruded from the wand and emitted a red laser beam. The doctors held the beam a few inches away from the wound and waved the wand over the injury. New tissue knit itself together sealing the wound.

"Nicely done," one doctor said to the other.

"I'll be back to see his progress." The doctor exited the plexiglass room.

"He's going to make it," the doctor said. "But we must keep Mr. Carter under surveillance for the next twenty-four hours, as this was an experimental procedure never performed before. The new rapid-healing serum we gave him is still in the testing phase, but it has shown great promise."

"What about Winston?" Becca asked. "Did he undergo the same procedure?"

"Come with me," the doctor said. He guided them to another room that was even more futuristic than the one they'd just left. Inside was a giant horizontal tube made of clear crystal. Winston didn't look good, as he lay unmoving in the tube.

"Unfortunately, Winston wasn't strong enough to undergo the same procedure as Mr. Carter. He's alive but in critical condition. This chamber is his lifeline and is designed to speed up the healing process from near death. This is an extremely dangerous experimental procedure that must be done in three phases. Due to his age and the severity of the wound so close to his heart, if we aren't careful, instead of speeding up his healing, we could speed up his death."

Becca stared at an almost lifeless Winston in the giant tube. She hated what she saw. She put her hand on the tube and said a quiet prayer.

"Only time will tell, I'm afraid," the doctor said. "No matter how advanced our technology, it always comes down to the body and will of the patient to survive."

The other doctor entered the room. "Mr. Carter's asking for you."

The main doctor turned to leave.

"Not you, sir. Them." He pointed to Becca, RC, and Vivian.

They hurried back to Mason's room and found him sitting up, tired but alert.

"Dad." RC sounded relieved and surprised.

"Leave us." Mason waved away the doctors.

They nodded and exited the room, leaving Mason with Falcon squad.

"How bad is it?" Mason asked.

"They got the bullet out, and your lungs weren't contaminated enough by the poison to do serious damage, though you still need time to heal."

"I didn't mean me. I meant the Griffins." Mason looked to Vivian. "How bad were we hit?"

"Cassie's working on that now. The team was able to connect fifteen headquarters across the globe that were intentionally hit to send us a message." Becca held up the iPad and showed Mason the fox emblem she'd drawn connecting the attacks.

Mason coughed violently. He may have been alert, but he still wasn't up to snuff. "Were you able to acquire the contact list from Chen?"

Vivian shook her head. "We were ambushed by the Brotherhood at Chen's mansion. They tried to burn us alive, including Chen. There was no time to acquire the list."

Mason sighed. "What else do we know? Are you tracking Sherylynn?"

"She ditched the tracker, left it in her bedroom. She's off-grid," Vivian replied.

"Of course," Mason said, annoyed.

"Dad, did you—"

"No. I never suspected her. She played us perfectly." Mason shifted in bed, but it was difficult for him to do so while being connected to so many machines. RC and Becca did their best to help him get as comfortable as possible. "Any other survivors?"

They all shook their heads.

Mason closed his eyes. "What are our options?"

Cassie knocked on the door. She stood there holding her open laptop.

Vivian motioned for her to enter. "You don't have to ask for permission to enter, Cassie."

"Sorry, Boss."

"What do you have?" Mason asked.

"It's not good, sir. They've stolen our DIANA interface. They got half of my Eye software, but I was able to erase the other half before they could download it. Still, they have enough of our tech to build upon it and do even more damage than they already have."

"Looks like you'll be fighting a version of yourselves now," Mason said.

"Sir?" Vivian asked.

"You're going back out there, into the field. The job isn't done."

"With all due respect, sir, we need to regroup and make plans. We don't have the resources to be as effective as normal," Vivian said.

Mason looked at Cassie. "What do you need to start rebuilding DIANA and your Eye program?"

"Time, sir. More than we can afford."

"Every second we wait, Sherylynn is out there doing God knows what with the most lethal hidden force the world has never seen," RC said.

"If she has control of our resources, she could topple governments without them ever seeing it coming in, what, a year?" Becca said.

"Eight to ten months by my calculations," Cassie said.

Mason looked behind Vivian at a news report that floated high up the wall opposite the bed. A reporter stood in front of the Carter mansion. The chyron read:

CARTER & ROMANOV FAMILY PRESUMED DEAD IN TRAGIC GAS ACCIDENT

"Volume level twenty," Mason said.

"It is unclear how the gas leak happened," the reporter said, "but authorities have identified the bodies of Sherylynn Carter, Mason

Carter, their son, Reed Alexander Carter, and friends Vivian Lake Romanov and her daughter, Rebecca Hunter Lake Romanov."

"They're missing about five hundred other bodies in this report," Becca said, frustrated.

Mason sighed and winced with pain. "Sherylynn just provided the perfect cover story for her escape."

"And our way to retaliate," Becca added.

Cassie typed on her laptop. "I'm contacting Scout to let him and Dex know the truth."

"Don't," Mason said. "Don't contact them yet. We're still under surveillance. All of us."

"The Brotherhood hasn't found our bodies," RC said. "This news report is their distraction to the public and a threat to every remaining Griffin. It's a victory lap for Sherylynn."

Becca did her best to think of what they could do to reclaim some sort of upper hand, but nothing triggered her mind. The surprise attack hit them so hard, she didn't know if they would actually be able to recover from the massive blow. She shook away the negative thought. There was only one option. They had to recover from this somehow, someway.

"Our options are so limited." Becca looked at her mother. "Cassie's the only member of Falcon squad not declared dead. Even Dex and Scout are supposed to have died in the fire at Chen's estate. That's got to be a plus for us." Becca faced Cassie. "Sorry to put pressure on you."

Cassie shrugged. "The Griffins are my home. So, put me in, Boss."

"You don't have the necessary field experience," Vivian said. "It's too risky."

"It's never too late to gain experience," Mason said. "We've all been declared dead." He looked at each member of Falcon squad. "Congratulations. Time to use it."

Mason's words added to the endless fire that burned inside Becca's soul from the loss of Barry. Her hatred for the Brotherhood now had a face, a target to unleash her rage on now that it was no longer hidden in the shadows. The same enemy for Mason, RC, Vivian, and every Griffin who still lived throughout the world. They had limited resources now and one giant advantage: They were still alive, and the Brotherhood didn't know it and had no reason to hunt for them.

Mason looked at RC, Vivian, and Cassie. With more emotional pain than Becca had ever seen on his face, Mason looked into her eyes and gave her the biggest vote of confidence she'd ever received from him.

"Take her down."

LEAGUE OF GRIFFINS TATTOOS

Griffin Beak-Leader of the organization
Griffin Claw-Attack squad
Griffin Talons-Assassins
Griffin Wings-Information gatherers
Griffin Feather-Trusted advisors

ABOUT THE AUTHOR

Barb Goodwin worked for years as a flight attendant for a major international airline. While flying she found a passion for writing novels. The Lost Treasures series, about famous, still-missing treasures, was born. Barb has two sisters, one an identical twin, and they are all best friends. Her wonderful nephew is her coauthor for the Lost Treasures series, and he always brings laughter to their writing sessions. She lives in California.

f

ABOUT THE AUTHOR

Doug Penikas is an actor, dancer, and filmmaker. He has performed in numerous films and television shows for many years, as well as music videos and live musicals. He is passionate about storytelling in all forms and is thrilled to be a coauthor with his aunt on the Lost Treasures series. Doug lives in California.

ALSO BY BARB GOODWIN & DOUG PENIKAS

Lost Treasures

Secrets of the Royal Danish Egg